Praise for Jenna Black's
THE DEVIL INSIDE

"A sassy heroine who's not afraid to do what it takes to get the job done or to save a loved one's life. Add to that a sexy hero, great secondary characters and a story line that keeps you reading, and this one is definitely a keeper."
　　　　　　　　　　　　　　　　　　—Keri Arthur

"[Black's] got a winning heroine, a well-crafted contemporary world where demonic possession is just a part of life, and a nice balance of mystery, action and sex, making this light but engaging novel an urban fantasy series kickoff full of promise."　　　　　　　—*Publishers Weekly*

"Talk about your odd couples! The delicious irony of trapping a sexy demon and a cranky exorcist in the same body gives rising star Black lots of room for conflict and action. It's inventive in the extreme! 4½ stars. Top pick!"　　　　　　　　　　　　　　—*Romantic Times*

"Another great paranormal book by Jenna Black [who] weaves a new world and new concepts into every story she writes. . . . Morgan is a strong heroine who will have you cheering her along."　　　—NightOwlRomance.com

Praise for Jenna Black's
WATCHERS IN THE NIGHT

"Clever plotting and terrific supporting characters elevate this novel into a first-rate romantic thriller."
　　　　　　　　　　　　　　　　　　—*Romantic Times*

P9-DTT-622

"Jenna Black has crafted a fine story with *Watchers in the Night*. She supplies deft handling of plot, characters, and genre, and I enjoyed the novel tremendously. I see many more fascinating novels coming from this author in the future!"

—Heather Graham, *New York Times* bestselling author of *Kiss of Darkness*

"You'll want to bare your throat to Jenna Black's enthralling heroes. This cleverly plotted romantic tale will leave you hungry for more!"

—Sabrina Jeffries, *New York Times* bestselling author of *Only a Duke Will Do*

"Jenna Black's *Watchers in the Night* is a sexy, fast-paced, totally engaging read. She's built an exciting world of vampires and added a 'to die for' hero and a kick-butt heroine! This is a book you can really sink your teeth into!"

—Ronda Thompson, *New York Times* bestselling author of *The Untamed One*

"Mystery, magic, and vampires! In *Watchers in the Night*, Jenna Black has created a fresh and fascinating vampire universe. What more could any lover of the paranormal ask for?"

—Lori Handeland, RITA Award–winning author of *Midnight Moon*

"Jenna Black's *Watchers in the Night* is sexy, suspenseful, and what a great read! Vampire Gray James hits the top of my Hot-O-Meter from the moment he comes back from the dead to save his girlfriend, Carolyn Mathers—who just happens to be a kick-ass PI able to take care of herself. Just the right mix of mystery, vampires, romance, great characters, and underworld shenanigans to keep me happy. I can't wait to see what happens next in the world of the Guardians!"

—Tess Mallory, author of *Highland Fling*

"Inventive, sexy, sassy twist on the vampire mythos. These are not your mother's vampires; Black serves up a strong heroine and plenty of delicious humor as well as a sly twist on the clichéd 'tortured hero.' Very enjoyable! It struck me as kind of a Stephanie Plum Meets Old Anita Blake."
—Lilith Saintcrow, author of *Working for the Devil*

"Grabs you from the very beginning and doesn't let you go until the very end. Even then, you're hoping for more. Peopled with an intriguing supporting cast, and a plotline that twists and turns like a maze, Ms. Black does a wonderful job creating a world where you're never sure what's going to happen." —Vivi Anna, author of *Hell Kat*

Praise for Jenna Black's
SECRETS IN THE SHADOWS

"Paranormal romance at its finest! Black writes the kind of hero I want to date!"
—Gena Showalter, author of *The Nymph King*

"[A] gripping supernatural drama." —*Romantic Times*

"The best new vampire twist to hit the shelves."
—RomanceJunkies.com

"Jenna Black has done a remarkable job of taking an old myth—vampires—and spinning it into a fabulous new world, at once good and evil." —FallenAngelReviews.com

Praise for Jenna Black's
SHADOWS ON THE SOUL

"Dark, magical and deliciously brooding, just how I like them!" —Gena Showalter, author of *The Nymph King*

"Black hits a note-perfect combination of romance, vengeance and passion. Her best book to date. 4½ stars! Top Pick." —*Romantic Times*

"Vampires should be mysterious and erotic, and these vampires are top of the line." —SFRevu.com

"*Shadows on the Soul* is an awe-inspiring dark vampire romance with tortured characters and an exciting plot. I highly recommend it." —OnceUponARomance.net

ALSO BY JENNA BLACK

The Devil Inside
Watchers in the Night
Secrets in the Shadows
Shadows on the Soul

THE DEVIL
YOU KNOW

JENNA BLACK

A DELL SPECTRA BOOK

THE DEVIL YOU KNOW
A Dell Spectra Book / August 2008

Published by Bantam Dell
A Division of Random House, Inc.
New York, New York

This is a work of fiction. Names, characters, places, and incidents
either are the product of the author's imagination or are used
fictitiously. Any resemblance to actual persons, living or dead,
events, or locales is entirely coincidental.

All rights reserved
Copyright © 2008 by Jenna Black
Cover art © Vince Natale
Cover design by Jamie S. Warren Youll

If you purchased this book without a cover, you should be aware
that this book is stolen property. It was reported as "unsold and
destroyed" to the publisher, and neither the author nor the
publisher has received any payment for this "stripped book."

Dell is a registered trademark of Random House, Inc., and
the Dell colophon, Spectra, and the portrayal of a boxed "s" are
trademarks of Random House, Inc.

ISBN 978-0-553-59045-6

Printed in the United States of America
Published simultaneously in Canada

www.bantamdell.com

OPM   10 9 8 7 6 5 4 3 2 1

For Gayle, one of my first critique partners, whose courage and positive attitude have truly been an inspiration

Acknowledgments

Many thanks to Anne Groell, my fabulous editor, for helping me make this a better book, and just for being fabulous in general. Thanks to Miriam Kriss, my agent, whose enthusiasm always helps keep me motivated. And my heartfelt thanks to the Heart of Carolina Romance Writers, who are, in my admittedly biased opinion, the most talented and supportive group of writers on the planet.

Chapter 1

There's no denying Dominic Castello is a treat to look at—the classic tall, dark, and handsome. Soulful hazel eyes framed by thick lashes, warm olive skin, muscles in all the right places . . . But on seeing him standing in my doorway, my first impulse was to slam the door in his face.

He must have read my expression, for he wedged his foot in the door and smiled at me. He has a sweet, disarming smile that would turn most women to jelly, but I'm not most women. Besides, his equally good-looking boyfriend was the sadomasochistic demon host who'd shot my brother. That put Dominic near the bottom of the list of people I wanted to see, with only his boyfriend, Adam, and pretty much my entire family below him.

Unfortunately, with him being over six feet tall and at least two hundred pounds, I wasn't keeping him out of my apartment now that I'd been stupid enough to open the door in the first place.

Giving in to the inevitable, I moved away from the door, letting him enter—though I didn't actually invite him in. I headed to my minuscule kitchen, where a half-full pot of coffee left over from breakfast still sat on the warmer.

"Wanna cup?" I asked without looking at him.

"Sure. Thanks."

I filled two mugs, noticing that the coffee was dark as ink and smelled stale. If it were just me, I'd make a fresh pot, but I didn't want Dominic staying that long.

"Cream and sugar?"

Dominic looked at the tar-scented swill in the cup I handed him and shook his head. "I doubt it would help much."

That almost made me smile. "So, what brings you to this part of town?" I took a sip of the coffee to prove it was drinkable and tried not to gag when I discovered it wasn't.

When Dominic didn't immediately answer, my nerves went on red alert. Apparently, this wasn't a social call, which I suppose I'd known all along.

"Maybe we should sit down for a bit," he suggested.

I really hated the sound of that—and the way he wouldn't quite meet my eyes. My stomach gave an unhappy gurgle, and my fingers clenched on the coffee cup. I put it down before I took a sip by reflex.

For the last few weeks, I'd been trying my best to live under a rock. I'd had enough stress lately to last me a lifetime—or three. Realistically, I knew my problems were far from over, but I'd been determined to hold them at bay for as long as possible—ideally, until I was on my deathbed.

See, here's the thing. I'm an exorcist. My calling in life, my very raison d'être, is to kick demon ass. Only the ones who possess unwilling hosts or who commit violent crimes, of course, but in reality I don't like legal demons much better. So as you can imagine, my life became a little complicated when I found out I was possessed by the king of the demons, who was embroiled in a war for the throne of the Demon Realm.

For reasons neither of us understands, the demon king, Lugh, can't take control of me the way a demon normally dominates a host. Even though I'm possessed, I remain in total control of my body. For the most part, Lugh can only take command when I'm asleep, and can only communicate with me through dreams.

From the moment I'd found out I was possessed, my life had shot straight to hell and stayed there. My best friend had tried to kill me. My house was burned to the ground. I was thrown in jail for murder. My boyfriend, Brian—actually, he's my *ex*-boyfriend now, though I have yet to convince him of this fact—was kidnapped and tortured in an attempt to get to me. And to win his aid in rescuing Brian, I'd let Dominic's boyfriend whip me bloody for his own amusement.

All in all, I was desperately in need of some R&R. But since I wasn't getting Dominic out of my apartment through brute force, I figured the quickest way to get rid of him was to listen to what he had to say.

I'm sure I looked pretty sulky and mulish as I led him into my living room and gestured him toward my couch. I dropped into the love seat and suffered a momentary pang of yearning for the homey, comfortable furniture that had been destroyed when my house burned down. I'd rented this apartment furnished, and nothing in it reflected my tastes. This love seat, for example, was hard enough to numb my ass. I hoped the sofa would have the same effect on Dominic.

"So we're sitting down," I said, folding my arms across my chest. "Why don't you tell me why you're here?"

He put his cup on the coffee table—I don't think he'd been stupid enough to take a sip, like I had—then turned so he could face me full-on. I didn't like the intensity of his expression, so instead of looking at him, I idly tugged at a loose thread on the arm of the love seat.

"Adam has found out something he thinks you should know," Dominic said.

I pulled on the thread a little harder, and the fabric started to unravel. With a grunt of disgust, I stopped fidgeting and gave Dom my best steely-eyed glare. "If Adam thinks I should know, why isn't *he* the one sitting here?"

Dominic grinned. "He thought I was more likely to get through your door."

I couldn't help a rueful chuckle. There have been times when I've said some terrible things to Dominic, but he's never deserved them. When I'd first met him, he'd been a willing demon host, and I had despised him for being the kind of weak-minded, suicidal fool who was willing to give up his entire identity to host a demon. Because the human personality was (in all cases except my own) completely buried beneath the demon's, I'd considered the human hosts as good as dead. Many people—including my entire family—considered those who sacrificed themselves to host "Higher Powers," as they called demons, to be great heroes. Because demons are so much stronger and so much more resilient than humans, the hosts can take on extremely dangerous tasks. But I'd always considered them sheep.

After some of the things he had done for me—and for Brian, a man he didn't even know—I now believed Dominic was a genuine hero, even without his demon. And despite my feelings about Adam, I had to admit that, most of the time, I rather liked Dom.

"Adam could have tried phoning," I said, attempting to maintain my grumpy demeanor.

Dominic just laughed. "And you would have hung up on him and taken the phone off the hook."

Probably true. "All right, you win. Tell me what he

found out. I assume it's important or you wouldn't be here."

The humor faded from his face. "Yeah." He cleared his throat, and once again his eyes slid away from mine. "This is going to be kind of awkward."

"Great."

"Adam's been doing some, er, investigation."

Along with all his other sterling qualities, Adam is also the Director of Special Forces, the branch of the Philly police department responsible for demon-related crime. The fact that he's hosting a demon himself has never seemed like a conflict of interest to the Powers That Be, though I wasn't the only citizen who questioned the wisdom of his appointment.

"What kind of investigation?" I prompted when Dominic seemed to be struggling to continue.

He huffed out a breath, and one corner of his mouth tipped up in a wry smile. "I can't think of a way to tell you this without risking bodily injury, so I'm just going to blurt it out." And honest to God, the man tensed up as if ready to defend himself. "He's been investigating you and your family."

I blinked a couple of times as I let that sink in. A low simmer started in my chest, but either I was getting more serene in my old age, or Dominic had given the statement so much buildup that nothing he said could be as bad as I expected. Knowing me, the latter is more likely.

"Investigating how? And why?"

He was still watching me warily, which meant there was more to this story he didn't think I would like. "He's been wondering why Raphael chose *you* to be Lugh's host."

Dougal—Lugh's oldest brother and second in line for the throne—had hatched an insidious plan to take over as king of the Demon Realm. He'd planned to summon Lugh into a human host, and then burn that host alive, which, counter to popular wisdom, is the only way to kill a demon. Raphael, Lugh's youngest brother, had ostensibly been Dougal's accomplice, but instead of arranging for Lugh to take over the chosen host, he'd stuck Lugh in *my* body.

Turned out Raphael had always been on Lugh's side, and had summoned him into me to save his life. Somehow, Raphael had known Lugh wouldn't be able to take me over, and because of that inability, he would remain hidden from his enemies. Even when Raphael had revealed his true loyalties, he'd refused to tell Lugh how he'd known.

"I'm sure we've all been wondering that," I said cautiously. "What does my family have to do with anything?"

"You mean other than the fact that your brother was Raphael's host?"

I rolled my eyes. "You know what I mean!"

"Yes. Well. Adam figured that Raphael must have found out something interesting when he insinuated himself into your family, so Adam hoped to find out what that interesting something was."

My heart seemed to be beating louder than it should, but it was probably my imagination. "And? What did he find?"

Dominic looked even more uncomfortable. "I love Adam, but I wish he hadn't sent me to do this. . . ."

I made a little sound of frustration. "Just tell me, already! Waiting for the other shoe to drop is killing me."

Dominic clasped his hands in his lap and regarded them with concentration. "He found an old, buried police report from twenty-eight years ago. About a rape." He squirmed. "The victim was your mother."

The blood drained from my face. Never had my mother even hinted that she'd been raped. Of course, my mother and I had been at each other's throats since I was about five, so I guess it isn't surprising that she hadn't shared a confidence like that with me.

Still, I didn't know how to feel. I mean . . . damn! What a horrible secret to keep for all these years. How much had that rape affected my mother's life? And her personality? Was it possible that all the things I despised about her were symptoms of that terrible trauma in her past?

Then the other shoe dropped—though I was losing count of how many shoes it had been so far.

"Twenty-eight years ago?" I asked in a hushed whisper, and Dominic met my eyes this time. His chin dipped in a barely perceptible nod, and the sympathy in his expression made my throat ache. "Then there's a chance . . ." I couldn't say it. My pulse was pounding in my ears, my world tipping sideways once again.

Dominic sighed. "Not just a chance, I'm afraid," he said gently. "Adam also found the record of a paternity test."

My heart clenched in my chest, and it was all I could do to hold myself together. "I guess that means my father isn't really my father, huh?" I tried for something like nonchalance and was sure I failed.

Dominic shook his head. "I wish there were some good way to tell you this."

He looked so miserable that I was able to pull myself up by my bootstraps, at least temporarily. "You did fine," I assured him. I could only imagine how Adam would have delivered the news. He doesn't like me any more than I like him. In my more generous moments, I admit that I've given him good cause to dislike me. But my generous moments are few and far between.

Still, I guess this unpleasant truth about my origins explained a bit about my less-than-stellar relationship with my parents. I'd always assumed they favored my brother for his willingness to host a demon. My parents are members of the Spirit Society, a group that practically worships these demons. To them, there can be no greater glory than to sacrifice oneself to host a demon. The fact that they hadn't been able to brainwash me into hosting had inspired boundless animosity, but now I had an insight into what else they held against me. And it wasn't pretty.

"Not to be shitty or anything," I said, "but is there some burning reason you and Adam felt it necessary to tell me this? I mean, I've gone twenty-eight years without knowing, and I'd have been happy to go twenty-eight more."

Dominic shrugged. "Lugh can't gain control of you. There's got to be a reason, since Raphael had no trouble taking over your brother. Don't you think the fact that you and your brother have different fathers might have something to do with it?"

I leaned back into the stiff, uncomfortable cushions of my rent-a-couch and brooded a bit. I wasn't sure how I felt about this revelation. There was definitely an element of shock. I mean, how could I not be shocked? But I think I would have been more devastated if I were actually close to my dad.

Christ! Why had they done it? Why had my mother decided to keep her baby under the circumstances? Yeah, she was the pro-life type, but even if she wasn't willing to have an abortion, that didn't mean she had to keep me after I was born! Had my father known all along that I wasn't his?

The questions circled like sharks, and I didn't want to deal with them.

"Okay," I said, "let's say you're right and my biological father"—man, did that sound weird—"has something to do with why Lugh can't get a foothold.

What does that gain us? We don't know who he was, do we?"

Dominic shook his head. "No. Your mother didn't even give much of a description in the police report. But the strange thing is that, after she made the initial report, nothing happened."

"What do you mean?"

"I mean, no one made any effort to investigate the case. It just kind of sank out of sight, and your mother never made an inquiry. I can't help wondering why."

I had to admit, that was pretty strange. But I also had a sneaking suspicion where this was going, and I intended to nip it in the bud. "If you think I'm going to question my mom about it, you can forget it."

"Now, Morgan—"

"No!" I snapped. "I do everything I can to avoid her, even in supposedly pleasant situations. No way in hell am I asking her about a rape she never bothered to tell me about."

I was too agitated to sit still, so I stood up and paced. I wanted to pull the blanket of denial up over my head again. After all the shit I'd been through, I needed more time, damn it! Bad enough to have to deal with royal intrigue and assassins and the fate of the human race—which, according to Lugh, could turn seriously ugly if Dougal managed to grab the throne—but to have to deal with my family issues on top of all that . . .

Nope, not ready for it.

Dominic's a pretty smart guy, and his instincts are good. He took one look at my face, then swallowed whatever argument he'd been about to make.

"All right," he said, standing. "I can certainly understand your position. Adam will keep poking around the old files. He'll let you know if he finds anything important."

I'm not the most polite person under the best of

circumstances, which these weren't, so I couldn't manage much better than a curt nod of acceptance. Still, I did walk him to the door, which I felt was rather decent of me.

"If you ever need someone to talk to," he said before he left, "give me a call. I'm a good listener."

I couldn't help a little snort of laughter. Dom looked hurt.

"Nothing personal," I hastened to assure him. "I'm sure you're a *great* listener. But I'm a lousy talker." Which I bet he knew already. He hadn't known me all that long, but he was far too sensitive not to have picked that up.

Dominic smiled faintly. "All right. But the offer stays open."

"Thanks," I said, and then there was nothing else to say.

After Dominic left, the apartment seemed ominously empty and quiet. Just the kind of atmosphere to encourage a round of brooding melancholy and self-pity. I decided hanging around would be a bad idea, so I stuffed my Taser in my purse and headed out.

Tasers are one of the few weapons that actually work against demons. The electricity fucks up their ability to control the host body and leaves them essentially helpless. Normal weapons, like guns, might be able to kill the host, but the demon would just return to the Demon Realm. And if it ever managed to get back to the Mortal Plain, you'd be high on its shit list.

It used to be that I rarely carried my Taser when I went out. By the time I'm called in to do an exorcism, the demon has been well and truly contained and is no threat to me. Now, with Dougal's unknown minions wanting to kill me, I wouldn't go to the lobby to pick up my mail without the Taser on my person.

I didn't actually have a plan for where I wanted to

go, but as I walked the streets of Philadelphia, trying not to brood or even *think*, I found myself heading toward The Healing Circle. That's the hospital-cum-nursing home where my brother currently resides. The demon Raphael abandoned my brother's body after Adam shot him. My brother managed to survive the gunshot wound, but as is usually the case when a host loses his demon, his mind didn't survive. He's in a state of catatonia, probably permanently.

For many years, I'd despised Andrew as much as I'd despised the rest of my family. But in the horrible moment when Adam shot him, I'd realized that, despite all our troubles, I still loved him. And so, even when I was otherwise trying to keep my head firmly buried in the sand, I made sure to visit Andrew on a regular basis. Usually, I tried to time my visits to miss my other family members. Visiting spur of the moment like this was dangerous, but I guess after the disturbing news I felt the need to connect to the one family member I felt comfortable with.

The fact that I could talk to Andrew without him talking back might also have been a plus.

The gods decided to have mercy on me—for once!—and Andrew had no visitors when I arrived. My parents were well-off enough to afford a private room—only the best for their favored son—so I closed the door behind me and pulled up a chair.

Naturally, Andrew had lost a lost of weight since he'd gone catatonic. He was too tall and big-boned to look frail, but he certainly didn't look like the strong and powerful big brother I'd once known.

"Hi, Andy," I said, reaching out to clasp his limp hand. My voice came out a bit raspy, and the stinging in my eyes said I was on the verge of tears. I blinked until they went away.

Andy didn't move or blink. His eyes were open,

but they stared fixedly ahead. I swallowed hard. Those few demon hosts who'd recovered after being in this state said they were conscious and aware during their catatonia, even though they couldn't move or speak. Knowing that, I always tried to talk to him, keep him up-to-date on the news, maybe even read to him. Anything to keep his mind from atrophying inside his useless husk of a body.

But tonight, my own mind was in too much turmoil to manage banter, and I didn't want to tell him what I'd learned from Dominic. There was always the possibility he knew, but I kind of doubted it. He would have been only three years old when the rape happened—too young to understand what was going on around him, even if he had heard whatever discussions my parents must have had as they decided to keep me.

Instead, I just sat there holding his hand. It felt strangely peaceful, and I let my eyes slide shut.

I guess I hadn't been getting all that much sleep lately. Either that, or the stress of Dominic's revelation had sapped the last vestiges of my energy.

Whatever the reason, I must have drifted off, because when I next opened my eyes, I wasn't in my brother's room anymore.

When I'd first met Lugh in my dreams, his control of even my unconscious mind had been tenuous at best. I'd met him in a barren white room with no doors or windows. As his control had gotten better, the room had gotten homier.

He'd embellished it since the last time I'd been here, adding a simple geometric rug under the coffee table and a frothy potted fern on a plant stand between the sofa and love seat. I gave these details about a half-second's attention before I gave in to the inevitable and let my gaze rest on Lugh.

Dominic is nice to look at. Lugh is every woman's

sexual fantasy come to life. His skin is a beautiful burnished bronze, his hair is a silky, shiny jet black and reaches to his shoulder blades when unbound, and his eyes . . . They're an intense shade of dark amber, and there always seems to be a hint of light glowing behind them. And let's not even talk about his incredible body!

Of course, demons are actually incorporeal, so that body was nothing but an illusion—and since Lugh has access to all my deepest thoughts and feelings, he knows exactly what buttons to push to make my mouth water. But knowing that doesn't ever seem to stop me from drooling when I see him.

He was sitting on the middle seat of the sofa, his long arms stretched out along the back, his ankle resting on his knee as he watched me ogle him. His sensuous lips curved into a hint of a smile. I made an unladylike grunting sound and plopped into the love seat. I didn't particularly want to talk to my own personal demon right this moment, but it would take me a while to close my mental doors to him. So . . .

"Long time no see," I said, fighting the urge to cross my arms over my chest in my trademark defensive gesture.

"I've been trying to give you some space," he answered.

His low, rumbling voice always seemed to vibrate through my nerves. Goose bumps rose on my arms at the sound of it, and I had to fight a shiver.

"Very considerate of you." My voice sounded too breathy for the attempt at sarcasm.

"But in light of this evening's news," he continued, "I think it's time for us to do some investigation."

I suppressed a groan. "Let Adam do all the investigating he wants! That's not my area of expertise, and

I'd rather spend time with my gynecologist than my mom." I tried a little harder to close my mental doors.

"There's only so long you can go on pretending none of this is happening. You know Dougal's people have been up to no good while they've walked the Mortal Plain, and you know the fate of your entire race may lie in the balance."

"Thanks for reminding me!" I snapped, allowing another wave of self-pity to break over me. "I might have forgotten all about it otherwise."

He sighed quietly. "I can apologize again for dragging you into this against your will, but my apologies don't seem to do either one of us any good. The only chance you have of returning to your 'normal' life is to help me defeat Dougal. Until then, you'll never know when one of his supporters might find out you're hosting me and try to kill you."

His words stung. "Do you really think the only reason I might help you is to save my own ass?"

"Of course not," he answered with reassuring promptness. "I just thought the reminder might hurry you up a bit."

I was working my way up to a smart-ass reply when I finally managed to shove those mental doors closed and wake up. I entertained a few less-than-complimentary thoughts about Lugh for a moment before I remembered where I was.

My hand was still clasped in Andy's. With a start, I realized that his fingers were actually curled around mine instead of lying limply in my grip. A shot of adrenaline burst through me, and I sat up abruptly and opened my eyes.

Andy's head was turned toward me, and when our eyes met, I could see the recognition and intelligence in his gaze. Without a moment's warning, I burst into tears and bowed my head over our clasped hands.

Chapter 2

Eventually, I stopped bawling. Andy held my hand the whole time, neither speaking nor moving. I could have used that hand to wipe away the tears, but I wasn't any more eager to let go than he was.

Sniffling like a baby, I pulled myself together as best I could and met his gaze once more.

"How ya doin', bro?" I asked.

He managed a faint smile. "Better than about thirty minutes ago," he said, his voice little more than a whisper. His eyes closed for a moment, and worry stabbed through me.

"Andy?"

He opened his eyes again, and I noticed for the first time the haunted expression in them. He didn't speak, and I couldn't think of anything to say.

I hadn't spoken to Andy, the *real* Andy, for ten years. The last time I'd spoken to him, I'd let him know in no uncertain terms that I hated his guts for volunteering to host a demon. For years, I'd believed that. Not until Adam shot him had I realized how untrue those words had been.

Thinking about that awful moment reminded me

of some problems I'd rather have ignored. Like the explanation we'd given the police for what had happened to Andy, which had been a complete work of fiction. God, I hoped he was willing to go along with the story, even though it painted his demon, Raphael, in the worst possible light.

How much did he know? I'd gotten the impression Raphael had made a habit of blocking Andy out to keep him from overhearing state secrets. Did Andy remember anything about the confrontation that led to his temporary death? Perhaps not. Perhaps all he knew was the official story, which he had surely overheard multiple times during his stay here.

But I wasn't about to bring that up now. Maybe I couldn't think of anything to say to my brother after his ten-year absence from my life, but I wasn't going to dump problems on him to break the awkwardness. At least, not yet.

"Thanks for coming to visit," Andy said, his voice weak and sickly. "I always knew you were here, even if I couldn't talk."

I gave his hand a squeeze. "Hey, in spite of our differences, you're still my big brother."

He smiled, though the expression didn't reach his eyes. "You told Raphael I was dead as far as you were concerned."

I winced and looked away. "I know." Remembering some of the other things I'd said to Raphael, I squirmed with guilt. I'd been very, very hard on Andy.

"It's okay," he assured me. "Raphael was a real son of a bitch, and I'm the one who brought him into your life."

I raised my head, surprised at the bitterness in his voice. The only other demon host I knew who'd lost his demon and was still functional—Dominic—had been so attached to his demon that I'd expected Andy to be the same way. Although I had to admit, I had a hard time imagining anyone being attached to Raphael.

"So you're not sorry he's gone?" I asked.

He shuddered. "No. Adam did me a real favor by helping me get rid of him." Well, that answered the question of whether he knew what had really happened.

His jaw clenched, and he let go of my hand. He shifted position in the bed, then winced. "God, I feel weak as a newborn. And I'm more than ready to lose the diaper. Could you go let the nurses know I'm back?"

I didn't want to leave his side, especially with all the questions and regrets that swarmed me, but I knew if I'd been in his position, I'd be in a hurry to regain my dignity, too. I wanted to hug him, or kiss him, or even ruffle his hair, but his body language didn't invite affection.

"I'll be right back," I told him around the lump in my throat. He merely nodded, not looking at me. I didn't know if he was angry at me, or at Raphael, or at Lugh, or just at the situation in general. But there'd be time to talk about that later.

Knees feeling a bit wobbly, I went to the nurses' station and gave them the good news. Looking genuinely delighted, a nurse and an orderly hurried to his room, telling me to stay put while they helped Andy get cleaned up and dressed.

"Here," the remaining nurse at the station said, pushing a phone toward me. "I'll let you be the one to give your parents the good news."

I made a face. I didn't want to talk to my parents under ordinary circumstances. After what I'd learned this afternoon, I wanted to even less. However, it would probably take more energy than I had to talk the nurse into taking the phone back, so I gritted my teeth and made the call.

Naturally, my mother was beside herself with glee,

and I knew she and my dad would be at the hospital as soon as humanly possible. I'd have given everything I owned to get the hell out of there before they made their grand entrance, but I couldn't walk out on Andy like that. Not after he'd been gone for so long.

I took a seat in the depressing waiting area and tried not to chew my lip raw. Eventually, the nurse came to get me, beaming. "You can go back into the room now," she informed me, and I tried to smile at her.

Don't get me wrong—I was thrilled that Andy had awakened. But I was such an emotional mess myself that I couldn't manage the giddy excitement I thought I should be feeling. Andy and I had been estranged, at best, when he'd gone to the ceremony that drew Raphael into the Mortal Plain, and now he'd been dormant inside his own body for ten long years. The man who awaited me in that room was a stranger.

I stood in the doorway a moment, struggling against my cowardly impulse to flee. Then, with a deep breath, I pushed the door all the way open and stepped inside.

Dressed in blue jeans and a black T-shirt that hung loosely on his gaunt frame, he sat in a wheelchair, eyes fixed on his hands, which were clenched in his lap. He didn't seem to notice me entering the room.

"Andy?" I asked hesitantly. "You okay?"

He blinked and looked up at me. "Yeah. Fine." He tried a smile, but it was a sorry effort. "Apparently, it's going to take me some time to regain my strength," he said. His voice still sounded weak and raspy, but then his vocal cords were out of practice. "It was all I could do to stand up long enough for them to get the pants on."

I bit my lip. "I'm sorry."

He raised his eyebrows. "What for?"

I sighed. "Everything?"

He laughed briefly. "That certainly covers all the bases."

The awkward silence threatened to return, and I rushed to fill it. "Mom and Dad are on their way."

To my surprise, he grimaced. He and my folks had always gotten along famously, what with him being the golden boy and all.

He saw my surprise and shook his head. "They're going to expect me to exonerate Raphael, and obviously I can't do that."

As far as everyone except myself, Adam, and Dominic knew, Raphael had gone rogue, kidnapping and torturing my boyfriend to punish me for the bad blood between us. My parents had always refused to believe that. They loved Raphael as if *he* were their true son, not Andy.

"How much do you remember?" I asked.

He closed his eyes. "Exactly as much as Raphael wanted me to. He made sure I knew the party line before he left me. Just in case I'd ever be a functional human being again." He sighed. "How much do you want to bet Mom and Dad are going to try to convince me that there must be some kind of misunderstanding?"

I frowned. "I know they won't be happy, but surely once you confirm the story, they'll have to believe it."

He snorted. "You're underestimating the power of their denial. They might not argue with me, but I doubt they'll really believe me."

Of course, since the story wasn't true, it was hard to blame my parents too much for not believing it. But no worries—there were plenty of other things I could blame them for.

I longed to ask Andy if he knew anything about my real father and the circumstances of my birth, but I knew it was too early for that. I needed to give him time to recuperate, to readjust to life as an independent human being. So I'd wait until tomorrow to ask.

I was once again struggling against my urge to run away when I heard the excited babble of my parents' voices and realized it was too late.

"You want to hide out in the bathroom until they're gone?" Andy asked me, and for the first time since he'd awakened I saw a spark of life and humor in his eyes.

Sad to say, that offer actually tempted me. But I scraped up what maturity I could and stayed right where I was.

My mom came through the door first. She's the kind of woman who won't set foot outside her house until her face is meticulously painted to hide any hint of blemishes or wrinkles and her hair has been sprayed until it didn't dare move even in a gale-force wind. She wields her iron with fanatical zeal, and even when she wears linen, you'll rarely see a crease anywhere.

Tonight was no exception, though how she managed to look so perfect when she'd obviously rushed out of the house, I had no clue. Maybe she was really a demon-possessed mannequin. But I'm being uncharitable. So what else is new?

She put her hands over her mouth when she caught sight of Andy, stifling a sob as her eyes shimmered with tears. Then she walked past me without even a sidelong glance and reached out her hand toward my brother. Andy took the offered hand and forced a smile. My mother couldn't speak through her silent tears, and for that I was grateful.

My dad wouldn't know a tender emotion if it bit him in the ass. He stepped through the doorway and gave me a brief nod, then moved to stand by Andy's wheelchair, looking like being reunited with formerly catatonic sons was an everyday occurrence for him. I wondered if anyone would notice if I just slipped out the door.

"How are you feeling, son?" my dad asked.

"Much better," Andy said. He tried to withdraw his hand from my mother's grasp, but she didn't let go.

"We're so grateful to have you back," my mom said, her voice quavering. "And now you can tell us what *really* happened on the night you were shot."

Andy and I shared a look. Now as you might have gathered, there's no love lost between me and my mom, but even *I* had a hard time believing she could be this callous. My mouth went on autopilot.

"You haven't talked to the real Andy in ten years, he's been catatonic for weeks, and the first thing you say to him is how grateful you are that he can tell you R—" I stopped myself before Raphael's name left my lips. Demons adopt their hosts' names when they walk the Mortal Plain, and they rarely divulged their own names. In all likelihood, my parents didn't know the name of the demon who had possessed Andy, and we were all better off if it stayed that way. "Raphael" might not be his True Name, but there were probably others who knew that was the king's brother's name.

I cleared my throat, trying to disguise the slip as a cough. "Hoping he can tell you his demon isn't the bastard everyone else has said?"

My mother's back stiffened, and my dad glared at me.

"Morgan," he said, "if you don't have anything nice to say, then I'd suggest you not say anything at all."

What was I, five? My hackles rose even higher. "I might say the same of the two of you! Are you even marginally happy to see Andy restored, or is that god-damn demon the only thing you care about?"

My dad's glare became even more icy. "Watch your language."

Unbelievable! I'd always thought of Andy as their favored son. I'd known it was because he'd agreed to host a demon, but I didn't realize until this moment how little regard they actually had for him as a real person.

"Let's not argue, okay?" Andy said weakly. "I don't have the strength for it."

I immediately felt like shit. Yeah, I thought my mom was a callous bitch, but surely I had enough self-control to keep my opinion to myself for a few minutes while he and my parents got reacquainted.

"Sorry," I mumbled. I was apologizing to Andy, but my parents seemed to think the apology encompassed them as well, and I saw no reason to disillusion them. My dad turned away without a word, and my mom had never looked my way in the first place.

"Of course we're very glad to see you recovered," my mom assured Andy. "I can't imagine what these last few weeks must have been like for you." She sniffled daintily, and Andy forced another smile.

"It's been rough," he admitted, "but that's over."

My mom finally let go of his hand and pulled up a chair, my dad standing behind her like some kind of bodyguard. Surely he was feeling *something*—other than his distaste for me, that is—but you wouldn't know it by looking at him. He's one of those super-uptight men who thinks showing emotion is girly. I doubt a tear had dared leak from his eye since well before puberty.

Leaning forward slightly in her chair with her earnestness, my mom asked, "So tell us what happened."

Once again, Andy and I shared a look, but this time I managed to bite my tongue and let him talk. He shook his head and met my mother's gaze.

"I'm really sorry, Mom, but I'm afraid you already know the truth. My demon went rogue, and there was nothing I could do to stop him." He shuddered visibly, and my mom sat back in her chair looking dumbstruck.

"How can that be?" she whispered, eyes wide and incredulous.

Andy shrugged. "Not all demons are the same. I just happened to draw one of the bad ones."

My mom didn't say anything, but anyone with half a brain could see she wasn't convinced. I really don't get her. She *has* to know that there are bad demons out there. Even with the thickest, rosiest-colored glasses imaginable, she had to have seen reports of rogues (demons who commit violent crimes) and illegals (demons who possess unwilling hosts). Why was it so impossible for her to imagine Andy getting saddled with one?

"Well," my dad said with false cheer, "even if that's the case, I'm sure things will go better next time."

My jaw dropped open, and I felt like I'd been punched in the gut.

I should have known my parents would want him to host again. Hell, they'd probably wished they could summon another demon to take him over while he was catatonic. However, even though he'd signed the consent forms the first time around, he'd have to do it all over again if he wanted to host another demon.

I'd just gotten my brother back after a ten-year absence. I didn't want to lose him again!

Then an insidious thought wormed its way into my mind. If Andy was going to host another demon, why shouldn't that demon be Lugh? My heart tripped over itself. Andy had always wanted to be a hero, and I never had. It would be perfect! I'd get rid of Lugh and go back to as normal a life as I'd ever had. And Andy would get to be the hero who saved the world.

But before I got too excited about the idea, I saw the ghastly white color of my brother's skin, saw the horror in his eyes, and knew that my faint hope was already dead.

Still pale, his hands gripping the arms of the wheelchair, Andy shook his head. "There won't be a next time," he declared, his voice slightly wobbly. "Once was enough for me."

My mother put a hand to her breastbone in shock, and my dad was momentarily rendered speechless. He recovered quickly.

"That was insensitive of me," my dad said, and I swallowed a laugh. "I'm sorry, son. I didn't mean to rush you. The first thing you have to do is get your strength back. We can talk about your future later."

Once again, my brother shook his head. "We can talk about my future, but I'm telling you now, that future won't involve becoming a host again. I know you think I'm traumatized and will change my mind when I get better, but don't get your hopes up."

My dad looked like he had something else to say to that, but my mom beat him to it, leaning forward and putting her hand on Andy's shoulder.

"Of course not, dear," she said. "You know we'll support you one hundred percent, no matter what you choose to do."

I had to swallow bitter laughter. And ugly though it might be, I couldn't suppress the surge of jealousy. Of course they'd support him no matter what. It was only *me* that they left hanging out to dry if I didn't exactly what they wanted me to.

But given what I now knew about my origins, could I really blame them?

I smiled grimly to myself. You bet your ass I could. I'd been doing it all my life. Why should I stop now?

Chapter 3

The doctor on call wanted Andy to stay at the hospital at least one more night for observation. My parents were disappointed, but far be it from them to argue with the doctor. Not when he was another Spirit Society member whom they obviously respected.

I left them to get reacquainted with their real son. I would call Andy when he was out of the hospital and my parents were nowhere to be found. *Then* he and I could talk some more.

It was nearing dinnertime when I stepped out of the elevator into the hospital's lobby. My stomach was growling at me for skipping lunch, but when I considered my various options for dinner, none of them seemed terribly appealing.

All thoughts of food fled my mind when I saw Adam standing at the information desk.

Being gorgeous was something of a job requirement for a demon host, and Adam was no exception. He was a little shorter than Dominic, though his swagger always made him look like the biggest guy in the room. If Dominic was tall, dark, and handsome, Adam was tall, dark, and dangerous. No matter how much I didn't like him, I couldn't say I minded the view. Now if I could only put up a wall of bars between us and duct-tape his mouth shut, I might almost be happy to see him.

As it was, the sight of him made a hard day even worse. I scowled at him as he grinned and met me halfway to the exit. I had managed to avoid him ever since the night he shot my brother, but apparently my lucky streak was at its end.

"What are you doing here?" I growled, my hand itching for the Taser I didn't dare draw. "You sure as hell better not be following me!"

He gave me a look of mock innocence. "Who, *moi?*"

At my savage expression, Adam dropped the phony innocence and shook his head. "Actually, the fact that you're here, too, is merely a happy coincidence."

I snorted and headed for the door, not at all surprised when he fell into step beside me.

"I heard the news about your brother," he said. "I'm glad he's doing better."

"No thanks to you," I muttered, then wished I'd kept the thought to myself. This wasn't a conversation I was anxious to have with Adam. I glanced at my watch. "It's been less than an hour. You must have a damn good informant."

It figured Adam would have someone keeping an eye on Andy. If my brother had blown our cover story, Adam would have been in the worst trouble of us all.

He shrugged benignly. "It was in all our best interests to know if and when he snapped out of it, and I couldn't count on you conveniently being by his side when he did." He held the door for me like a gentleman, and protesting would have been more trouble than it was worth. I stepped out onto the sidewalk just as a bus was pulling away from the stop in a cloud of exhaust fumes, reminding me why I'd always preferred living in the suburbs.

Before I had a chance to start walking toward my apartment, Adam took hold of my arm and steered me in the opposite direction. Naturally, I tried to jerk my arm out of his grip, but he didn't let go.

"What do you think you're doing?"

"It's time for you and me to have a talk," he said, still gripping my arm.

Now I *did* reach for my Taser, though it was an awkward reach with Adam holding my right arm. He noticed what I was trying to do and rolled his eyes.

"Don't assault a police officer, love. You could get in trouble for it."

True, but I was still mighty tempted. "Let go of my arm."

To my surprise, he did. "Better?" he asked, turning to face me.

It was still rush hour, and the tide of pedestrians wasn't happy that the two of us had stopped. They walked around us, but I was aware of the dirty looks cast our way as we disrupted the flow of traffic.

I didn't answer him, but I started walking in the same direction he'd been leading me. "So, where are we going?"

"How about to my car? I believe Dom said he was cooking chicken cacciatore tonight. I'm sure there'll be enough for three."

I hated my traitorous stomach for growling the way it did, but I knew from personal experience that Dominic was a fantastic cook, and I couldn't help but be tempted. Until I thought about hanging around with Adam and Dom together. I have no problems with gay people—I have a lot of prejudices, but that isn't one of them. What I *do* have trouble with is public displays of affection, and I swear Adam loves nothing more than making me squirm. Dom's a little more modest, but not so modest that he ever refuses Adam's advances. They'd probably be all over each other the moment the door closed.

"Thanks, but no thanks," I said, hoping I wasn't blushing at the mental images that came to mind, trying to pretend that it was their making out itself that made me uncomfortable around them, rather than my own involuntary reactions to it. Because, you see, no matter how uncomfortable they made me, they were both seriously sexy guys, and seeing them together never failed to arouse me, and to create fantasies in my mind that I'd rather not acknowledge. That was the last thing I needed right now, with my hormones already bitching at me for being celibate since I'd broken up with Brian.

For once, Adam resisted the urge to tease. "It's important for us to talk. I promise Dominic and I will be on our best behavior."

I flashed him a sardonic grin. "And with you that means what? You'll keep your clothes on while you paw each other?"

He laughed. "We do have some self-control, love. I think we can avoid the temptation to make you blush for one evening, no matter how much fun it is."

I gritted my teeth against a retort. Both Adam and Brian got quite a kick out of making me blush. With Brian, it was because he found it funny that a tough broad who wears a total of seven earrings and has a tattoo on her lower back blushes like a schoolgirl at sexual innuendo. Adam just does it because he knows it pisses me off.

"Why should I trust you?" I asked instead.

"Because whatever you might think of me, I've never done anything to betray your trust."

He didn't say "unlike you," but we both knew that's what he was thinking. Admittedly, I had called the police on him and accused him of murder. But then again, he had actually murdered someone—my former best friend, Val, who'd turned out to be part of the conspiracy to kill me. With a little time and emotional distance, I had to admit to myself that he hadn't had much choice at the time. But I would never admit that to *him*.

I once again annoyed the harried pedestrians by bringing us both to a stop. I looked up into Adam's eyes and tried to decide whether I was up to dealing with him and Dom tonight.

"If I say no, will you actually let me go, or am I going to find myself in handcuffs?" I finally asked.

He didn't give me the evil grin I was expecting. "You'll have to talk to us eventually," he said. "You know that as well as I. But no, I won't drag you along by force. Not tonight, anyway."

Maybe I was being a pushover, but I believed him. And because I believed I had free will, I found myself able to agree.

"All right," I said. "I'll come with you on one condition." He raised an eyebrow and waited. "Let me enjoy Dom's cooking in peace. We can talk business *after* dinner. Deal?"

He smiled. "Deal."

Adam has more money than I can explain for a government employee. His house is huge, by Center City standards, and doesn't share walls with the houses around it. Which is a good thing, considering just what his neighbors might hear if they were too close.

The scent of garlic and peppers and Italian spices hit me as soon as I stepped through the doorway, and

I took a deep, appreciative breath. My mouth started watering immediately, and I almost forgot the distasteful price of admittance.

Dominic was in the kitchen, naturally. I saw the kitchen table was set for three, and I gave Adam a dirty look.

"You were that sure I'd come, huh?"

He grinned. "Only an idiot would pass up the chance to eat Dom's chicken cacciatore."

At the stove, Dominic chuckled. He was modest by nature, but I knew how much he appreciated the praise.

"It's almost ready," Dominic said over his shoulder. "Want to pour the wine, Adam?"

"None for me, thanks," I said, holding up my hands. I've never been able to figure out the appeal of fermented grapes.

Adam poured for himself and Dom, then pulled out a chair for me. I gave him another dirty look—I was good at those. He shrugged and took his own seat. When Dom brought the food to the table, I followed like a dog desperate for table scraps.

I should have known Adam wouldn't honor our agreement to wait until after dinner to talk shop. Unpleasant conversations never seemed to sully his appetite, unlike mine.

"I presume Andrew isn't contradicting our story, or you would be in a more agitated frame of mind," he said.

I stuffed my mouth with chicken so I didn't have to answer right away. And I took my time chewing, too. I probably should have kept right on eating. He couldn't *force* me to talk when I wasn't ready. But then, maybe I'd find talking to him easier with Dominic's cacciatore to help it go down.

"He knows how important it is to keep the truth to himself," I said when I finally swallowed.

"Good." Adam shared a look with Dominic. One of those looks that suggested they knew something I didn't.

"How much did you get to talk to him?"

I narrowed my eyes. "Why don't you come right out and ask me what you want to know instead of beating around the bush?"

He shrugged. "Okay. I was wondering how much he knows about what Raphael learned during their years together."

That thought didn't exactly bring a smile to my face. It hadn't even occurred to me to ask, but of course there were many questions we had for Raphael—questions he hadn't been willing to answer. Odds were, he'd kept Andy from learning anything he didn't want him to know—a demon could prevent its host from seeing or hearing when it wanted to. But then Raphael had expected to be in Andy until Andy died, so perhaps he'd been careless. Of course, Andy hadn't volunteered any information.

"I don't know," I admitted. "Things were kind of awkward and emotional." Especially once my parents made their appearance. "We didn't really talk much about what happened."

Adam and Dom shared another one of those looks, and I had to grit my teeth to resist the smart-ass comment I wanted to make. It was never a good idea to let Adam know when he was getting to me.

"It's occurred to me that we aren't the only ones who might suspect Andrew knows more than he should," Adam said.

The delicious chicken turned into a lump of lead in my stomach. "You think he's in danger?"

Adam shrugged. "Maybe. It's hard to know. We

have every reason to believe that we've wiped out the cell that Raphael had infiltrated. If that's the case, then there's no one who knows just what a VIP Andrew was hosting. And what that VIP might have wanted to keep secret."

My stomach cramped again. "Except Raphael."

Raphael had returned to the Demon Realm when he'd fled my brother's body, but he'd intended to find another host and return to infiltrate another cell of Dougal's revolutionary army. While Raphael was on Lugh's side, and therefore technically one of the good guys, I didn't exactly trust him. He wasn't what you'd call a nice guy, and I somehow doubted he and I shared the same moral code. He'd also made it clear that he knew more than he'd been willing to have me hear, and when Lugh refused to block me out, Raphael had clammed up.

Adam nodded. "Exactly. You might want to ask Lugh tonight what he thinks the chances are that Raphael will come after Andrew."

I didn't need to wait until night, because at that moment pain stabbed through my head, a nasty ice-pick-in-the-eye sensation that—so far—was the only way Lugh could communicate with me while I was conscious. Before I even had a chance to wince, the pain was gone.

"I'll take that as a yes," I mumbled, and Adam gave me an inquiring look. "Lugh can give me a headache when I'm awake," I explained. "He just did it, so I'm guessing that means he thinks Andy could be in danger." I frowned, realizing once again how little I, as a supposed demon expert, really knew about demons. They were incredibly secretive by nature, which is one of the reasons I've always distrusted them.

I knew demons were summoned to the Mortal Plain via a ceremony where the potential host spoke a kind of incantation. I also knew that if you learned a demon's True Name, you could summon it specifically. But I had no idea how the demons determined who would answer a generic summons, assuming it was more than just random luck of the draw.

"How would Raphael go about finding a new host?" I asked, and as I did, I also realized how thoroughly I'd tried to shut out the realities of my new life in the last several weeks. There were so many questions I should have asked before now, but in my desperate quest for denial, I'd suppressed them all. "And do you think he's already back in the Mortal Plain?"

Adam shifted uncomfortably and stared at the tabletop. "I can't answer that," he said. "Not without Lugh's permission."

I grunted in frustration. "If you want me to cooperate with you, you're going to have to give up some of your precious secrets."

He met my eyes. "I can't. Not without Lugh's permission. He's my king."

Lugh wasn't giving me any headaches at the moment, but I decided that was because he knew Adam wouldn't believe me if I said he was. But you can bet your ass I'd have a bunch of questions to ask him tonight—assuming I ever managed to fall asleep.

"Can you at least answer my second question about whether you think Raphael could be back yet?"

Adam nodded. "It's possible."

"Then how do we keep Andrew safe?"

"For tonight," Adam said, "I've put a guard on his room at the hospital. That's why I was there. Running into you was only a happy coincidence." He gave me a cheesy smile, and I snorted.

"Yeah, as evidenced by the fact that Dom made dinner for three."

The cheesy smile remained in place. "Perhaps a not-unexpected happy coincidence."

"So for tonight, he has a guard. What about tomorrow?"

"That's the big question," Adam said. "He can't just go back to his apartment, and I doubt he'd be any safer staying with your parents."

I sighed, realizing where this was going. "You want him to stay with me."

Adam shrugged. "You do have a guest room in your new digs, right?"

"It's not like I'd be much use as a bodyguard. Not against a demon, at least."

"You would be if you let Lugh take charge."

I shuddered, and every hint of appetite fled. I shoved my plate away from me, then pushed back from the table, fighting an urge to run like hell.

I had let Lugh take control of my body when I was about to be burned at the stake, but though he'd been kind enough to give me back control when everything was over, I still remembered with a shiver of panic the terrifying minutes when I was a helpless passenger in my own body. Being possessed, being helpless, had always been my worst nightmare—there was a reason I'd chosen exorcism as a profession—and though Lugh had saved my life by taking possession, it was not an experience I hoped to duplicate. Ever.

The panic continued to beat at me, and I rose to my feet. I think I would have run away if Adam hadn't grabbed hold of my arm.

"Sit down, Morgan," he said. His voice was conspicuously gentle. His ability to be gentle when he usually had such a hard edge to him always surprised me. The surprise lessened my panic, and I lowered myself back into the chair. "It was just a suggestion," he continued. "But even if you're not willing to let Lugh take control, Raphael might hesitate to attack your brother if he's staying with you."

I supposed that was true. Raphael might not realize that I wouldn't voluntarily allow Lugh to surface. Besides, while there was admittedly bad blood between the brothers, Raphael appeared to have at least a modicum of respect for his king, and he might consider Andy staying with me as a sign that he was under Lugh's protection.

"I'll see if I can arrange it," I said, wondering if Andy would even be willing to stay with me. We had established beyond a shadow of a doubt that I still loved him, but that didn't mean things were ever going to be easy between us.

The enticing scents of dinner coaxed my appetite out of hiding, and I began to eat again. Dominic smiled knowingly at me, and I gave him a light kick under the table.

"Yeah, you're the world's greatest chef," I said with my mouth full. "Don't get a big head over it." Adam chuckled, and I heard the double entendre in my words. I probably blushed, but luckily for everyone Adam let it go.

It wasn't until after I'd eaten the last crumb of Dominic's homemade tiramisu that Adam brought up the subject I'd been dreading since the moment I'd laid eyes on him. He got out the words "So are you going to talk to" before I cut him off.

"No!" I snapped. "I told Dominic no, and I'm saying the same thing to you. My mom and I are barely on speaking terms, and I'm not going to question her about whatever it was you dug up."

His face darkened. "You know how important this is."

"I don't care," I said stubbornly. "Even if I asked

her, she wouldn't tell me anything, I can guarantee that. And that's my final answer."

Adam's cheeks flushed with anger, but Dominic laid a soothing hand on his arm. "Let it go," he advised. "We'll just have to find our answers some other way."

I looked at him suspiciously. He was a hell of a lot nicer and had better people skills than Adam, but I knew from experience that he could also be a sneaky little bastard. His easy agreement suggested to me that he had something up his sleeve, but if he did, it wasn't showing in his face.

Adam's face clearly said he didn't like it, but he let the subject drop. Dominic flashed me an innocent smile, and my gut knotted with worry.

It could be that he was really on my side, that there was no hidden meaning behind his words, no hidden agenda. But I knew unease would be clawing through me for the foreseeable future as I wondered if the two of them were up to something I didn't want to know about.

All told, I suspected I should have resisted the unbearable temptation of that free, home-cooked meal.

Chapter 4

I went home with a lot to think about, but once I stepped through the door of my apartment and turned on the light, all the things I *should* have been thinking about fled my mind, and I hurried to the kitchen to check my answering machine.

The machine claimed I had two messages, and I held my breath as I hit the Play button.

"If you would like to make a call, please hang up and try again," the machine said, and I hit the Erase button with a curse, waiting for the next message. "Hello!" a mechanical voice said. "I'm trying to reach—" I cursed again and erased the non-message.

It was now officially one week since Brian had last called. I'd told myself the cute, endearing messages he'd left on my machine every day were annoying. Not that it had stopped me from listening to them, mind you. When I'd been having a particularly bad day, I'd save his messages and play them over and over.

Maybe he was taking a vacation, on a cruise ship somewhere with no access to a phone. A lump formed in my throat. I swallowed hard. It was supposed to be a *good* thing if he'd finally gotten the message I'd been trying to shove down his gullet. Too bad my heart couldn't seem to keep that in mind.

Missing the sound of his voice, the feel of his naked skin against mine, the taste of his tongue in my mouth, I went to bed. And lay there wide awake, tossing restlessly, my mind unable to shut down for the night.

My nerves felt twitchy, my skin oversensitive. Memories of cuddling up with Brian after a spectacular bout of lovemaking assaulted and aroused me. My hand slid down my belly toward my panties, but I jerked it away at the last moment. I knew it was incredibly silly, but I didn't want to have an orgasm without Brian. I'd cave eventually, the physical need too strong to deny, but for the moment, I humored the part of me that still hoped I could make things work between us. If we did somehow, miraculously get back together, our reunion would be even sweeter if I'd been starving myself the whole time we were apart.

The last thing I remembered before I finally fell asleep was raising my head and glaring at the glowing numbers on my clock that told me it was three AM. Somewhere around one, I'd gotten up and played umpteen million games of Spider Solitaire to try to quiet my mind, but it didn't seem to have worked. When I saw how late it was, I was tempted to give the night up as a lost cause, but I decided to give sleep one last shot. I should have known there was no rest for the wicked, because the minute I finally drifted off, I awakened in Lugh's imaginary living room.

I crossed my arms over my chest and glared at Lugh, who sat on his couch smiling at me, his amber eyes twinkling with humor. He'd gone with his S&M poster-boy look tonight, which he tends to do whenever I've had impure thoughts about Adam and Dominic, and was wearing something that was either a shirt cobbled together from black leather straps or a complicated bondage device I wanted no part of—despite the fact that the shirt/bondage device framed his nipples in the perfect, mouth-watering display, and the fact that my hormones couldn't help taking in the golden, almost tawny color of his skin and the ripple of muscles beneath it.

Damn, I sure was missing the healthy sex life I had enjoyed with Brian. I mean, I'd have to be *dead* not to be turned on by Lugh, but if I were getting any in real life, surely it wouldn't feel so . . . urgent.

Even though he can't control me as well as most demons control their hosts, Lugh does have full access to my thoughts and memories. He knows when I'm aroused, no matter how much I might want to hide it. Which was no doubt the source of that damn smile on his face.

I stomped over to the chair across from him. He might know how much I liked the view, but that didn't mean I had to admit it. "Why couldn't you just let me sleep?" I griped.

His laugh was low and sexy and made every cell in my body thrum. "I was under the impression you had some questions for me."

That was true, but it would have been easier to remember the questions if he weren't dressed like that. I stared down at my hands, rather than at him. My hormones calmed, though I remained hyper-aware of his presence.

"Could Raphael be back on the Mortal Plain yet?" I asked.

"Certainly. If he was trusting enough to give someone on this plain his True Name, they could have summoned him back immediately."

My gaze drifted away from my hands. "Do you think he is? Trusting enough, I mean."

An expression crossed Lugh's face that looked

suspiciously like bitterness. "No. Only *I* was naive enough to reveal my True Name to anyone. But it was a long time ago, and relations between myself and my brothers weren't so strained yet. At least, not outwardly. When they both reneged on the promise to reciprocate, I had my first inkling that all was not well between us. I'm sure Raphael has learned from my mistake. But even if he didn't reveal his True Name, rank has its privileges, and he could have made his way back by now. Especially with Dougal's help."

Until I'd met Lugh, I hadn't known anything about True Names, hadn't even known they'd existed. I *still* knew very little—only that someone who knew a demon's True Name could summon him specifically to the Mortal Plain. Questions tumbled over themselves in my brain trying to get out, but Lugh didn't wait for me to sort through them.

"Don't you think you should speak to your mother?" The look on his face told me the change of subject was deliberate—and nonnegotiable.

I was tempted to press, despite my conviction that it wouldn't do any good, but I managed to resist. "You're not going to lay a guilt trip on me, are you? Because you have to know my mom isn't going to tell me anything even if I cave and talk to her."

"I know you believe that. I don't know if it's true."

My head jerked up, and I opened my mouth to say something scathing. Lugh stopped my words with an imperious gesture.

"But I also know," he continued loudly, "that the more anyone tries to talk you into doing it, the more you're going to dig your heels in."

That effectively shut me up. He was right, of course, though I wasn't completely comfortable with the admission. It made me sound kind of childish.

"So if you didn't bring me here to persuade me to

do what you want, and you're not going to answer all the questions I have, then what are you actually up to?" I asked. I realized my eyes were roving over the exposed areas of his chest, and I once again dropped my gaze to my own hands. They were much less interesting.

"Would you believe I was just hoping we could get reacquainted?"

"No."

He laughed again, tricking me into looking up. God, he was gorgeous! His hair was unbound today, framing his face in a raven's wing halo. My skin remembered how silky that hair was to the touch. Not that we'd ever had any sexual relationship, nothing above some very aggressive flirting on his part—and some rampant desire on mine.

He cocked his head at me. "You're not dating Brian anymore. Why are you still so uncomfortable with your attraction to me?"

I tried not to squirm. "Hey, you're the one who can see into all the nooks and crannies in my mind. *You* tell *me*."

He looked terribly amused. "Would you actually listen to anything I told you?"

Of course, he knew the answer to that, too. "Is there any chance we could just stick to business?"

He leaned forward on the couch, letting his hair flow over his shoulders to drape over the skin of his chest. I pressed my thighs together and reminded myself of the unfair advantage he had in the seduction and manipulation department.

"Your emotional well-being *is* my business," he said. "You're my host, and yet I'm utterly dependent on you. It is not the most comfortable of situations for either of us. The better you cope with the reality of our relationship, the better off we'll both be."

I shook my head. "None of that means you have to keep coming on to me!"

He met my mutinous gaze. "Do you think I'd keep doing it if you weren't responding to me?"

"Since this is a dream and you control everything about it, you can make me respond whether I want to or not."

He smiled, the expression equal parts amusement and exasperation. "Keep telling yourself that, if it makes you feel better. You are, after all, the admitted queen of denial."

"And proud of it, too."

He laughed, the sound like warm black velvet gliding over my skin. Goose bumps peppered my arms, and Lugh's unique scent—a blend of musk and spice like nothing I'd ever smelled before—tickled my nose. I might deny to him that I felt any genuine attraction, but it was getting harder by the minute to deny it to myself. I closed my eyes, willing myself to wake up, to escape.

Lugh interrupted my thoughts. "As a prince among demons, I have rarely had the opportunity to walk the Mortal Plain. You are only my third host in a very long life. But I've never seen—or even heard of— someone who keeps so much of herself walled off from the outside world."

My eyes popped open. "What are you, my therapist?"

He smiled. "You, my dear, would drive a therapist to drink."

I couldn't help my reluctant laugh. He definitely had me pegged. "My parents made me see a therapist when I was a teenager. And if I didn't drive him to drink, it wasn't for lack of trying."

"I know," Lugh reminded me, and I scowled. He

gave me an apologetic shrug. "I can't help that I see inside your mind. Should I pretend I don't?"

I sighed. "No, of course not. But I'm sure you see well enough to know how uncomfortable I am with the idea."

He nodded. "I do. And I'm sorry. But I can't help it."

It seemed to me we were at an impasse, and I desperately hoped that meant he was about to let me wake up—or, better yet, drift off into dreamless slumber.

No dice.

"There is one part of your mind I can't see into," he said.

That sure as hell got my attention. "What do you mean?"

"I mean there are some memories that are so solidly walled off that I can't breach your defenses even when I try."

I instantly knew what he was talking about, but fascinating though it might be to know there was anything in my mind he couldn't read, I still latched onto what—to me—was the most important thing he'd said.

"You've been *trying* to breach my defenses?" My voice had risen and sounded shrill. I tried to take it down a notch. "And here you were apologizing for what you couldn't help seeing! For an apology to count, you have to actually mean it."

"I *do* mean it. But you can't expect a demon not to be fascinated when he finds a part of his host's mind that he can't penetrate."

"Sure I can!"

He sighed and shook his head. If I was lucky, I'd drive *him* to drink.

"So you're not at all interested in this fact yourself?"

he asked. "You aren't even mildly curious as to why I can't see into that dark corner of your mind?"

I shrugged. "I don't know that it's any great mystery. If I don't actually remember it myself, then why should you be able to see it?"

He gave me a knowing look. "Because the memory's in there. Nothing that happened to you damaged your memory itself—you've just repressed it with frightening ferocity."

I scowled at him. "I was drugged to the gills the whole time I was at the hospital! I don't think it's unusual that I wouldn't have much memory of the time."

I had just turned thirteen when I was diagnosed with encephalitis, a rare but potentially life-threatening inflammation of the brain. I'd been suffering from headaches and fever and a stiff neck, and my parents had rushed me to the hospital fearing that I had the much more common meningitis. By the time I was admitted, I was delirious, and I don't remember a thing from that time until I got out of the hospital.

I'd spent more than a week at The Healing Circle, much of the time on a ventilator, fighting for my life. My parents told me I was unconscious throughout most of it, and that when I was conscious I suffered from delusions and hallucinations. The doctors determined that I'd gotten sick from a mosquito bite. Unbelievable how much trouble such a tiny insect can cause.

Yeah, there were times when the idea that I'd lost a whole week of my life as if it never existed was freaky and strange. But most of the time it seemed easy to explain away.

Lugh looked like he was deep in thought, but of course he didn't let the conversation die a natural death.

"I don't know if I can explain it to you in a way

you'd understand," he said. "Maybe you have to be able to see as intimately into another's mind as I can for it to make sense. But believe me, whatever's going on with your memory is not normal, and it's not just because of drugs. You were drugged when Raphael tricked you into summoning me. I can feel a . . . blank spot, for lack of a better term, in your memory from where the drugs damaged it. The time you were at the hospital isn't blank, it's walled off. There's a difference." He licked his lips as if nervous. "Something happened to you in that hospital. Something your subconscious is desperate to forget."

I shivered. "If my subconscious is that desperate to forget it, then there must be a damn good reason."

"Indeed," Lugh agreed. "And the fact that whatever it is happened at The Healing Circle, a demon-run hospital, makes me extremely curious."

"That makes one of us," I growled. "I have enough problems *now* without digging up shit from the past. Just let it go."

He opened his mouth on a protest, then closed it before he actually said anything. "All right. I'll let it go for now." He smiled at me. "I should take my own advice about not causing you to dig your heels in deeper."

I sighed in relief, though I knew I hadn't heard the end of this topic. "Thanks."

He acknowledged that with a nod. "I suppose I should let you get some more peaceful sleep."

"Thanks," I said again.

"Sweet dreams." He gave me one last smoldering look before my eyes slid closed and the dream dissolved.

The next morning, I awoke in sleep-deprived grouch mode. I had an exorcism scheduled at ten-fifteen, but when I called the hospital to check on Andy, I found out he was being released at nine-thirty. He wasn't in his room when I called, but the nurse I talked to confirmed my suspicion that he was planning to go home with my parents. I decided I had to show up at the hospital before they did and use my boundless charm to convince Andy to come with me instead. I had a feeling this whole mess would make me late for the exorcism, but protecting Andy was a higher priority. I doubted the state of Pennsylvania would agree, but I'd deal with that later.

I showed up at the hospital at eight thirty-five—way too early in the morning for my tastes—and found Andy alone in his room, sitting in the wheelchair and staring off into space. He didn't notice when I stood in the doorway, so I rapped lightly on the door. He blinked as if just waking up, then turned to look at me. If he was surprised to see me, he didn't show it.

Feeling awkward, I stuffed my hands into my pants pockets and resisted the urge to scuff my feet. "How are you doing this morning, bro?"

He shrugged. "I'm going to live with Mom and Dad until I get my strength back. How would you feel in my shoes?"

I grimaced. "Like a prisoner about to be executed."

He didn't seem to have the energy to muster a laugh, but he smiled at least. "All right, I'm not quite that bad. But I'm not exactly looking forward to it."

I stepped all the way into the room and shut the door behind me. Andy raised his eyebrows at that.

I cleared my throat, leaning my back against the door to make sure there would be no interruptions. "Maybe you'd be better off staying with me until you're ready to make it on your own," I suggested.

When he started laughing, I felt a sudden, almost irresistible urge to throttle him. Heat flooded my face, a combination of anger and hurt coursing through my veins.

Andy stifled his laughter and shook his head at me. "Don't look so murderous! Can you really blame me for laughing at the image of you as nursemaid?"

I glared at him. "Hey, this is *me* we're talking about. I can blame you for the sky being blue if I want to." But secretly I had to admit, he had a point. I'm not exactly what you'd call a motherly sort.

He laughed again, but it didn't sting so much this time. "Good point. But I still think we'll get along better if we aren't living in the same house."

"Apartment," I corrected, and the hurt was back even though I knew he was right. "But we'll also get along better if Raphael doesn't kill you."

I saw my shot hit home and wished I'd presented my argument more tactfully. Andy's hands clenched into fists, and his face—already pale from too many weeks in the hospital—went white.

Mentally giving myself a swift kick in the ass, I moved farther into the room and sat on one of the visitors' chairs, pulling it around so I could face my brother.

"Do you know anything he might want to kill you for?" I asked.

"No," he answered, too quickly. "He kept me shut off from the outside world much of the time, when he was hiding something or we . . . disagreed." He shivered. "It wasn't anything like what I was expecting."

My heart ached for him. Yeah, he'd been a volunteer, and technically it was his own fault that he'd been miserable, but he'd only been twenty-one when he'd invited Raphael into this world and into his body. That's awfully young to make a decision that in theory would be irreversible for the rest of your life. He had known the risks, but *knowing* the risks and *understanding* them were two different things.

I'm not the touchy-feely sort, but I reached out and clasped Andy's hand anyway. His fingers wrapped tightly around mine, as though he were hanging on for dear life.

"I'm sorry," I said, feeling completely inadequate. Surely there should be *something* I could say to lessen his pain, to chase that haunted expression from his eyes. But there was nothing.

A perfunctory knock on the door interrupted the silence. Neither one of us said anything, but the door swung open anyway, and a distinguished-looking man about fifty years old walked in.

"Am I interrupting?" he asked, looking back and forth between me and Andy. He wore a traditional white lab coat, and I could see from the ID badge clipped to his lapel that this was Dr. Frederick Neely. I had never met him before, but I knew he was one of the doctors who had been treating Andy. Reluctantly, I let go of Andy's hand.

"Would it matter if you were?" Andy asked.

The doctor laughed, and I gave my brother a sidelong glance. That sounded like something *I* would say. Andy was usually polite to a fault.

Correction—the Andy I'd known ten years ago had been polite to a fault. Even ten years of *normal* life would have changed him. Ten years with Raphael might have warped him beyond recognition. Only time would tell.

"I just need to give you a final checkup before discharging you," Dr. Neely said. He looked at me pointedly. "If you would excuse us please, Morgan."

I blinked in surprise. I'd never seen this guy before, so how did he know who I was? "Have we met?" I asked, though I knew the answer.

Dr. Neely shook his head. "No, but the nurses told me you were here." He reached out his hand. "I'm Dr. Neely," he said, putting on a charming smile.

I shook his hand. We had a brief who-can-squeeze-harder contest, but since The Healing Circle was crawling with demons, I decided I'd better give up before I learned the hard way that Dr. Neely was one of them. He didn't quite have the physique of your stereotypical host, but he was close enough to make me cautious. There was a glint of amusement in his eyes that told me he knew *exactly* what I was thinking, and I decided on the spot that I didn't like him one bit. Andy's body language showed me he shared my opinion.

"Pleased to meet you," I said, my voice oozing insincerity.

"Likewise," Dr. Neely answered. He sounded more sincere than I did, but not by much. "Now, if you wouldn't mind excusing us?"

"Never mind," Andy said. "I'm ready to get out of here. Morgan's here to take me home."

Dr. Neely raised an eyebrow at that. No doubt he knew Andy was supposed to go home with our parents, but he didn't comment. "Just as soon as I've had a chance to examine you."

But Andy shook his head. "No. Now. I've been in this place long enough."

Dr. Neely looked stern. "I'm afraid I can't discharge you without examining you first."

"I don't need your permission to leave." Andy gave me a significant look, and I took the hint. I took hold of the handles of his wheelchair as he released the brake.

Dr. Neely frowned. "This is medically inadvisable," he said, blocking the doorway.

Andy didn't answer, and I started pushing him

toward the door. I'd have been happy to run over Dr. Neely if necessary. I wasn't sure what I was going to do if he called the nurses and orderlies to stop me, but I'd cross that bridge only if I had to. He had no legal right to keep Andy here against his will.

Dr. Neely held his ground until we were almost on top of him, then took a quick step to the side. I bent close to Andy's ear as I pushed him down the hall.

"We're leaving without your personal effects," I pointed out.

"I don't care," he said tightly. "Just get me the hell out of here."

I was happy to oblige.

Chapter 5

By the time I got Andy properly installed in my spare bedroom, I wasn't only late for the exorcism, I'd missed it entirely. I'd called the courthouse to let them know that a family emergency had come up. The judge kindly refrained from slapping me with a contempt of court charge, but she assured me I'd used up my one and only get-out-of-jail-free card. I was very polite and professional—don't laugh!—and rescheduled for mid-afternoon.

My parents weren't so easy to defuse. They were furious with me for taking Andy away from them—I think they were hoping that they could brainwash him into hosting again if they got to spend lots of "quality time" with him. My mom demanded I allow her to speak with him, but he communicated to me with a shake of the head that he didn't want to. I told her he was sleeping.

After the phone call from hell, I made lunch for Andy and me. I'm not much of a cook, so this elegant lunch consisted of peanut butter and jelly sandwiches washed down with skim milk, but Andy didn't complain, and I figured PB&J counted as comfort food. Something we both needed.

Afterward, I helped Andy drag himself to the living room couch. I should have set out for the courthouse, but instead I sat beside him on the couch. He looked at me warily, and I cleared my throat.

"I was wondering," I started, then almost talked myself out of the question. But the fact was that Lugh's comments last night continued to ricochet across my brain and I wouldn't rest easy unless I asked. Of course, I wasn't likely to rest easy even if I did.

Andy raised his eyebrows, but otherwise waited patiently for me to continue.

"You remember when I was thirteen, and I spent a week at The Healing Circle?" I asked. Andy was three years older than me, so I figured there was a chance he might know something I didn't.

"Yeah," he said cautiously. His caution immediately triggered my suspicious nature.

"Did anything . . . weird happen while I was there?"

He frowned at me. "You mean other than you almost dying?"

Don't ask me why, but something about the look in his eyes or the expression on his face made me think he knew exactly what I was talking about. My first impulse was to go into overdrive and demand he tell me whatever it was he knew. But though I'd always thought of Andy as a strong, tough guy, the man sitting in my apartment was not the big brother I'd once known. There was something distinctly fragile about him, and it wasn't just his gaunt frame. I did my best to rein myself in and be gentle.

"I mean I don't remember a thing about my stay," I said, and I think I managed not to sound impatient. "Lugh says there's something hinky about that. He says that he can't access those memories, and that it has nothing to do with me having been drugged to the gills."

Andy shrugged and shifted uncomfortably on the sofa. "Every time I saw you, you were too out of it to even recognize me," he said, his gaze fixed on the floor. "I don't think it's surprising that you don't remember."

I narrowed my eyes at him, but since he was so fascinated with my exciting beige carpet, he didn't notice. "*Lugh* thinks it's surprising."

Another shrug, and still he didn't look at me. "Maybe it is. Or maybe he's got some hidden agenda." He finally raised his eyes to mine. "Once upon a time, I trusted the demons. Now I know better."

The haunted look in his eyes made me long for the opportunity to beat the crap out of Raphael.

"What did he do to you, Andy?" I found myself asking, though I wasn't sure I wanted to know. "He seemed pretty convinced he was one of the good guys."

Andy laughed bitterly. "Yeah, right." He shook his head. "He knows exactly what he is, and he doesn't give a damn. Never make the mistake of trusting him, even when he seems to be on the same side."

"Do you have to talk in riddles? Can't you just tell me what the hell happened?"

Andy shook his head again, and his chin took on a stubborn set with which I was intimately familiar. "I don't want to talk about it."

It took a lot of tongue-biting, but I managed to let the subject drop, reminding myself that he'd been through ten years of hell and maybe he needed me to give him a break for the time being. Besides, I'd told Lugh I didn't want to know if anything fishy took place while I was at the hospital.

Too bad just knowing that my memory was fucked

up in a way even a demon couldn't understand made me too uneasy to let the questions go.

I managed to be late to the rescheduled exorcism, which didn't exactly endear me to the judge. I held my breath, fearing I was about to be fined to within an inch of my life, but she let it slide. It was my lucky day.

The exorcism went smoothly, my power easily forcing the demon out of its unwilling human host. And to top it off, the host was one of the lucky twenty percent whose mind remained intact after the exorcism. Traumatized as all hell, probably needing some serious therapy, but alive and sane. I wished I didn't know the truth about demons, wished I didn't know that exorcism didn't actually kill them, just sent them back to the Demon Realm. It meant the son of a bitch who'd possessed this poor guy could come back to the Mortal Plain for fresh meat anytime he felt like it.

One of the many unpalatable truths I'd learned from Lugh was that, while possessing a human host against his or her will was most definitely illegal in our world, it wasn't in the Demon Realm. That was the status quo Lugh had vowed to change when he'd ascended to the throne, and it was the reason Dougal and his supporters had staged their palace coup. I might not feel like much of a hero, but I truly believed that in helping Lugh, I served a worthy cause. Of course, I was also in it for self-preservation, seeing as Lugh's enemies wanted him dead.

I made a couple of stops on my way home, to pick up Andy's things from the hospital, and to stop by his apartment to pack up some clothes and other essentials. I rushed through everything, feeling edgy even as I told myself Raphael couldn't have found Andy this fast, even if he *was* on the Mortal Plain.

When I let myself into my apartment, I was not what you'd call pleased to discover that, while I was right and Raphael hadn't killed my brother while I was gone, Andy did have a visitor.

I let the door slam closed behind me, tossing my keys onto a side table and counting backward slowly from a hundred. I took another look at Adam and decided to start at a thousand instead.

"What are you doing here?" I asked, ever the gracious hostess. Habit and longing made me glance quickly at the answering machine, my baser nature hoping Brian had called no matter how much I told myself I didn't want him to. But there were no messages.

Adam had made himself at home, settling into the couch, helping himself to one of my bottles of expensive birch beer, and propping his feet on my coffee table. Andy, tension radiating from his every pore, sat on the love seat with his arms crossed over his chest and his gaze fixed on the carpet.

At least Adam hadn't shot him again, I thought sourly as I once again fantasized about Tasering the hell out of Adam. He liked pain, but he felt it was far better to give than receive, and I was sure he wouldn't enjoy the Taser. Certainly he hadn't seemed to the last time I'd used it on him.

Adam swung his feet off the coffee table and sat up straight, but he drained the remains of the birch beer before answering. He sighed in satisfaction as he put the empty bottle down. "Almost as good as a *real* beer."

I started counting backward again, this time from a million. I figured I could go all the way down to zero without feeling much less irritated.

"Unless you'd like me to practice some innovative uses for empty bottles," I growled, "you'd better tell me what the fuck you're doing in my apartment." I gave Andy a dirty look, wondering why he'd let Adam in.

Andy held his hands up in surrender. "I didn't open the door," he said. "Your *friend* got a key from the super."

Adam's eyes gleamed, and he ignored the interplay between me and my brother. "Just what kind of innovative uses do you have in mind?"

Naturally, I blushed like a little girl. "Cracking it on your head seems like a good idea."

He exaggerated a frown. "And here I thought you were creative."

"Adam . . ."

"Come sit down," he said, patting the couch beside him.

I figured I had two options. I could Taser him and drag him out into the hall, or I could sit and listen to whatever he had to say. I'd prefer the Taser option, but since he'd gotten into the apartment once without my help, I supposed he'd be able to do it again, so all I'd accomplish was to piss him off.

I took a seat next to Andy, who still showed no inclination to acknowledge Adam's presence. I put my hand on his shoulder.

"You all right, bro?" I asked softly.

He nodded, but didn't answer. I couldn't blame him for being reticent around the man who'd shot him. Of course, I also knew the level of brutality Adam was capable of. If he suspected Andy knew things he wasn't telling . . .

I gave Adam my best marrow-freezing glare. "If you ever hurt my brother again . . ."

He gave me another one of those faux-innocent looks in return. "I can't imagine what you're talking about."

I gritted my teeth. "Like hell you can't! Now tell

me what you're doing in my apartment before I get impatient with you."

He snickered. "I don't have a time machine."

"You're in *my* place—I'm the only one who gets to be a smart-ass here."

His expression told me he was sorely tempted to continue the comedy routine, but he managed to control himself. "I have news for you."

The way my life was going, I subscribed to the "no news is good news" theory, but I was running out of excuses to bury my head in the sand. Tension thrumming through my body, I sat up straighter and waited for him to continue.

"This may have nothing to do with us, or with Lugh," Adam said, "but we've had a rather . . . strange case come up."

"By 'we,' do you mean Special Forces?" I asked.

He nodded. "This isn't anything we're sharing with the general public, so I hope you'll be circumspect and keep it to yourself." He waited for me to nod my agreement before he continued. "A brandnew demon host was found in an alley late last night. The ceremony to invite his demon in was only two days ago, but he was found catatonic, very obviously no longer possessed."

I shivered in a nonexistent chill. "What happened to him?"

"Good question. I interviewed his family to see if there was anything unusual about his situation. I found out the Grand Poobah of their chapter of the Spirit Society had instructed the host to invite a specific demon, using his True Name."

By "Grand Poobah," I assumed Adam meant the Regional Director, a man by the name of Bradley Cooper. A close personal friend of my mom and dad, and one of the slimiest bastards I'd ever met who wasn't a politician or a lawyer. But for all that I couldn't stand the guy, I'd never heard of him taking that kind of a personal interest in one particular member of the Society. Nor had I ever heard of him wanting to summon a particular demon by name.

"You think it's Raphael," Andy said in a voice barely louder than a whisper. "You think he's come back and abandoned his host so no one will know who he's in."

Adam shrugged. "The thought has occurred to me."

"Lugh didn't think Raphael would trust his buddies enough to tell them his True Name," I said.

Adam frowned at me. "Lugh must know it, and if *he* knows it, then I can't imagine Dougal doesn't."

I cocked my head curiously. "Why *must* Lugh know it?" I asked, racking my brain to remember whether Lugh had out and out denied knowing, or if he'd just led me to believe he didn't.

"Because he's the king," Adam replied, as if that were all the answer I needed.

"And the king is omniscient?"

But Adam seemed to realize he was on the verge of volunteering information and gave me a tight-lipped glare. "The number of demons who have True Names is relatively small. Only the truly extraordinary—like the royal family—earn them."

"Have you?" I asked before I had time to think better of it.

He smiled. "If I had, I doubt I'd tell you. We may be working together, but you don't exactly have my best interests at heart."

"Like you have mine, you mean?" I retorted instantly.

He gave me one of his coldest looks. "As you know perfectly well, I don't give a shit about you. But I do

The Devil You Know   59

have *Lugh's* best interests at heart, and you're his host."

I really hated the hurt that stabbed through my chest at his words. It wasn't like he was telling me anything I didn't already know. And it wasn't like we'd ever been anything even resembling friends. I didn't really care if he liked me or not, but the calculated indifference stung, and it took everything I had to keep from lashing out.

"Unfortunately," Adam continued as if he hadn't just taken that nasty jab at me, "with the original host catatonic, we have no idea who's hosting Raphael now—if it really is him—and we don't know what exactly he's up to. He no longer has any reason to keep us in the dark about his plans, so you'd think he'd have contacted us as soon as he crossed to the Mortal Plain—unless he was up to something he knew Lugh wouldn't approve of."

Yeah, that sounded like Raphael, all right. "Better to ask forgiveness than permission?"

"Something like that."

I frowned. "But Raphael agrees with Lugh's stance on possessing unwilling hosts, right? So why would he come into the world in one body and then transfer to someone else?"

To my surprise, it was Andy who answered. "Because he's a demon," he said bitterly. "He might agree with that idea in theory, but if he thinks it's to his advantage to misplace his morals, he's more than happy to do so."

Adam raised an eyebrow at him. "I gather yours was not a blissful union?"

Andy just scowled at him.

"I'm sure you know perfectly well we're not all the same, just like all humans aren't," Adam said. "Don't assume we're all like Raphael."

"But you are," Andy countered. "You all believe the end justifies the means. You'd cut out the heart of your dearest friend if you saw the angle in it."

Adam had as much as admitted that to me once before, but now he shook his head. "It isn't like that." He saw my incredulous look. "It isn't!" he insisted. "Yeah, we're more pragmatic than humans, and Andrew's right, we do believe the end justifies the means. But that doesn't mean we have to plow through every obstacle in our way. There's always more than one way to reach an end. Raphael has always had a tendency to choose the easiest way and damn the consequences. Some of us try a lot harder than that."

Andy leaned forward in his seat and glared at Adam. "Oh yeah? What would your host say about you if he was ever allowed to speak?"

Adam glared right back. I was glad to see I wasn't the only one who was able to inspire that furious look on his face. "My host and I have our differences now and again just as any two human beings would. But he's never regretted hosting me."

"So you say, but we only have your word for it."

Adam's face was turning red with rage. Apparently, Andy was really hitting a sore spot. There was a time when I thought Adam didn't have much of a temper, but I knew now how terribly wrong I'd been to think that. I didn't want to stand up for him, but I was afraid if I didn't, things might get ugly.

"You can't know how Adam and his demon really get along," I said, "but you *can* know about Dominic and Saul." It occurred to me suddenly that although I knew the names of Dominic's and Andy's demons, I had never once asked Adam what his demon's name was. After all that had happened, I felt like I knew him pretty well—and yet, I didn't even know his name. I shook the thought off.

"From everything I can tell, Saul seems to have treated Dominic decently," I finished.

Andy frowned at me. "Since when do you defend demons?"

I feigned a casual shrug. "I'm not going to make a habit of it. I'm just saying that Adam's probably right and they aren't all like Raphael." What I didn't say was that there was a big part of me that was really hoping *Lugh* wasn't like his brother. You see, despite the fact that he'd possessed me against my will, I couldn't help liking Lugh. I hoped like hell my warm fuzzy feelings toward him were genuine and originated from inside of me, rather than being constructs of his manipulations. But there was no way to tell, and I would be forever aware of that.

Andy's face told me I hadn't convinced him of anything—not surprising, since I hadn't actually convinced myself, either.

When in doubt, change the subject. "So, if Raphael is back and he's in an unknown body, what do you think he's up to?"

I directed the question at Adam, but it was Andy who answered. "I thought we'd already established that. He's coming to kill me. I don't think it's a coincidence that he shows up in the Mortal Plain the day after I come back to myself."

Adam shook his head. "Not true. He came back into the Mortal Plain a couple of nights ago. It was last night that he changed bodies. If he was really coming after you, I suspect he would have done it as soon as he got here. It wouldn't have mattered to him if you were catatonic or not. He knew you could recover at any time."

"So you don't think he's here to kill Andy?" I asked.

"I wouldn't go that far. I'm just saying there might

be other possibilities. I'm going to try to interview the family members again, and I'm definitely going to have a word with Bradley Cooper. I doubt he'll tell me anything, but it's worth a shot."

I frowned. "Why wouldn't he tell you anything? You're a demon—doesn't he worship the ground you walk on?" Cooper was one of those people—like my parents—who acted shocked when anyone used the word "demon." To them, "demon" was an ethnic slur. Adam and I were possessed not by demons but by "Higher Powers." It made me want to gag. It also made me want to ask if we should start calling the Demon Realm the Higher Power Realm, but fanatics like Cooper never found my jokes funny.

Adam stood up, and I was relieved to realize that meant he was leaving. "Mr. Cooper respects me as a demon, but my profession makes my loyalty to the cause questionable in his eyes. However, I'll see what I can do. Maybe I'll get lucky and he'll tell me who he ordered Henry Jenner to summon. And why."

That line of questioning spawned a slew of other questions in my mind, but I stifled them. I doubted Adam would answer, even if he knew. Besides, if he was really about to leave, I didn't want to give him any excuse to stay.

"Meanwhile," Adam continued, "if you're unwilling to talk to your mother about who your real father might have been, maybe you'll find that Andrew can give you some more information."

Out of the corner of my eye, I saw Andy's jaw drop. I think my own heart stopped beating in shock. Adam grinned to show how much he'd enjoyed dropping that bombshell—and Andy's and my reaction to it—then let himself out.

Chapter 6

"I guess I should have followed my first instinct and Tasered the hell out of the son of a bitch," I muttered under my breath.

Andy neither laughed nor smiled. He merely sat rigidly in his chair and stared straight ahead. I couldn't tell whether he was shocked because what Adam had said had come as a complete surprise, or whether he was shocked because Adam knew. Earlier, I'd assumed Andy knew nothing about the circumstances of my birth, but now I wasn't so sure. He said Raphael had kept him from learning any deep, dark secrets, but I couldn't say I really believed him. Maybe it's just my natural, suspicious nature. Or maybe my Spidey senses were telling me something was off. Hard to tell.

I didn't want to sit next to Andy again, so I took a seat on the couch. It was still warm from Adam's body, and against my will I noticed the faint scent of spicy aftershave that lingered in the air. I really wished Adam weren't so goddamn sexy—it sure would make it easier to hate him. I watched the struggle on my brother's face and wondered what it was about.

Wondered if he would tell me. Wondered if I would believe him if he did.

He finally glanced at me, but his gaze quickly slid away. I tried not to squirm.

"So, care to comment?" I asked him when it became obvious he wasn't going to volunteer anything without prodding.

He gave me a closed, shuttered look. "No."

I ran a hand through my hair, scrubbing at my scalp as if that would make everything suddenly make sense. It didn't work. "Do you know anything about my biological father?" I blurted.

The look on his face didn't change. "Dad is your real father."

He sounded firm and sure, but if he were so sure it was true, he wouldn't be guarding his expression so carefully. What did he know? And why wasn't he telling me?

"Whatever it is you're hiding, you know you can tell me," I reminded him. "Right?"

He gave a bark of bitter laughter. "I'm not hiding anything. But if I were, I'd be happy to share it with you." His gaze pierced me, his expression filled with intensity. "Of course, I can't share anything with you without sharing it with Lugh, too."

I cursed under my breath, annoyed with myself for how easily I could forget that I was inextricably bound to my own personal demon. And yet . . . "Lugh's one of the good guys," I told my brother.

Andy looked away yet again. "Lugh has his own agenda. It won't always mesh with yours."

I couldn't disagree with his words, though I wanted to. I'd never been much good at trusting anyone, and there was a part of me that longed to let go of my constant suspicions, my constant search for ulterior motives. I wanted to trust Lugh with not just my body, but my soul. And I knew I could never do it, no matter how much I liked him, no matter how much I believed in his cause. It's hard enough for a person to really know another human being all that well. It's impossible for a human to really understand a demon.

I didn't know what else to say, so I let the subject drop.

Andy and I had settled into an uneasy silence. He turned on the TV and stared at CNN while I puttered around the apartment trying not to notice the awkwardness. I wanted nothing more than to get the hell out of there, but after Adam's disturbing report, I didn't dare leave Andy alone. Even if I sort of wanted to kill him myself for being such a pain in the ass.

It wasn't that I didn't understand his reasons for not talking to me. It's just that I have approximately zero patience. I wanted to find out what the hell he knew, and I wanted to find it out *right now*.

At around six, I ordered a pizza for dinner. Andy wasn't up to going out, and I wasn't up to cooking. At six forty-five, the security desk called to let me know the pizza guy was on his way up. I muttered under my breath about the delights of cold pizza as I rooted through my purse for cash.

I was still digging through the purse when I opened the door, scraping loose change off the bottom in my quest to cobble together a decent tip. I expected the pizza guy to wait impatiently for me to get the money out, but instead he pushed past me into the apartment.

"Hey!" I yelled indignantly, dropping the purse and the money as it occurred to me that something most definitely wasn't right.

The intruder tossed the pizza box onto the nearest table, and I prepared for battle as he turned to face me. It took me a moment to recognize him, and when I did my head spun with confusion.

"Dr. Neely?" I said, blinking at him. He'd been carrying the pizza box, and he wore a baseball cap with the pizza place's logo on it, but how anyone could have mistaken him for a pizza delivery guy was beyond me.

He doffed his cap and bowed. "At your service."

I was still a couple of steps slow, trying to figure out a) why the doctor was here, and b) why he was pretending to deliver pizza.

The TV went silent, and I glanced over at Andy, whose face had gone pale.

"Raphael," he said, and there was a tremor in his voice.

Dr. Neely smiled and performed another fancy bow. "In the flesh, as it were."

I might have been slow on the uptake at first, but now that I understood what was happening, I moved damn fast. Before Raphael had risen from his bow, I closed the distance between us and jerked my knee up, catching him squarely in the nose. He howled in pain and clutched his face, blood seeping between his fingers.

I glanced over at Andy again. "Is he one of those demons who gets off on pain?" I asked. Being incorporeal in their own world, some demons find physical sensation so fascinating that they greatly enjoy even unpleasant sensations—hence Adam's fascination with pain, both his own and others'.

Andy chuckled, and there was more life in his eyes than I could remember seeing since he'd awakened. "No."

"Oh, good," I said, then planted my fist in Raphael's gut. He made a loud "oof," then collapsed to the floor. He couldn't seem to decide whether to clutch his nose or his stomach. As he was thinking about it, I made a dash for the coat closet where I kept my Taser, arming it in record time.

I put a respectable amount of distance between myself and Raphael, assuring myself I'd have time to pull the trigger if he launched himself at me when he'd recovered. Then I waited.

Being a relatively smart guy for a son of a bitch, he remained on his knees even after he got his breath back and the bleeding in his nose stopped. In Neely's body, his eyes were an arctic blue, and before he managed to pull himself all the way together again, he gave me a look that froze my marrow. Then he pulled his usual urbane mask on and smiled ruefully at me.

"You'd think I'd have learned by now what kind of reception to expect from you," he said, sounding so amused I could almost forget the way he'd just looked at me before he'd regained control of himself.

My finger tightened on the trigger of the Taser as I remembered all the shitty things Raphael had done to me and to people I cared about. Never mind that he'd actually saved my life in the end. He and I were never going to be anything resembling friends.

"Is there any particular reason I shouldn't Taser you into a quivering mass of Jell-O?" I asked.

His smile faded and he sighed. "If that's what you want to do, I'm in no position to stop you. When you've finished torturing me, though, we need to talk."

He sounded so damn calm and rational that some of my fury faded. Yeah, I knew he was a cold-blooded bastard even if he was marginally on my side. But I figured if he were here to bulldoze his way past me to kill Andy, he'd have done it before either of us had realized who he was. I hadn't exactly been on my guard when I'd opened the door.

Idiot, I chastised myself. Suspicious as I was by nature, I hadn't been suspicious enough.

I kept my distance but lowered the Taser. Like I said, Raphael was a pretty smart guy—he didn't even try to get up, and he kept his hands open and splayed over his thighs where I could see them.

"What do you want?" I asked. "And how long have you been in Dr. Neely?"

"I took Neely last night, after I heard that Andrew had recovered."

The hand with the Taser started rising again almost like it had a will of its own. "Then that poor bastard Adam found in the alley last night really was your former host."

Raphael looked puzzled. "No. I'm not sure who you're talking about, but I can guarantee no one has found my former host in an alley."

Andy made a strangled sound in the back of his throat, and Raphael gave him a penetrating look. "No, I didn't kill him, if that's why you look like you swallowed a live frog."

Andy managed to look scared and skeptical at the same time. "So there's someone out there who knowingly summoned you to the Mortal Plain, knowingly transferred you into an illegal host, and has lived to tell the story?"

Raphael's ice blue eyes fixed on Andy in a chilling stare. "He won't be telling anyone anything, but not because I did him any harm. Amazingly enough, it's possible for someone to host me for a couple of days without hating me."

Andy's lip curled in a sneer. "Or becoming an animated turnip?"

For someone as scared of Raphael as Andy seemed to be, he had quite an attitude, but I had the feeling I'd stepped into the middle of a long-standing feud. I fig-

ured it would do no one any good if I let the hostilities
escalate, so I interrupted before Raphael could retort.

"All right," I said, "so the vegetable Adam told me
about wasn't your former host, and you hate each
other's guts. Why don't you tell me what the hell
you're doing here? Or is that a deep, dark secret?
Because if you're here just to pick fights with my
brother, I'm going to pump you full of electricity and
let him work out some of his hostilities on you." I
pointed the Taser for emphasis.

Raphael gave me an unfriendly look. "You really
are a cast-iron bitch, you know?"

"Your point being?"

That drew what sounded like a reluctant laugh. He
shook his head and quickly sobered. "When I returned
to the Demon Realm, I told Dougal that you were no
longer hosting Lugh. I told him you'd managed to
ditch him into a different host, one whose face I never
saw."

"Oh, thanks a lot!" I said, appalled. "Now I'll
have every demon in existence after me."

He shrugged. "I had to tell him *something*. He was
mad enough at me already for not just letting his people summon Lugh into the sacrificial host. If I'd refused to tell him who I'd chosen to host him, I
wouldn't have been in any position to help you right
now." I supposed he had a point, but I still didn't like
it. "Dougal's sent me back to the Mortal Plain with a
twofold mission—to find out from you who's now
hosting Lugh and to eliminate Andrew, who by all
rights should have been dead the night I left the
Mortal Plain."

My Taser hand sprang back to the ready, but
Raphael showed no sign he was about to attack.

"Don't worry. I'm not going to do it. You may find
this hard to believe, but I do respect Lugh, even if he

and I will never be the poster children for brotherly love. If you would let him surface, I know he'd command me not to kill your brother, and I would respect that command."

I snorted. "Yeah, like you respected his command to tell him what the hell you know about Dougal's activities?"

He shrugged. "I have my reasons for that." He turned his head to look at Andy. "Besides, Andrew knows me well," he said with what I could only describe as an evil smile. "I'm sure he has some idea what the consequences would be if he said something inadvisable."

Of course, Raphael had been living in my brother for ten years before he'd fled back to the Demon Realm, which meant *he* should have known *me* pretty well by now, too. While he was giving Andy the evil eye, my finger tightened on the Taser.

I didn't consciously decide to shoot him, but somehow the pressure on the trigger became just enough. The Taser popped, and the probes rocketed across the room and buried themselves in Raphael's back. He screamed and collapsed, his muscles quivering helplessly. I worked hard to resist the urge to go beat on him some more while he was down.

Over the distance between us, Andy's and my eyes met, and he smiled faintly. "Remind me never to get on your bad side."

"Too late," I quipped back, ejecting the Taser cartridge and reloading while I waited for Raphael to pick himself up and dust himself off. It would take a while. Demons take Taser shots even harder than humans do. "That was a gentle warning," I told Raphael, who glared at me as he lay twitching on the floor. "Not only are you forbidden to hurt my brother, you're forbidden to threaten him."

He bared his teeth at me like a dog. He was either growling at me or gritting his teeth in pain. I hoped it was the latter.

We all waited in silence until Raphael regained control of Dr. Neely's body. "That was unnecessary," he said when he had the breath to spare.

"Maybe. But it was fun."

He shook his head at me and sat up. "You're supposed to be pleased I'm not here to kill Andrew. Instead, you shoot me."

"Am I supposed to feel sorry for you?"

He sighed. "I suppose not. Do you want to hear what else I have to say, or would you rather punish me some more?"

I couldn't claim to be real anxious to hear anything else he might have to tell me, but I figured it wasn't something I could avoid. "Why don't you just shoot me an e-mail?" I grumbled, but he knew I was caving.

"It wasn't me who left an empty host behind for your buddy to find."

"Adam is *not* my buddy," I retorted, though I knew how unimportant the distinction was.

Raphael gave me a knowing look. "Whatever. It wasn't me."

"I heard you the first time." Then I noticed the concerned look in his eyes, and I frowned. "Are you telling me you know who it is?"

"I have a suspicion."

That worried the hell out of me. "Who is it?"

He smiled condescendingly. "No one you know."

"Do you want me to shoot you again to loosen up your tongue?"

The smile faded. "You and Lugh make a great couple. I saved your life, remember?"

I couldn't help laughing. "You don't get credit for saving my life when you're the one who put it in danger in the first place, asshole. And you tortured my boyfriend, and God only knows what you did to Andy in the ten years you were with him. I don't owe you a goddamn thing."

It didn't look like he appreciated that at all. He scowled at me, then rose to his feet despite the fact that I'd rearmed the Taser.

"Fine," he snarled, moving toward the door. "Maybe I don't owe *you* a goddamn thing, either. You're more trouble than you're worth."

"Tell me who just entered the Mortal Plain!" I demanded, but Raphael kept moving toward the door.

"Fuck you," he said, and jerked the door open.

My finger twitched on the trigger, but I stopped myself from shooting him again. Yeah, it might get him to hang around, but somehow I didn't think it would inspire him to talk.

"I'm sorry," I said, belatedly realizing I should have kept a muzzle on my temper.

In case I didn't get the message the first time, he gave me the finger. And he slammed the door behind him when he left.

Chapter 7

I had a hell of a hard time falling asleep that night. Too much on my mind, I guess. Too many secrets hovering outside my grasp, too much turmoil in my heart, too much fear for my future. And not enough trust to fill a thimble. Andy was lying to me. Raphael was only marginally one of the good guys. Adam tolerated me only for Lugh's sake. Lugh—nice as he was, for the most part—would do whatever was necessary to further his cause, no matter what happened to me or those I cared about in the process. And it had been over a week since Brian had made his last overture. It looked like he had finally given up on me.

Which was exactly what I wanted, I told myself as I flopped around in my bed and punched the pillow. He had suffered enough on my account, and I hadn't been good for him even before I'd acquired Lugh.

My chest tightened as a wave of loneliness crashed over me. I'd known almost since the first time I'd met him that I was in love with Brian. I'd known it would hurt like hell to let him go. But no amount of knowing could have prepared me for the desolation I felt now as I realized I might well have gotten my wish.

Eventually, sleep dragged me down, but I wasn't at all surprised when I found myself in Lugh's living room. I almost wished I could communicate with him while I was awake, just so I could get a good night's sleep. But if I could communicate while awake, it would mean he was gaining more control, and that wasn't something I allowed myself to wish for.

He was wearing the S&M getup with the black leather straps again. My hormones hummed their approval, and it felt like every cell in my body was straining to cross the distance between us.

"You lied to me," I accused, hoping an argument would keep my cravings under control.

He looked surprised. "About what?" And then he must have gleaned the source of my annoyance from my mind. "Adam was wrong. I don't know my brothers' True Names." He grimaced. "I thought by not forcing them to reveal their True Names when I took the throne, I might mend some fences."

"Huh?"

He gave me one of those penetrating looks of his, then decided to let me in on another closely held secret. "True Names are granted by the king. As Adam said, it's a rare 'honor' "—I could hear the quotes he put around the word—"granted only to the extraordinary." He shook his head. "The hidden meaning behind the honor is that you're powerful enough to be a potential threat to the king. So he grants you a True Name, which really is considered an honor—but it also allows the king to summon you from anywhere in the Demon Realm at a moment's notice. A collar and leash, as it were. That it allows us to be summoned to the Mortal Plain as well is merely a side effect."

It sure would have made our lives easier if Lugh had put that collar and leash on his brothers.

"As king," Lugh continued, "I should know the

True Names of all my subjects who have them. Most gave them voluntarily as soon as I took the throne. When my brothers refused, I could have used my power to force them to tell me, but I didn't. Which probably cemented Dougal's opinion that I was too soft to lead the Demon Realm."

His image started to go fuzzy around the edges, like it did when I was starting to wake up from one of these dreams.

"Don't wake up yet," he urged, then blinked out of existence. I thought I was going to wake up despite his urging, but then some sixth sense told me where he was, only a fraction of a second before the warmth of his breath tickled the back of my neck. "I haven't finished with you."

His hands came to rest on my shoulders, his grip firm enough that with only the tiniest bit more pressure, he'd leave bruises. I tensed, but something in my center tightened in anticipation. The room solidified around me as his touch pulled me back down into sleep. His hands slid down my arms until they cuffed my wrists, and then he pressed his chest up against my back.

My throat went dry as I realized that somewhere along the line he'd lost his decorative leather straps— and I'd lost my shirt.

His skin was warm and smooth against mine, and the silky locks of his hair draped over my shoulder when he planted a soft kiss on the side of my neck.

"What are you doing?" I gasped, but though my mind urged me to pull away, I found myself holding very still, my heartbeat ratcheting up as my breath came suddenly short.

His chuckle tickled my ear. "I don't think it's terribly mysterious." He emphasized his point with a little bump-and-grind action that let me feel the entire length and breadth of him. It seemed he'd lost his pants now, too.

I clenched my thighs together against the surge of my desire. I'd been attracted to Lugh since the first moment I'd laid eyes on him, but I didn't dare let myself act on that attraction. *Not* because I was saving myself for Brian, I mentally insisted.

"Relax, Morgan," Lugh whispered in my ear. "I'm not going to make love to you. I know you're not ready for that yet."

I tried to muster a protest at his use of the word "yet," but my tongue appeared to be glued to the roof of my mouth, and I had too many brain cells focused on the pulsing heat at the small of my back to unstick it.

He rubbed his chin over the top of my head. I don't think it was an accident that the motion caused his hair to sweep over my breasts, teasing my nipples into pebbles.

"But you're desperately in need of some stress relief," he continued. "I can give you the release you crave without making love to you."

Once again, I opened my mouth to argue. And once again, not a sound came out. Lugh's arms swept around my waist, holding me even more tightly against him.

Suddenly, we weren't alone anymore. A sound finally escaped my throat, but it wasn't the protest I'd been planning; it was a low, urgent moan.

Adam, bare-chested and wearing nothing more than a pair of shrink-wrap-tight jeans faded to white in some interesting places, flashed me one of his feral smiles as Dominic molded himself against his back. Already, Adam's impressive erection strained against the confines of those tight jeans, threatening to burst through the thin fabric, but he visibly swelled even more as Dom's hands slid down his chest, tweaking his nipples on the way.

"Stop it," I managed to gasp, but I was swimming in arousal and suspected I would expire of frustration if Lugh really did stop the illusion.

I'd both seen and heard Adam and Dom having sex before. The time I'd heard them going at it in an adjoining room had been one of the most erotic forbidden thrills of my life, though I still hated to admit it to myself. The time I'd *seen* them had been entirely different. They hadn't been willing, though Adam had managed to muster just enough enthusiasm to get the job done. Adam's fury and Dominic's humiliation had robbed the scene of all erotic potential for me, but I had a feeling Lugh was about to create a visual that would linger in uncomfortable fantasies long after this night was over.

One of Dom's hands continued to play with Adam's nipple, while the other smoothed over the bulge in Adam's pants. Adam moaned in appreciation, his head falling back against his lover's shoulder. Dominic gave me a saucy wink—which he never would have done in real life, being far less comfortable with public displays of affection than Adam.

"Don't do this," I begged Lugh, but we both knew how my body thrummed in anticipation.

"Just a dream," he murmured in my ear as Dominic slid Adam's zipper down.

Moisture trickled down the inside of my thigh when Adam's enormous erection sprang free. My body clenched as I wondered what a cock of that size would feel like inside me, stretching me to my limits. Lugh's tongue flicked out and tasted the shell of my ear, and I fought against a cry of pleasure.

"You're allowed to enjoy this," he whispered.

At that point, I didn't have much choice.

Dominic wrapped one hand around Adam's cock, stroking him from base to tip, milking out a shiny drop of pre-cum. My mouth watered at the sight, and once again Dominic gave me a very un-Dominic-like smile, a devilish glint in his eye as he brushed his middle finger over the head of Adam's cock. I watched in spellbound fascination as Dominic brought that finger to his mouth and sucked it.

I knew what he was going to do then, and while a part of me still frantically fought my arousal, I was helpless against it. Lugh held me tight, his own erection a constant heat at my back, as Dominic positioned Adam for optimum viewing convenience then dropped to his knees.

I shook my head, but couldn't muster any more strenuous protest as Dominic cupped Adam's magnificent ass and then enveloped him in his mouth. Adam and I moaned in sync as Dom began to suck, his cheeks hollowing with each forceful pull. I licked my lips, and I could almost taste him in my mouth.

No. It wasn't *Adam's* taste that burst over my tongue. It was *Brian's*. The sensory memory overwhelmed me, and when I drew in a breath and let it out on a moan, I could have sworn I smelled Brian's unique scent all around me. Watching Adam and Dom was almost unbearably exciting, but it was Brian I ached for, Brian I longed to have filling me.

Urged on by the grip of Dom's hand on his ass, Adam began to thrust into Dom's mouth. Dom showed every sign of loving it, his face awash with pleasure. I imagined Brian plunging into me as I watched them, and I almost came just from the mental image.

Lugh took my hand and guided it to the juncture of my thighs. I was still wearing a pair of jeans and some underwear, but the button and zipper were open. I fought against Lugh's urging for about half a second, then couldn't stand the arousal anymore. I didn't want to give in, didn't want to let Lugh win this mini battle of wills, but the stimulation was just too much. I felt like I had to come or I would break into tiny little pieces, never to be put together again.

Dominic was oblivious to me now, sucking Adam's cock like his life depended on it. I slipped my hand into my panties and stroked myself in time to Adam's thrusts.

Within the first few strokes, I erupted like Mount Vesuvius. I heard a howl start to rise from Adam's throat as my vision flashed white with pleasure. The howl was cut off abruptly, and my eyes popped open to stare up at the ceiling of my darkened bedroom. The tail end of the orgasm rippled through me as I realized I was awake and one hand was between my legs.

Muscles quivering in the aftermath of the massive release, I lay on my bed and breathed like a runner at the end of a marathon. For a long, breathless moment, I gloried in the warmth of the afterglow, knowing I was going to feel humiliated when the glow faded, and not caring. Then I noticed the phone clutched in my other hand.

The warmth fled, and I sat bolt upright and stared at the evidence.

What the fuck had Lugh been doing with my body while he distracted me with sex? I glanced at the clock beside me and confirmed it was oh dark-thirty in the morning, but I hit the Redial button anyway. The number that was backlit on the phone was an unfamiliar one. Holding my breath, I waited for an answer.

"Uh-oh," said an all-too-familiar voice on the other end of the line. "Did big brother get caught with his pants down?"

My hand tightened on the phone, and at that moment I was pretty sure I'd cheerfully kill both Lugh and Raphael if I had the chance.

Raphael laughed at my outraged silence. "Don't get your panties in a twist, as the saying goes. I have been ordered to cooperate with you."

I snorted. "Like that means anything."

"It's true, I'm not great at following orders, especially when they come from Lugh. In the Demon Realm, he could punish me for my insubordination. Here, he just has to swallow it. However, I did agree with him that it's in everyone's best interest that I finish telling you what I'd come to tell you earlier tonight. Please forgive my fit of pique, but you have to know you are a sore trial for anyone's patience."

I started to retort, but he spoke right over me.

"The demon that was summoned into the Mortal Plain and left that body in the alley is known as Der Jäger."

I'd taken enough German in high school to translate the name. "The Hunter."

"Indeed. He's an unusual creature. He has a unique ability to recognize demons in the Mortal Plain—and to hunt them. That's how he earned his True Name. He is also the demon equivalent of a sociopath. His entire life revolves around the hunt and the kill. For the past three hundred years, he's been imprisoned in the Demon Realm, but Dougal has offered him his freedom if he can find and kill Lugh.

"The good news is that since your aura overwhelms Lugh's, Der Jäger can't seem to catch his scent. Everyone's quite puzzled by the phenomenon, though I suspect they'll be even more puzzled after tonight. Der Jäger will no doubt have sensed Lugh's presence while he and I spoke, but I'm certain he won't have been able to home in on it in so short a time."

"How do you know he hasn't been able to catch Lugh's scent?" I asked.

"Because I'm one of the bad guys, remember? That's the whole reason I went back to the Demon Realm in the first place, to infiltrate another cell. I'll feed you what information I can, but I'm also going to keep my cover."

I heard the warning in his words and instantly bristled. "I told you before, if you ever hurt Andy again—"

"Good night, Morgan. Sweet dreams."

He hung up on me, and it took every ounce of my self-restraint not to throw the phone across the room in frustration.

I wasn't surprised when I woke up at around ten in the morning, groggy and bleary-eyed, after several hours of uninterrupted sleep. Funny how Lugh hadn't felt like speaking to me after my little chat with Raphael. I'd been more than ready to give Lugh a piece of my mind for driving my body while I was asleep, but apparently he wasn't overly eager to hear what I had to say about it.

I was left at something of a loss as to what to do with myself. Obviously, I couldn't leave Andy alone and undefended, but I wasn't going to learn much hanging around the apartment babysitting him. In the light of early morning—after getting a few hours of much-needed sleep—it was clear to me that ignoring my problems wasn't going to make them go away. My mental vacation was well and truly over, and it was time to start getting some answers.

The only thing I could think of to do for Andy was

to call Adam to come keep an eye on him. Andy really hated the idea, and who could blame him? But we both knew I couldn't just sit around the apartment and hope everything went away.

I think my face was beet red the entire time I was in the apartment with Adam—which, considering my inability to block out the dream images Lugh had implanted in my mind, and my extreme discomfort with those images, was all of about five minutes. He gave me a curious look, but otherwise refrained from questioning me.

I had three major issues I could deal with—or *not* deal with, as the mood hit me. There was the question of my parentage. There was the question of my repressed memory. And, because I needed another nightmare in my life, there was Der Jäger.

What I wanted to do more than anything was hunt down and exorcize Der Jäger. Unfortunately, I hadn't the faintest idea how to do it. I didn't know what body he was in. And even if I did, the last thing I wanted was to draw his attention when he had no idea that I was hosting Lugh.

That left the unpalatable choices of digging into my mom's past or digging into my own. Since I knew what the first step would be to learning about my mom, and since I hadn't a clue how to find out what happened to me—if Lugh was right and it was something other than what I'd been told—I supposed I was stuck.

I showed up at my parents' house just after lunchtime, having spent the entire morning procrastinating, finding one excuse after another to avoid doing what I knew I had to. My inner chickenshit prayed that she wouldn't be home so I could put this off some more, but she came to the door before I had a chance to get my hopes up.

Her eyes widened in surprise to see me, her plucked-to-within-an-inch-of-their-life eyebrows arching hugely. I had to stifle a laugh, though admittedly I couldn't remember the last time I'd come here when it wasn't the mandatory Christmas or Thanksgiving dinner.

No doubt about it, there were parts of me that would have loved to disown my parents completely. Those holiday dinners were about as much fun as a yeast infection, and we'd probably all have a better time if I didn't show up. But like it or not, this was the only family I had, and I did reluctantly love them—the man who wasn't really my father, and my mother the Stepford wife.

"Are you going to invite me in, or are you going to keep catching flies?" I asked when my mom just stood there.

Her jaw snapped shut, and her lips pursed into her usual disapproving frown. "You could try giving me a hint of respect every once in a while."

I refrained from reminding her that respect had to be earned. I again had to fight against my urge to flee, but now I was getting annoyed at myself, too. All the terrible things that had happened to me recently, and I was turning into a total wuss over a *conversation*? I mentally recited the "sticks and stones" adage and forced myself to soldier on.

"I need to talk to you about something," I said. "I'll try my best to be civil, and I hope you'll do the same, but we both know we can't talk to each other without a little sniping, so let's just agree to ignore it."

She sighed dramatically, but opened the door and let me in.

My mother is the last of a dying breed, the honest-to-God fifties housewife. She'd married my dad right out of college, and hadn't worked a paying job her entire life. Her life revolved around cooking, cleaning, and being beautiful. Her children came in a distant fourth, though I knew she loved us in her own way. There wasn't an aspect of her life I didn't rebel against, which might explain why I was a single, work-obsessed, fiercely independent tomboy.

The house I grew up in is beautiful, always freshly cleaned, and decorated with impeccable taste. And it has the warm, homey atmosphere of a walk-in freezer. It was impossible to step inside and not become instantly conscious of my ungainliness as I joined my mother in the formal living room. The house has a den, too, but it's not any more relaxed than the living room. I found myself demurely crossing my legs at the ankles when I sat. Of course, as soon as I noticed I practically slapped myself on the forehead and forced myself to relax.

"Shall I make us some tea?" my mother asked.

I was proud of myself for not rolling my eyes. "Thanks, but I'll skip it." I squirmed a bit as I tried to figure out how to get started. I mean, really, how do you ask your mom about a rape she'd never even hinted she'd suffered? Not that I'd have expected Mrs. Perfection to discuss such a distasteful topic with *anyone,* much less her daughter.

Prim and proper as a headmistress, she sat on the edge of a chair, her back arrow-straight. When she did the ladylike ankle-cross, she stayed that way. "What is it we need to talk about?" she asked. "Might I hope that you've persuaded Andrew to come home?"

You can hope all you want, I thought but didn't say. See, I am capable of editing myself for content every once in a while. "He's going to stay with me for the time being. You and Dad didn't exactly make him feel welcome when you were in such a rush to have him host again."

My mother's spine lost a little of its starch, and she looked away. Of course, the push to have Andy host again wasn't the reason he was staying with me, but if I could shovel a heap of guilt onto her shoulders, I was more than happy to do so.

"We made a mistake," she admitted. That might have been a first. "We were so excited to have him back—"

"So excited to have him back you tried to get rid of him immediately?" I interrupted, my voice going up an octave or two.

She sat up even straighter. I wouldn't have thought that was possible. "We just wanted things to go back to normal. And I guess we didn't want to know that he'd been unhappy to host a Higher Power. It was what he'd always wanted, and we'd always wanted for him. We thought he was living his dream . . ."

"*Your* dream, you mean." My dad wasn't attractive or well-built enough to meet the Society's standards for a demon host, and when my mom had been young enough to volunteer, the Society had still been too sexist to consider women worthy hosts. Three cheers for progress!

Mom winced at the accusation, but didn't contradict me.

It occurred to me that I knew where I'd inherited my talent for denial. The epiphany tasted sour in my mouth, and I made what I felt sure was an ugly face. "Remind me not to nominate you for Mother of the Year."

Her cheeks reddened—whether from anger, or guilt, or a combination of the two, I couldn't tell. "If the only reason you've come is to talk about my inadequacies as a mother, then I have nothing more to say to you."

If I were there to talk about her inadequacies, she'd

die of old age before I was finished, but I refrained from voicing that opinion. "I'm here to ask you about my real father."

She jumped like she'd just stuck her finger in an outlet, and even through her perfect makeup, I could see the color drain from her face. "What are you talking about?" she gasped.

"You know perfectly well what I'm talking about. It's written all over your face."

Her face went from white to red, but, not surprisingly, she continued to stonewall. "Believe what you want, but you've known your real father from the day you were born."

Usually, my mom isn't much of a liar, which is why she's so bad at it. She sounded more confident now, but I caught on to the lie she was telling herself. "All right, then. Tell me about my *biological* father."

Realizing her tactics weren't working, she went for slamming the metaphorical door in my face. "I think it's time you leave."

I sat back on the couch and crossed my arms over my chest. "I don't think so. I think you owe me an explanation."

Her gaze frosted over. "I don't owe you anything! Certainly I have no reason to feed this ridiculous fantasy of yours."

Maybe if I shoved some more information in her face, she'd realize how pointless it was to deny the truth. "Twenty-eight years ago, you filed a rape report with the police. You never pursued it, and as far as I can tell the case died before it took its first breath, but you did a paternity test on me. And Dad is not my biological father." He wasn't much of a *real* father, either, but that was beside the point.

Her eyes glistened like she was on the verge of tears, and lines of strain were etched into her face. I almost felt sorry for her, though I carried too much anger to let the pity take charge.

"Why did you never tell me?" I asked, and was pleasantly surprised when my voice sounded gentle, rather than accusatory.

She sighed and shook her head. "What good would it have done? It was better for all of us if we just . . . pretended it never happened."

Yes, pretending was one of my mom's greatest skills. "Do you think it was better for the other women he might have raped after you?" I couldn't keep the sharp edge out of my voice, though intellectually, I knew how hard a rape charge can be for the victim, especially that long ago.

My mom's lips pressed together in a thin, hard line. "We . . . I did what was best for my own family. I don't expect you to agree. It's not like you understand the meaning of the word 'caution.' "

"But you *did* file a charge, at least initially."

"I didn't have a choice at the time. The police found me after . . ." Her hands fisted in her lap, perfect nails digging into her palms.

I forced myself to gentle my voice. "Tell me what happened."

I didn't really expect her to answer, so I was startled when she started talking.

"I used to do volunteer work at The Healing Circle when Andrew was young. One evening when I was leaving, a man dressed in scrubs accosted me in the parking deck. He forced me at gunpoint to drive him out into the suburbs. Then he . . ." She swallowed hard and wrung her hands. "He left me tied up in the backseat when he was finished, and that was how the police eventually found me. The Healing Circle said they'd had a John Doe they'd been examining in the psych ward, and that was probably the man who attacked me. But they never found him, never figured out who he was."

Yeah, and apparently Mom never made a peep after that initial report. I had a strong suspicion she knew more about this John Doe than she was telling. But there was another question I burned to ask first.

"Why on earth did you and Dad keep me under the circumstances? It's not like you ever loved me."

Damn it, I hadn't meant to say that. The last thing I wanted was to admit to my parents that they had the power to hurt me. But perhaps it wasn't such a bad thing after all, because my mom's face softened, and some of the angry tension faded from her posture.

"Of course we love you. *I* love you. You're my daughter, and no amount of fighting will change that." She offered me a smile, but I didn't smile back.

"Tell me why you kept me," I insisted, glomming on to the question that troubled me the most. "Even if you do love me in your own way, you have to sort of hate me, too. I'm a constant reminder of what happened to you. How could you look at me every day after that?"

I could see the denial on her lips. But she must have seen how pointless it was, because she gave up the fight. "It wasn't always easy," she admitted. "But I'm your mother, and that's what mothers do. They love their children unconditionally."

"You could have put me up for adoption. It seems like the sensible thing to do. Why did you keep me?" I hoped that the third time I asked would be the charm, but I should have known better.

"I'm just not the kind of mother who can give up her child. What my attacker did to me isn't your fault, and neither I nor your father—your *real* father, the one who raised you—has ever held it against you."

That was bullshit, but I'd never get her to admit it,

so I let it drop. "Tell me the truth this time. Who *was* my father? Because I don't believe for a second that you don't know."

And with that, it seemed that our special mother/daughter chat had come to an end. "I've said as much as I'm going to say. Your father and I kept you for your own good, and that's all you need to know."

"Like hell it is!"

The softness that I'd seen was completely gone now. "Well it's all I'm going to tell you."

I looked daggers at her. "I'm not leaving until you tell me what else you know about my biological father."

She raised one shoulder in a dainty shrug. "Fine, then. Make yourself comfortable."

And then she got up and left the room as if I weren't even there.

Chapter 8

I hung around the house for about an hour, making a nuisance of myself, hoping she'd cave. But she carried about her business without giving me a second glance.

I almost gave up. Then I realized that there was more than one way to get information out of her. If she was going to ignore me, then I had free range of the house—including my dad's study, where I swear he keeps every piece of paper that has ever crossed his path filed, indexed, and cross-referenced.

When my mom went to the kitchen to start dinner—which, seeing as she was Suzie Homemaker, was three o'clock in the afternoon—I didn't follow her.

Being anal as hell, my dad had always kept his study door locked. When Andy and I were kids, we'd briefly made a game of trying to breach the fortress of the Forbidden Zone. That had ended when I was six and Andy was nine. We'd finally found a way to get in, Andy having appropriated a copy of Dad's key. While Dad was at work, we let ourselves in. There wasn't a thing in there that was of any interest to children our age, but it was such an exciting, forbidden thrill to be inside that we'd stayed far too long. Long enough for Dad to come home and catch us.

Now I don't want you to get the impression that my dad is abusive. Really, he's not. But he definitely believes in the old "spare the rod, spoil the child" philosophy. At age nine, Andy had thought himself far too old for a spanking. He found out the hard way he was wrong. It was an impressive thrashing that discouraged him from sitting down for a couple of days, but it wasn't the pain that had made the strongest impression on him—it was the humiliation of it all, being spanked at that age, and in front of me.

Even at six years old, I was something of a stoic. I watched Andy struggle not to cry, and eventually lose that struggle. My own eyes welled with sympathy as I waited my turn, but when Dad took me over his knee, I was determined to be brave.

In the end, I'd broken just as my brother had, but I'm sure my dad was surprised at how hard he had to work for it. Andy was cowed by the whole experience, his spark of childish mischief extinguished. You can't say the same about me.

Since there were no children in the house anymore, I was gambling my dad no longer locked the door. Even so, I held my breath as I tried the knob, letting out a sigh of relief when it turned in my hand. I slipped inside and closed the door behind me. Hopefully, if my mom started to wonder where I was and came to check on me, she'd assume I'd gone home like a sensible girl.

I smiled faintly as I looked around the room, realizing I still felt a thrill at doing the forbidden.

There's hardly a bare patch of wall anywhere in my dad's study. Two walls are taken up by floor-to-ceiling bookcases, the shelves crammed to bursting with books, grouped by subject matter, then alphabetized by author name, because this is Anal-Retentive Man we're talking about. The other two walls are dominated by his massive mahogany desk, and more file cabinets than you'd see in a lawyer's record room. These, too, were grouped by subject matter, with convenient labels on the outside so that prying eyes like mine could find the most likely candidates for interesting reading.

His personal files were on the bottom, right next to the door. I wasn't entirely surprised to discover there was one entire drawer devoted to each member of our immediate family.

For some reason, my palms went clammy when I imagined pulling my own file open, so I started with Andy's. Inside, there were folders for every aspect of my brother's life. His birth announcement. A yellowed piece of paper with tiny baby footprints on it. Even the ID bracelets he and my mother had worn in the hospital. Then there was a file of all his report cards starting with kindergarten. Art projects that in a normal home would have been tacked up on the refrigerator but in ours had gone straight from Andy's hand to storage. The homemade Christmas cards he'd given our parents every year until he turned twenty-one and was lost beneath Raphael's personality.

I stopped myself from looking any further, feeling like a voyeur. My throat felt strangely tight as I realized that for all of Dad's deficiencies, for all his coldness, he must love Andy somewhere deep down. Otherwise, why would he keep all this stuff?

I slid Andy's drawer closed, then wiped my sweaty palms on my pants legs before taking a deep breath and opening my own.

I wasn't surprised to discover my drawer was very different from Andy's. That didn't stop the hurt that stabbed through me when I saw that whereas Andy's file was so full of memorabilia you could barely pull anything out, mine was positively sparse. No birth records. No cutesy, childish art. No report cards, though I could hardly blame him for that. I don't think there's a report card in existence that didn't mention how much of a pain in the ass I was, even though I was smart enough to get good grades without having to work too hard.

The first thing of interest I found was the record of the paternity test, which was conducted when I was about a month old. I saw in black and white that Dad and I were not related. I swallowed hard and shoved the folder back in the drawer.

My files, being much duller than Andy's, were organized by year rather than subject matter. I skipped forward to the year of my possibly mysterious hospitalization. I laid the file open on my lap and started flipping through it, looking more carefully than I had at anything previously. My hand—and my heart—came to a stop when I found a letter with the Spirit Society's logo emblazoned at the top. It was from Bradley Cooper, although he hadn't risen to his exalted rank of Regional Director yet and was merely a Team Leader.

Dear Mr. Kingsley,

We are sorry to hear about the difficulties you and your wife are experiencing with the child. We understand your frustration, and thank you again for the heroic efforts you have made for the Cause.

Our suggestion is that you have the child speak with one of our psychiatrists. He will examine her and make a determination as to the likelihood that she can be turned at this late age. It is possible that the resistance you are experiencing is nothing more than the rebellion of a normal teenager. If so, we would ask that you continue on as you have at least for the next couple of years until we can make a determination as to whether she will join with us of her own free will.

If our doctor determines that she is, in fact, intractable, then other, more desperate measures may be needed. We will discuss those measures when and if they become necessary so that we may come to a mutually acceptable arrangement.

Once again, I thank you on the behalf of the entire Society for your loyalty to our Cause, and for service above and beyond the call of duty. If you are amenable to our suggestion, please give me a call and we will set up an appointment.

My stomach flopped like a fish out of water. I could only assume this "teenage rebellion" of which Cooper spoke was my insistence that I would never, ever host a demon.

My parents had begun the recruitment effort on my twelfth birthday—the same age that they'd started working on Andy. But while Andy had immediately succumbed to the allure of becoming an all-powerful hero, I had balked. And more than a year of dragging me to Society meetings and shoving Society propaganda in my face had only made me dig my heels in deeper.

I remembered that trip to the psychiatrist. It had been the first of many. With trembling fingers, I turned to the next page, and saw the psychiatrist's report. I was still reading through it, simultaneously fascinated and appalled to read this stranger's impressions of me, most of which seemed surprisingly accurate, when the study door opened and my dad walked in.

For a long, breathless moment, we were both too shocked to move or speak. Inwardly, I cursed myself for getting so absorbed in my reading that I hadn't heard him coming. If I'd heard him, maybe I could have stuffed some of the more interesting pages into my pockets for later perusal.

Dad snapped out of it first, stepping fully into the room and slamming the door behind him. I winced at the sound, then reminded myself that I was an adult, not a six-year-old girl.

With what I hoped was cool aplomb, I closed the folder and tucked it back into the drawer, then stood. I was a full head taller than my dad, and we looked nothing alike. When I'd been a kid, people had always commented to my mom that I was her spitting image in everything but height. No one had ever said I looked like my dad, but I'd always assumed that was merely a gender thing. Now I realized the true reason. Even so, as I stood there and watched him trying to absorb the indignity of my intrusion upon his *sanctum sanctorum*, he still *felt* like my father to me. The little girl in my core wanted to apologize, to finally see a hint of approval on his face, but it wasn't going to happen.

"You have some nerve," he said when he recovered enough to talk. His voice was highly controlled, but I could hear the fury in it anyway.

I crossed my arms over my chest and leaned back against the cabinets behind me, pretending to be a hell of a lot more relaxed than I was. "Nice to see you, too, Pops," I said.

I think I saw a wisp of steam rise from his ears. "What is the meaning of this?" he demanded, and the look on his face said he was seriously considering taking me over his knee again.

I managed to swallow the laugh the mental image conjured and just shook my head at him. "You know the meaning as well as I do, assuming you spoke to

Mom before you came in here. And if you're planning to go the denial route, don't bother. You conveniently kept the results of the paternity test filed for me to find."

His face turned red with anger, but it seemed he wasn't in the mood for a good knock-down, drag-out. "Get out" was all he said.

"What else is in those files?" I asked, not about to budge. "I saw Cooper's letter about the 'desperate measures' the Society would take if you decided the brainwashing wasn't working. And I can't help connecting those desperate measures to my stay at The Healing Circle that very same year."

"I said get out!"

"I heard you. But like I told Mom, I'm not leaving until I get the answers I came for. So you're either going to answer my questions, or I'll help myself to the contents of my file." Or both, actually. It wasn't like I'd trust anything he told me under the circumstances. Still, I wouldn't mind getting the *Cliffs Notes* before I got started on the heavy reading.

When he didn't start talking, I began to bend down for the drawer. He grabbed my arm and yanked me back.

"You're leaving now," he informed me, and tried to pull me toward the door.

"The hell I am." I spread my legs and flexed my knees to give myself more leverage, and he couldn't budge me.

Anger still flashed in his eyes, but the expression on his face turned to stern paternal disapproval. "Don't make this any more difficult than it has to be. You have no right to paw through my personal records."

"They're *my* personal records, from what I could see. And yes, I definitely do have a right to see them.

Now let go of my arm before I show you how difficult I'm capable of being."

His grip tightened to painful proportions. "There's nothing in there you need to see. Let the past stay in the past, where it belongs."

Was that a hint of desperation I saw in his eyes? I didn't much care. With a twist and a hard yank, I freed my arm from his grip and once more bent for the drawer.

"Morgan, stop it!" he said in his most commanding voice, but I ignored him.

My fingers had just closed on the folder when my dad grabbed my arm again. I whirled on him with a snarl.

And turned my head right into the fist that was coming for my face.

I doubt I was out very long, but apparently it was just long enough for my dad—possibly with my mom's help—to drag my unconscious body out onto the front stoop. I was just struggling back up through the blackness when the door slammed loudly, followed by the sound of locks clicking shut.

A couple of passersby in the street gave me curious looks, but this being the city, they kept on walking. A sweet little old lady stopped to ask if I was all right and offered to dial 911, but I managed a smile and declined her offer. Behind the closed door, I could hear my parents' voices raised in argument, but I couldn't understand what they were saying. Just as well, no doubt.

Feeling disconnected with reality, I fingered the bruise that was forming on my jaw as I walked. Who knew my dad packed such a punch? Other than the occasional spanking when Andy and I were growing up, I'd never seen my dad hit anyone before. Never even seen any sign that he might be *capable* of hitting someone, even when he was madder than hell. My feelings might have been hurt if I hadn't remembered the sound of desperation in his voice. He'd tried everything he could think of to keep me from delving into those files, until he'd realized he wasn't getting me out of that room without resorting to violence.

And that told me that there was more in those files he wanted to hide. *Much* more, if he was that desperate to keep me from looking.

Unfortunately, I didn't think I was getting in that front door again. Not unless I *broke* in.

I wasn't opposed to bending the law here and there. But for all my wild, rebellious childhood and adolescence, I'd never broken into a house before. I hadn't the faintest idea how to go about it.

Of course, I did have an officer of the law I could call on for help. And I had no doubt Adam could get in the house if he wanted to. Hell, I could file a charge of assault against my father, and Adam could "investigate" it.

As tempting as the idea was, I nixed it before it took hold. I'd never had any warm, fuzzy feeling toward my parents, and I had even less right now. But I knew from cold, hard experience what could happen if I sicced Adam on them. My stomach tightened as I remembered Val's scream when Adam's whip had torn through her flesh. And I thought I might heave when I remembered the sickening crack of her neck breaking in his dispassionate hands.

No, the relationship between me and my parents wasn't all flowers and bunny rabbits. And yes, they possibly had information I *needed* to learn. But never again would I willingly give someone over to Adam.

Chapter 9

I stopped by a Chinese take-out place on my way home. My first inclination was to get two meals and kick Adam out of the apartment as soon as I got there, but I decided that was too bitchy. He had, after all, spent the afternoon babysitting my brother. I could muster up a scrap of gratitude in the form of a free meal.

I half-expected to find my apartment looking like a war zone, but everything was just about how it should be when I stepped in. Adam reported that the afternoon had been uneventful. No one had stopped by, and the only phone call had been from my mother, who wanted me to call back so she could apologize for Dad's behavior. Yeah, like *that* was going to happen.

I told myself I was relieved as I dropped the bag of takeout on the table and headed for the kitchen in search of plates. If Raphael had shown up, he probably could have beaten Adam in a fight. According to Lugh, he and his brothers were of an elite class, more powerful by far than most of the demons who walked the Mortal Plain—including Adam.

But though I was glad no disasters had occurred

while I was gone, I couldn't deny that my heart sank just a little lower on realizing that yet another day had passed without a word from Brian.

I took far longer than necessary to fish three clean forks out of the silverware drawer. My hands itched to reach for the phone, to call Brian's apartment and assure myself he was all right. After all, the enemy had gotten to him before. But in my heart of hearts, I knew he had made the conscious choice not to call me again.

The love of my life had finally given up on me. The thought made my chest ache and my eyes burn, even as I reminded myself that it was for his own good. I wished I could proudly and nobly make the sacrifice, but instead I found myself spinning scenarios in my mind where I could somehow free myself from Lugh and resume my interrupted life.

I guess I kind of spaced out for a while, because I didn't notice Adam joining me in the kitchen until he cleared his throat loudly. I jumped like a startled cat and barely kept from dropping the silverware.

"Do you have a concussion?" he asked, and for a moment I had no idea what he was talking about.

Then I remembered having my lights punched out, and I reached up to the swelling bruise on my chin. "I'm fine," I said, though I thought I detected a hint of hoarseness in my voice. I hoped Adam didn't hear it and couldn't recognize my distress, but his knowing look said he saw straight through me.

"You should put some ice on that. It's showy enough that Lugh can't afford to heal it without giving himself away."

I grimaced. I hadn't looked at myself in the mirror yet, but I took Adam's word for it.

"May I ask what happened?"

I laughed. "Ask whatever you want. Just don't expect me to answer."

Having recovered my composure, or at least some of it, I tried to move past him into what my landlord optimistically called my "dining room." As far as I was concerned, it was just a corner of the living room with barely enough space for a tiny table.

Adam stopped me with a hand on my arm. "Remember, we're on the same team, love. Being on the same team means working together, which means sharing information."

I narrowed my eyes at him. "Unless you'd like me to stick this fork into the back of your hand, I suggest you let go of me."

I never for a moment expected him to actually let go, but he sighed and his hand slid away. I was so surprised I stood there gaping at him like an idiot.

"Must we be constantly at war?" he asked.

This was a side of Adam I'd never seen before. Usually, he was as much into the "take no prisoners" philosophy as I was. Enough so that I didn't trust this apparent bid for truce.

"Let's review a few facts," I said. "You killed my best friend. You shot my brother. You tied me up and whipped me to within an inch of my life. How can you possibly expect us *not* to be at war?"

His eyes locked with mine as he enumerated his counterpoints on his fingers. "You exorcized my lover. You've repeatedly tried to drive a wedge between me and Dominic. And you tried to have me arrested and executed as a rogue demon. Neither one of us has any room to throw stones. The fact remains that we have a common enemy and a common goal. I spent a lot of time today talking with Andrew, and he's convinced me that trying to hurt one another isn't conducive to a successful working relationship."

His lips twitched up into a grin. "I can't imagine you waving the white flag, so I decided I'd be man enough to do it myself."

Everything he said sounded perfectly logical. He was even right. I mean, really, how well could we work together when we were both constantly taking verbal jabs at each other?

But I wasn't buying it. Although I hated to admit it even to myself, Adam and I were a lot alike in some ways, and our warm, forgiving natures weren't one of them. I didn't know what his angle was, but I was damn sure there was one.

"You can wave as many flags as you like," I said. "I have nothing to share with you. When I do, I'll let you know."

For half a second, his eyes seemed to glow, an effect I'd noticed before when he got really, really pissed. But the glow faded so fast I was almost able to convince myself it was my imagination.

He shook his head. "Fine. If that's the way it's got to be, then so be it. You'll only be needing two of those forks."

I went to bed that night thinking about Lugh, trying to will myself to fall asleep and wake up in his special room. I was seriously pissed at him for taking a joyride in my body last night, and though he already knew exactly how I felt about it, I was determined to tell him in my own words.

But I awoke the next morning from a long and dreamless sleep. When I got over the novelty of feeling rested, I cursed Lugh for what seemed suspiciously like a streak of cowardice. Grumbling to myself, I shoved the covers away and sat up. That's when I noticed the note by the bedside, written in my own handwriting.

> We'll talk when you've calmed down. We wouldn't accomplish anything useful in your present state of mind.

I crumpled the note and tossed it into the wastebasket across the room.

"Yeah," I muttered to the empty room. "Hijack my body again to write me a note. That's exactly the right way to make me calm down. I never took you for a chickenshit, Lugh."

Andy was still asleep when I got up, so I made myself a pot of coffee and sat at the table, examining my options for the day. It was Saturday, but Adam was on duty today so he couldn't stand guard over Andy. That left me in something of a quandary, because Saturday was meeting day for the Spirit Society, which meant there was a good chance my parents' house would be unoccupied for at least an hour and a half this afternoon. It seemed unlikely I would have a better chance to take another shot at my dad's study than that.

I was about halfway through the pot of coffee when Andy staggered out of bed. I was glad to see he'd gained enough strength to get from the bedroom to the dining room without leaning on me, though when he plopped into the chair, I could see that the effort had exhausted him.

Wordlessly, I slipped into the kitchen and poured him a mug of coffee, black with a teaspoon of sugar, just the way he liked it. I felt positively domestic. We sipped our coffee in companionable silence for about ten minutes, and I watched the caffeine banish the remnants of sleep from his face.

"What's the plan for today?" he asked when he was fully awake.

"Good question," I mumbled into my coffee cup.

"Are you going to go by Mom and Dad's place while they're at the meeting?"

I had told him last night about my adventure. He still maintained that he didn't remember anything unusual or suspicious about my hospitalization, but he had agreed that it might be a good idea to get a look at the rest of the files.

"The idea has possibilities," I admitted.

He nodded sagely. "But you're afraid to leave me alone, and Adam has to work today."

"There's also the fact that I'm not real good at breaking and entering," I said, trying to deflect any guilt he might feel about slowing me down.

He laughed. "It's not that hard. Especially when I have a key to the house."

I almost slapped myself in the forehead for that one. Of course Andy, as the favored son, would have a key to our parents' house. He was always welcome there, unlike me. So we were back to the problem of how to keep Andy safe.

"Just give me a Taser and lock the door behind you when you leave," he said. "I'll be fine."

"Not if Raphael breaks the door down," I said gloomily.

"If he does, I shoot him with the Taser and then call the police. Besides, he's not likely to attack in broad daylight. He may be a demon prince, but he'd die as easily as a commoner if he's convicted of going rogue."

That made a certain amount of sense, but I still hated the idea of leaving Andy alone and undefended when he was so weak. What if he ran out of energy and fell asleep? Raphael could be in the apartment and on him before he ever woke up. Not to mention that giving Andy my Taser would leave me Taserless myself. I wished I had more than one.

Andy saw my uncertainty and reached across the table to pat my hand. "Look, if I were going to tell you all kinds of crap Raphael doesn't want me to say, I would have done it by now. He knows that."

"Yeah, but he's under orders to kill you anyway."

Andy shrugged. "You may have noticed he's not too good at following orders." He smiled at me. "You two have that in common."

I couldn't think of a good comeback, so I just reached out and cuffed him on the side of the head. "Jerk."

"So are you going to go be a girl detective, or are you going to sit around the apartment being useless all day?"

I gave him a dirty look, but we both knew he'd won the argument. Fighting my reluctance, reminding myself that Andy was far more vulnerable than I, I handed over the Taser. I just hoped he was right about Raphael. If I came home from my little adventure and found out Andy'd been killed in my absence, I didn't know if I'd ever get over the guilt.

The Spirit Society meeting starts at three-thirty and usually lasts until about five. Many of the faithful go out to dinner together afterward, but I wasn't going to count on my parents spending the extra time.

The house was in one of the more heavily residential areas of the city, but there was a tiny grocery store across the street. I slipped inside for surveillance duty shortly after three o'clock—it would be pretty embarrassing to break into my parents' house and discover that they'd decided to play hooky this week!

I browsed aimlessly through the shelves, keeping an eye on my parents' house through the front window. I'd dressed in a conservative—for me—pair of jeans, with a light windbreaker that I kept zipped to cover the hint of belly that showed between the jeans and my blouse. I tried to be as unobtrusive as possible, but at five foot nine and with spiky red hair, it was kind of hard to miss me. I saw the geezer at the cash register watching my every move. The store was so small, it was hard to keep up the illusion that I was shopping for more than about five minutes.

Sensing that the guy at the cash register was getting more and more antsy, I snatched up a bottle of Tylenol, then went to the register.

"Will there be anything else?" he asked, still giving me the hairy eyeball.

"Nope, that'll do it," I replied cheerfully.

I watched my parents' front door out of the corner of my eye while he rang up my purchase. Then I made a big deal out of rooting through my purse looking for exact change. I was almost completely out of reasons to stall when the door finally opened and my parents stepped out. Mom locked up behind them, and they began walking briskly down the street in the opposite direction from my vantage point.

Sighing in relief, I pulled out a twenty and handed it to the cashier. He opened his mouth to say something, then shook his head and took the money. He shorted me on the change, but I figured I owed him the extra buck for rent.

I tried not to look furtive and sneaky as I climbed the three steps up to the door and slipped Andy's key into the lock. I'd been half-afraid the key wouldn't work, but the door opened easily, and soon I was inside.

The first thing I noticed was the way-too-strong

floral air freshener. I sneezed three times in rapid succession.

What was that all about? My mom usually kept small bowls of potpourri sitting around, but they wouldn't have this strong a scent. Then I ventured another sniff, stifling my need to sneeze again.

Under that cloying fragrance of pasteurized, processed flower product, there was something else. Smoke.

I had a bad feeling about this.

Ignoring Dad's study for the moment, I made my way to the den at the back of the house. The focal point of the den was an oversized fireplace. Sure enough, there was an impressive pile of ashes in there. When I got close enough, I noticed the air around the fireplace was still warm, and when I pulled aside the curtain, I saw a glowing ember or two.

Having a sneaking suspicion what I would find, I went to Dad's study.

Outwardly, it looked exactly as it had yesterday. But I wasn't a bit surprised when I pulled open my drawer and saw that it was empty. I slammed it closed and recited as many curses as I could think of. Then I gave the drawer a swift kick for good measure.

I supposed the only reasonable thing to do was to search through the rest of the files, hoping to find something Dad missed. However, I wasn't optimistic about my chances of success.

I was just bending to open Andy's file when I heard the front door open and close. I froze. *Now* what?

Footsteps moved down the hall, and I realized at once that whoever this was, it wasn't my mom or my dad. When they went to Spirit Society meetings, they went dressed in their Sunday best, which meant high-heeled pumps for my mom and leather-soled dress shoes for my dad. Whoever was in the house was wearing squeaky rubber soles.

Now I wished I'd brought the Taser with me, even if that would have meant leaving Andy vulnerable. My instincts insisted the intruder was one of the bad guys. I tried to convince myself I was just being paranoid because I was trespassing myself, but I didn't believe it.

The hair on the back of my neck stood up when I heard those footsteps coming closer.

There was no exit from this room save the door, which would lead me straight into the intruder's arms. And there were no closets or other convenient hiding places.

I backed to the far side of the room, searching frantically for anything I could use as a weapon. I almost laughed as I picked up the only thing I could find that was even remotely weapon-like—a letter opener. If I got attacked by a giant, rabid envelope, I was prepared.

The study door swung open, and an unfamiliar man stepped in. Dressed in faded, tattered jeans and a wife-beater that showed off about a zillion tattoos on each arm, he looked very much like your stereotypical city-dwelling predator. If this were someone else's house—and someone else's life—I might suspect he was a burglar, hoping to clear the place out while my parents were gone. But I knew that wasn't the case even before he smiled at me.

"Ms. Kingsley, I presume?" he asked, and the voice sounded strangely cultured in that decidedly déclassé body.

I blinked and brandished the letter opener, feeling vaguely ridiculous. "Who the fuck are you?"

His smile stayed in place. "I'll take that as a yes. And you might as well put your, er, weapon down. You won't find it terribly useful against me."

On the one hand, I couldn't expect him to be intimidated by a letter opener. On the other hand, something about the way he said that made me think he wouldn't be much more intimidated by a big-ass hunting knife. Which meant he was probably a demon. And considering what I'd learned from Raphael, I had a pretty good guess just which demon this was.

Of course, I wasn't supposed to know anything about Der Jäger, so I didn't let on that I had any idea who I was facing.

"I think I'll keep it, thanks." With my left hand, I rummaged in my purse, hoping to find my phone. I didn't think I'd have an opportunity to call in the cavalry, but I figured there was no harm in trying.

Der Jäger kept smiling at me, but it was an eerie, cold smile. "Put it down, or I'll be forced to take it from you. Trust me, you would not enjoy the experience."

"You seem to know who I am," I said as my questing fingers finally found the phone. I could hardly hear my own voice over the pounding of my heart, but bravado was so natural to me I was pretty sure I sounded less scared than I was. "If you know that, then you know I'm not just going to roll over for you."

His smile broadened. "Yes. I was counting on that."

I had just flipped open my phone when he flung himself at me. I was ready for him, so I made sure my makeshift knife was between us. He ignored it, slamming into me and knocking me to the floor, his own momentum forcing the letter opener in to the hilt.

My head slammed against the floor, and I wished my parents had opted for more padding under the carpet. Both my hands opened against my will. As I struggled for breath, Der Jäger grabbed my purse, flinging it across the room. The hilt of the letter opener protruded from his chest, just below his sternum, but though blood flowed from the wound, he didn't seem to mind.

When I had enough wind to manage it, I struggled weakly. Pain stabbed through my eyeball. *Don't you dare,* I mentally told Lugh. *He can't possibly know you're here, so don't give yourself away.*

It was quite a predicament. I was no use against a demon in hand-to-hand combat, but if I let Lugh take over—even presuming I was *able* to let him take over—we'd completely blow his cover. Unfortunately, if Der Jäger managed to kill me, not only would I be dead, but Lugh would be forced to abandon my body and return to the Demon Realm. Which would be all well and good if Dougal didn't know Lugh's True Name. But he did, so until we'd taken out Dougal, he could have his followers summon Lugh to the Mortal Plain at will—into a sacrificial lamb of a host who would be immediately burned at the stake, thus killing Lugh and letting Dougal claim the throne he coveted.

I kept struggling, but though I was strong and a passably good fighter, Der Jäger was unimpressed. He flipped me over onto my stomach, pinning my hands behind my back and sitting on me. His grip on my wrists was crushing, and I knew he could break the bones easily if he wanted to.

"Now that we've established that fighting me is not worth your while," he said, "let's have a nice chat." Holding my wrists easily with one hand, he plucked the letter opener from his chest and dropped it to the floor by my face. Blood dripped from the blade, soaking into the beige carpet.

"Who are you?" I asked, though it was hard to talk with his weight on my back and my face pressed against the floor.

"That is irrelevant. Suffice it to say I am aware that you were once the host of a demon known as Lugh. I would like you to describe for me the host you transferred him to. And, of course, tell me his or her name."

I could easily make up some bullshit description and name, but I had a feeling he would know it was bullshit if I gave in too easily. My stomach lurched as I wondered just how much abuse I would have to withstand before I could pretend to give him what he wanted. I certainly wasn't under the impression that he was just going to ask nicely and then go away.

"You aren't exactly endearing yourself to me. Why should I want to help you?"

His laugh was dark and made me shudder. "Do you have any idea what I can do to you if you annoy me?"

"I'm an exorcist, so yeah, I know what a demon is capable of. I also know there's no way in hell the Society would have accepted the body you're in as a host." The Society favored the fit and attractive as hosts—not street punks like this guy. "Which means you're an illegal. Which means you have the morals of a cockroach. Why should I believe talking will do me any good?"

My mind was still frantically searching for an escape route, but it wasn't looking good at the moment. I was thoroughly pinned, and I wasn't getting up until he let me.

Der Jäger slid lower down my body so that he was straddling my ass. He pressed down hard so I could feel that he was enjoying himself. I wished I could suppress my shudder, but I couldn't. Der Jäger laughed.

"This body is infected with any number of diseases. Were I planning to use it for the long term, I would fix it, but I have not bothered. If I were to rape you, you would get them all, and eventually they would kill you."

I closed my eyes and tried to control the panic. I didn't give a shit about the diseases, figuring Lugh could cure them, but while I was to some extent prepared to deal with pain, I wasn't so sure I could deal with rape.

If I blurted out a name and description now, would he believe me? Or did I need to let this go further before I caved? More important, would he actually let me go if I did? I remembered Raphael describing him as a sociopath, so if he was jonesing for me, he'd do whatever he damn well wanted to. A chill shivered through me as I realized the best way for him to get the information out of me was to transfer into my body and rape my mind. He didn't seem to have any compunction about leaving brain-dead hosts in his wake. What would happen when he tried it and couldn't get in was anyone's guess.

Apparently, I was quiet too long. I was brought back to myself when he grabbed one of my hands with his free hand.

"You will tell me what I need to know," he said, prying my clenched fingers apart and wrapping his hand around my pinkie. "If I'm pleased with you, I'll let you go. I will give you no guarantees, however, except that if you refuse to talk, I will make you regret that decision."

He jerked on my finger, hard, and I heard the bone snap at the same moment pain tore a scream from my throat. Sweat popped out over my whole body, and for a moment my vision swam. When it cleared, I still felt like I might barf. Who knew one tiny finger could cause so much pain? Lugh helped things along with another ice pick in the eye, but though I appreciated his desire to help me, I knew that keeping him hidden was far more important. No matter how pissed I was at him at the moment.

"Are you beginning to get the message?" Der Jäger asked.

"All right, all right. You win," I gasped. Tears burned at my eyes, and for once I didn't try to suppress them. I needed him to believe I was well and truly beaten, and if squirting out a few tears would help with the illusion, then I was willing to sacrifice a bit of my dignity.

"That was a foregone conclusion," he said. "Now tell me the name of the human you transferred Lugh into."

"Peter Bishop," I said, improvising. "But Lugh had to know someone would come looking for him, so I doubt he stayed in a host I could identify."

"Where might I find this Mr. Bishop? He may no longer be Lugh's host, but perhaps I can persuade him to tell me who is."

I was about to launch into a story about the fictional Mr. Bishop's probable location when the doorbell rang. Unfortunately, Der Jäger reacted faster than I did, clapping a hand tightly over my mouth before I could scream for help. I made as much noise as I could, but I had no illusions anyone standing outside the house could hear me.

The doorbell sounded again, followed by the pounding of the knocker. Followed by a shout announcing the persistent visitor as police. I didn't know what the police could be doing here—I was sure my parents didn't have an alarm system that I tripped, and even if someone had heard me scream and called the police, there wouldn't have been enough time for them to arrive.

Der Jäger continued to pin me and cover my mouth, his whole body tense. I suspect he was hoping the police would go away and let him go about his business, but the officer at the door knocked once again, and I heard a siren approaching. I tensed, even more sure Der Jäger was about to try to move into my body. And yet, he didn't.

One of the questions that Raphael had refused to answer was how he had known that Lugh wouldn't be able to control me the way demons can usually control their hosts. I was guessing that whatever that secret was, Der Jäger knew it, too.

"We will continue this discussion at some other time," Der Jäger said. Then he grabbed me by the hair—a neat trick when my hair was so short—and slammed my head into the floor.

I didn't lose consciousness, but my head swam. I felt the weight of his body leave my back. I made a feeble effort to grab at his ankle—with my left hand, where all the fingers were whole—as he moved past me, but it wasn't like I could have stopped him even if I'd managed to get a grip.

Dizzy and nauseated, I raised my head and watched as he made his way casually toward the back of the house, where no doubt he intended to slip out the back door. I pushed myself up onto my hands and knees, trying to find the strength and will to shout some kind of warning at the police, but I was too shaky, so I collapsed.

From the back of the house, I heard a shout, then a gunshot. I lay on my back on the floor and held my breath, knowing just how much effect a gun would have on Der Jäger. I flinched when I heard a man's high-pitched scream. Then I tried to get up again, and this time the blackness took me.

Chapter **10**

I came to seconds later—too fast for Lugh to fix anything—when the police broke down the front door. I would really have liked to get the hell out of there—I didn't think the police were a complication I much needed—but though I managed to push myself up onto my knees, I knew my legs weren't ready to hold me yet.

Nausea roiled in my stomach, and my broken pinkie throbbed like a sonofabitch. When I looked at it, I saw it was bent at an unnatural angle, and for a moment I seriously thought I would puke. Then I thought about what would happen if they took me to the hospital. Hours of my life ticking away while I waited my turn. X-rays. Poking and prodding. Realigning the bone, then splinting the finger. That didn't sound like a whole lot of fun, so I carefully slid that hand into my jacket pocket. Even that small movement made me whimper.

A gun-totin' policeman appeared in the doorway to the study. The moment he saw me, he aimed solidly at my chest and started shouting instructions at me— you know, the whole "put your hands on your head" routine. He looked seriously freaked out, like he might shoot me if I took a deep breath. I realized that with my hand in my jacket like that, I probably looked like I was going for a weapon.

I gave him woozy eyes for a moment, wondering if there was any way I could get out of showing him my hand. I was just determining the answer was no when Adam appeared in the doorway behind the cop.

"Stand down," he ordered. "I know her. This is her parents' house."

"Sir?" the officer asked uncertainly.

"Put your weapon away," Adam said more slowly.

The officer didn't look like he was too happy with the idea, but Adam outranked him, so he did as he was told. He kept a wary eye on me as he holstered his weapon and backed out of the doorway. I didn't look up, but I swear I could physically *feel* Adam glaring at me.

"You and I are going to have a long talk," he told me.

"Peachy," I said. I was so *not* looking forward to this conversation.

He came farther into the room, offering me a hand up. I ignored it and struggled to my feet. The motion jarred my finger, and the flash of pain almost took me back to the floor.

Adam frowned at me. "What's with the hand?"

I supposed it looked pretty suspicious, me keeping my hand buried in my jacket like that. I lowered my voice so that only Adam could hear me. "Broken finger, and I don't want anyone splinting it, if you know what I mean."

As long as no one knew it was broken, Lugh could fix it as soon as I got somewhere private and managed to lose consciousness. I'd have to put a splint or bandage on it so as not to let Der Jäger know I was possessed if—or, more likely, when—we met again, but I could do that after the break healed. More sirens approached. Adam regarded me with interest and speculation in his eyes. Frighteningly, I knew him well enough to guess what he was thinking.

"You turn me in to the EMTs, and I will feed you your balls."

He grinned. "It might almost be worth it." The grin faded. "But I don't think our little chat can wait until after the emergency room is done with you." He moved closer still, and I had to fight an urge to back away.

"Let's see how bad it is," he said.

I considered my options and realized there were none. Reluctantly, carefully, I extracted my hand from my pocket. Every movement brought a new wave of pain. I didn't want to look at the damage, but I couldn't seem to stop myself, even though seeing my finger bending that way made me want to pass out.

Apparently, I didn't know Adam as well as I thought—either that, or I was too addled by the blow to the head to guess what was coming.

He moved with lightning quickness, grabbing me, turning me around, and hauling me up against his chest. One hand clapped over my mouth, his fingers biting into the bruises Der Jäger and my father had left on me.

"Hold still," he hissed in my ear. "This'll be over in a second." Then, still covering my mouth, he reached for my injured hand. I tried to jerk away, but he was too much bigger and stronger than me. He pulled my arm up against my body, then used his other elbow to pin me there. I closed my eyes and gritted my teeth, knowing I would not win this battle.

A white light flashed behind my closed eyes like lightning when he straightened my finger, realigning the bone. I was glad he had his hand over my mouth, because despite my gritted teeth I would have screamed my lungs out if I could.

"There," he said, still holding me against him. "Now no one has to know it's broken."

He let me go, but not before I noticed he had a hard-on. And no, not because he thought I was such a hot chick that he couldn't help being turned on by the body contact. I wanted to tear into him, but at that moment another man in blue came into the room, and they started doing the cop-speak thing.

Adam pulled a lot of rank to hurry me out of there with only a cursory statement, which he "took down" himself. I was sure he'd fill me in later on what I supposedly told him. He extracted me from the crime scene, guiding me to his unmarked. I'd ridden in the backseat before, but apparently I'd gotten a promotion and now got to sit up front.

I looked back at the house as we were pulling away and saw EMTs swarming over something in the back. I remembered the scream I'd heard when Der Jäger escaped. I figured some poor guy had been covering the back door, having no idea that what came out of it wouldn't be human.

"Is he dead?" I asked Adam, craning my neck to keep the house in sight.

"No," Adam said brusquely, turning a corner. "Not yet, unfortunately."

I shuddered. I didn't really want to know, but I couldn't help asking. "What happened to him?"

Adam glanced at me from the corner of his eye, then fixed his gaze on the road once more. "He spilled his guts. Literally. Of course, he had some help."

My stomach roiled at the image, my face going first cold, then hot. "Stop the car!"

He didn't ask any questions, just pulled over to the curb and idled. I shoved the door open and puked into the gutter. I'm sure the nearby pedestrians were just thrilled with the show, but I couldn't help it. I heaved until there was nothing left in my stomach.

When I thought it was safe, I slumped back into the car and pulled the door shut. I was shaking and sweating, exhausted like I hadn't slept in weeks. And let's not forget the persistent, throbbing pain that pulsed in time to the beat of my heart.

Adam handed me a handkerchief. "Sorry I don't have any water to rinse out your mouth."

I closed my eyes and laid my head back against the seat. At the moment, I had absolutely nothing to say. I didn't even have the good sense to ask Adam where he was taking me. I tried to relax through my misery, hoping I could drift off long enough for Lugh to patch me up, but no such luck.

I didn't open my eyes again until Adam brought the car to a stop. I looked around and saw we were in a parking garage. I made the logical assumption that this was the garage for my apartment building, and I thought longingly of my bed.

But of course I still had to have my "conversation" with Adam.

"How did you end up showing up just in time to save the day?" I asked.

"A call came in about a possible burglary in progress. The caller said a six-foot, red-haired woman seemed to be casing the house, then snuck in when the occupants left. I recognized the address and made an educated guess who the six-foot woman was. I fig-ured whatever you were up to, it wasn't something the regular police needed to know about, so I thought I'd swing by."

I guess I hadn't been too subtle when I hung around that little grocery store. Not that subtlety had ever been one of my strong suits. "I'm only five-nine," I commented, but Adam didn't seem amused.

"What were you up to? And what went wrong?"

The cat was well and truly out of the bag, so I figured there was no point in keeping the information to myself. I told him everything—about my mysterious hospital stay, about the files, about the letter from Bradley Cooper, about the pile of ashes, and about Der Jäger. And I tried not to think about the scream I'd heard, the scream of a man having his guts torn out by a demon. I swallowed hard and thanked my lucky stars my stomach was already on empty.

Silence reigned when I was finished. I stared out the windshield at the gray concrete wall and concentrated on breathing. At least I tried, though the steady throbbing of my finger was something of a distraction. And I couldn't stop myself from thinking about Der Jäger's parting shot. He and I had unfinished business. Oh, joy!

"Why didn't you tell me any of this yesterday?" Adam asked. "We could have worked something out, gotten to those papers before your parents burned them."

I turned my head to look at him. "Maybe I didn't want to risk having my parents tortured to death if you weren't satisfied with what you learned."

"Ah," he said, "this is still about Valerie."

I reached for the handle of my door—with my left hand, of course—but Adam hit the locks.

"You're never going to forgive me for that, are you?" he asked. "Even though you know I had no choice."

I let out a heavy sigh. "My head knows you had no choice. My heart doesn't give a shit."

Would he figure he had no choice but to interrogate my parents now? And if he did, was there anything I could do to stop him?

I knew there wasn't. God, how I hated feeling helpless! And I'd been feeling helpless far too often lately.

Once again, I reached for the door, hitting the unlock button. But before my hand got to the handle, the locks snicked shut again. If I wanted to get out, I'd have to use both hands simultaneously, and I couldn't bear the thought of moving my right hand more than absolutely necessary. I glanced down at it and saw that while, thanks to Adam, the finger was straight, it was swelling up like the proverbial balloon.

"What are you planning to do now, Morgan?" Adam asked. "You can't just go back to your apartment and resume life as normal. Not with Der Jäger still hunting you."

I shuddered. "Like my life has been anything like normal lately."

"You know what I mean."

"Yeah, I know." I turned to face him. "What would you suggest? What can a puny human being do to protect herself from a rampaging demon?"

"Well for one thing, you can come stay with me and Dom."

My eyes widened. I'd gone that route before—not of my own free will, I might add—and I hadn't enjoyed the experience. "Yeah? And you're going to hang around and guard me 24/7? Might get in the way of your job just a bit, don't you think?" He didn't have a quick comeback for that one, so I continued to press. "Look, I live on the twenty-seventh floor. The only way Der Jäger can get to me is through my front door, right? He can't fly or climb up the outside of buildings like a spider."

Adam nodded his reluctant agreement.

"Remember, I have a Taser. And for the moment, I have a roommate. As long as we guard the door, there's no way Der Jäger can get to me without getting zapped."

Adam looked like he still really hated this plan—or lack thereof—but he didn't seem to have a better suggestion. "Don't leave the apartment without me," he ordered. "I'll come back as soon as I'm off duty and we'll see if we can cobble together a plan."

I didn't much like his tone of voice, but for once I managed to stifle my rebellious response. I wasn't stupid enough to think I could take on Der Jäger and win.

"Okay," I said.

Adam gave me a suspicious look. "That was too easy."

I shook my head. "I've met Der Jäger up close and personal. I *so* do not want to meet up with him again in some dark alley." I forced a bit of a smile. "Besides, I'm getting better about accepting help when I need it."

The look he gave me said he still didn't trust me, but this time when I reached for the door, he let me open it.

"I'll walk you to your apartment," he said, getting out of the car.

Again, I had to swallow the urge to tell him to back off. I reminded myself that I didn't have a Taser on me, and I didn't have a death wish.

"Thanks," I said through gritted teeth. Then, as we walked toward the elevator, a very disquieting thought struck me. "Could you beat Der Jäger in a fight?"

I looked at him out of the corner of my eye and saw the sudden tightness of his expression.

"I don't know," he finally answered. "But I could at least hold him off long enough for you to get away."

There wasn't much to say after that, so we walked the rest of the way to my apartment in silence.

Chapter 11

I discovered it's incredibly hard to fall asleep at five o'clock in the afternoon when you're in constant pain—even when I knew falling asleep would allow Lugh to heal the worst of it. I'd have to keep the bruise from yesterday's encounter with my not-father, but today's injuries could soon become nothing but an unpleasant memory. If only I could let myself drift off.

Outside my bedroom door, I could hear the TV going as it no doubt had been all day. I'd come home to find Andy sitting listlessly on the couch, staring at the TV but not really seeing it. He'd snapped out of it long enough to ask me what had happened during my ill-fated break-in, but when I'd stopped talking, the animation left him and he was back to staring. I had to hope he had enough brain cells functioning to shoot anything that came through the front door.

I was in too much pain to deal with his issues, so I'd gone to the bedroom to lie down. But as I lay there failing miserably at my attempt to sleep, I couldn't help worrying about him.

Andy might not be catatonic anymore, but he wasn't exactly back to normal, either. He had a fragile vulnerability that was so not in keeping with my mental image of him. Had Raphael damaged him irreparably? Was there anything I could do to help?

Eventually, I realized I wasn't getting to sleep without help. I raided my medicine cabinet and found an old, expired bottle of sleeping pills. I downed a couple, hoping they'd still be effective after the expiration date, then went back to bed and closed my eyes.

I don't know how much longer I lay there awake, my mind cycling through my impressive list of problems, but eventually I drifted off. I hadn't been sure if Lugh would talk to me now, or if he still thought I needed cooling-off time, but I awoke in another version of his dream world, one I had visited only once before, when he'd healed me after Adam had finished "playing" with me.

I lay on my back on a sumptuously soft bed, my body draped with a crimson silk sheet that clung to its contours like a wet T-shirt. Naturally, I was naked under that sheet, and I was keenly aware of the texture of the silk against my skin.

Lugh sat beside me on the edge of the bed. He'd toned down his wardrobe for this conversation, ditching the S&M getup for a plain black T-shirt that hugged his spectacular chest. He still wore his trademark black leather pants, but not the heavy black boots. One bare foot was tucked under the opposite leg, and I had the strangest urge to reach out and touch it. Then I remembered I was furious with him and nipped my arousal in the bud.

I glanced down at my body, noticing that despite my supposed anger, the thin sheet did little to hide my decidedly perky nipples. I scowled.

"Why do I have to be naked?" I grumbled. It was hard to have a good, knock-down, drag-out fight when you were naked as the day you were born. Then again, maybe that was Lugh's intention.

He smiled at my anger. "Perhaps because I like you that way?"

I struggled into a sitting position, clutching the sheet tightly against myself. "Well *I* don't! Put some clothes on me."

His smirk told me in advance things weren't going well. I no longer felt the sheet against the skin of my torso, but when I looked down I saw that I was wearing a barely there teddy in a sheer black mesh that didn't exactly hide anything. I shoved the sheet away, fighting down my embarrassment.

"Fine!" I snapped. "If you're going to be childish and take advantage of me again, there's nothing I can do to stop you."

His brows drew together. "In what way am I taking advantage of you? I reside within your body. I know what you look like naked. I even know what you look like in the throes of passion."

My blush burned my cheeks. There was little about these dreams to help me remember they were dreams—even when lingerie suddenly appeared out of thin air. I crossed my arms over my chest, hiding my breasts while the sheet hid the rest of me. I was letting him distract me from the real issue.

"Do you have anything to say for yourself?" I asked, and there was no way in hell he didn't know what I was talking about.

The teasing smile left his lips. "I needed to speak to my brother. Since you won't let me in when you're conscious, my only chance to do so was while you slept. But you started to wake up at an inconvenient moment, so I had to give you some incentive to stay asleep."

I swallowed hard, trying to blot out the images in

my mind of the distraction he'd conjured. "You could have just told me what you were going to do."

He laughed. "You're not fooling yourself with that argument any more than you're fooling me. If I'd told you what I was up to, you'd have awakened in a heartbeat. I'm sorry for the deception, but it was necessary."

He reached out and took my hand. I had the strong impression I should have tried to evade him, but I didn't. His grip was strong and steady, an anchor in the midst of my tumultuous life.

"Besides," he said, his amber eyes gazing into mine as he raised my hand to his lips, "you needed the release."

Once again, I urged myself to take back my hand, to resist the temptation of his touch. But though I willed my body to obey, I remained motionless and unresisting as his lips brushed over my knuckles.

That velvet touch sent a shudder through every cell in my body. Desire swamped my senses, and though he'd made me come two nights ago, it had been with the touch of my own hand, and that wasn't enough. I closed my eyes as his lips traveled from knuckles to wrist. Deep inside my belly, I ached for something I didn't dare let myself have.

His scent flooded my senses, and my skin felt the heat that radiated from his body as he pressed closer to me. His long, silky hair tickled my thigh, and I realized the sheet seemed to have slipped down past my knees.

I almost let it happen. Almost let my desire override my free will. Until I wondered just what he might be doing with my body in the real world.

I jerked away from him, my heart rate accelerating, my breath coming short. My hormones screamed in protest, but I ignored them.

"What the fuck are you doing?" I asked, and there was an edge of panic in my voice. I struggled to close my mental doors, but I was too freaked out to concentrate.

Lugh backed off, raising both hands in a gesture of innocence. "Easy, Morgan. I'm not doing anything. You're just lying in bed, recuperating."

I grabbed at the sheet, yanking it up to my shoulders and holding it there with both hands. "I don't believe you."

His shoulders drooped. "I haven't done anything to earn your distrust."

I laughed, a bit hysterically. "Newsflash for you—seducing me so you can drive my body uninterrupted is a violation of my trust."

He cocked his head to one side, looking genuinely puzzled. "I might have had more than one motive, but I did not coldly seduce you for only my own purposes. You have to know that my attraction to you is genuine."

The hysterical laughter wanted to come back, but I swallowed it. "I don't *have* to know anything. You can know everything I'm thinking, everything I'm feeling, everything that lies hidden under my surface. And I can know what you tell me. That's it! Am I just supposed to take it on faith that this isn't all some kind of game?"

He smiled ruefully, but if I didn't know better, I would have sworn there was a hint of hurt in his eyes. "I understand your point. And no, I would not expect you, of all people, to take anything on faith."

And with that, I jolted awake.

I lay in my bed a good fifteen minutes after I woke up. My finger was back to normal, and though I still sported the bruise my father had given me, the bumps and bruises I'd gotten this afternoon had vanished.

Lugh's words seemed to echo in my brain, as did the hurt look in his eyes. It made me feel like a cold-hearted bitch, and for a little while, I wallowed in my own inadequacies. Then I mentally slapped myself upside the head and sat up.

Lugh could lay all the guilt trip he wanted on me. The fact remained that he had seduced me under false pretenses. A familiar glow of indignation warmed my belly. I had every right to be upset with him!

Being possessed was such a pain in the ass.

I rubbed the remains of sleep out of my eyes, then taped my pinkie and ring fingers together. Probably more loosely than I would have if the finger had still been broken, but I hoped to leave myself at least a little mobility. Afterward, I wandered out into the living room just as my phone started ringing. Andy was still sitting exactly where I'd left him, CNN babbling unheeded on the TV. His eyes were on the screen, but there was a vacant expression in them that suggested he didn't see a thing. My heart contracted in my chest. Had he slipped back into catatonia? He didn't seem to be reacting to the ringing phone, even though it was about two feet from where he was sitting.

"Andy?" I asked, and I didn't realize how rigid every muscle in my body had gone until he blinked, and the tension seeped out of me.

Without a word to me, he turned to the phone and picked it up. He exchanged about four or five words with the caller, then hung up.

"Who was that?" I asked.

"Adam. The police found a catatonic man near the scene of the attack at Mom and Dad's house."

My knees felt a little wobbly, so I hurried over to the sofa and sat down. "Let me guess," I said, my voice raspy. "Young punk, ratty clothes, lots of tattoos on his arms?"

Andy nodded.

"Well, shit," I said, and that about summed it up. Der Jäger had now hijacked a new host. Which meant he could walk right up to me in an unfamiliar body, and I'd never know it was him.

A bolt of pure terror shot through me at the same moment pain stabbed through my head. The pain let up immediately—Lugh knew I'd come to the same alarming conclusion he had. Sweat suddenly trickled down the small of my back as I looked at Andy in horror.

"If you were Der Jäger, and you wanted to get to me, what would you do?"

I could tell from the pallor of his face the moment Andy figured out what I was thinking. "Since he doesn't seem to care how many hosts he goes through, he'd want to take over someone who was already close to you."

I was diving for the phone before the sentence was even out of his mouth.

I called Adam back first, fearing Der Jäger might go after Dominic. Then I retreated to my bedroom, the phone clutched in my hand, my heart hammering.

Maybe Brian was in no danger whatsoever. After all, I hadn't seen or talked to him since Der Jäger had entered the Mortal Plain. But I didn't dare take any chances. Mouth dry, palms sweaty, I dialed his number. I had to remind myself to breathe as the phone rang.

There was no answer. Brian often worked tons of overtime, so I tried his office number. No luck.

Finally, I resorted to dialing his cell phone. I hoped like hell I wasn't interrupting a date. Of course, since I'd cut him loose, I should theoretically be happy if he'd moved on with his life and found a new woman. *Theoretically* being the key word.

The phone rang three times, and I was afraid I was about to be dumped into voice mail. Then the voice I'd missed more than I could express said, "Hello, Morgan."

My mouth was so dry that I couldn't even answer him at first. I tried to interpret the tone of his voice. Was he furious with me? In dire pain? Or had he found a measure of acceptance? I couldn't figure it out from two words.

"Morgan? Are you all right?"

Five more words, and I still couldn't figure it out. But I found a scrap of my voice. "Yeah." I realized with a jolt of alarm that I had no idea what to say to him. Though he had suffered dreadfully on my account, he had no idea why. He knew only the police interpretation.

"Are you going to speak to me, or are you expecting a monologue?"

I cleared my throat, my mind still frantically searching for what to say. "Sorry," I said. My voice sounded crackly, and I cleared my throat again. When in doubt, stall. "Look, something's come up and I need to talk to you. Can you come over?"

There was a moment of silence as he processed that. "What kind of 'something'?"

"I'll tell you all about it when you get here." I wondered if my nose was growing longer.

He chuckled. "You never tell me 'all about' anything. And I'm kinda busy right now."

I hated the way my stomach clenched as I imagined just what "busy" might mean. *Please, God, don't let him be on a date*, I thought, then hated myself for it.

"It's important."

He sighed dramatically. "You do love keeping your

cards close to the vest. I still love you, but if you expect me to drop everything and come running without anything more to go on, I'm afraid I'm going to disappoint you."

I couldn't tell if hearing that he still loved me made me feel better, or worse. "It's too much to explain over the phone." Especially when I hadn't the foggiest idea what I was going to say. "But I think you may be in danger. I couldn't bear it if you got hurt because of me again."

He was silent for a long moment, and I held my breath. Then he sighed again and said, "I'll be there in about a half hour."

There was nothing more to say after that, so we hung up. When I wandered back into the living room, the TV was finally off. Andy watched me as I plopped down on the love seat and curled my feet up under me.

"What are you looking at?" I asked, folding my arms across my chest.

His lips twitched in a hint of a smile, quickly banished. "What are you going to tell him?"

I hunkered down lower in the love seat. "I haven't the faintest idea."

"And your plan to keep him safe from Der Jäger is . . . ?"

"See previous answer." I closed my eyes, laying the back of my head against the back of the love seat. Why did everything always have to be so fucking complicated?

"You might want to work something out before he gets here."

I opened my eyes and glared at him. "Thanks for the tip, Einstein."

My snarkiness didn't seem to bother him, which wasn't much of a surprise. After all, I'd probably been snarky in the womb, and he'd known me all my life. He met my glare with a neutral expression.

"And have you considered the possibility that Der Jäger might have gotten to him already?"

"No!" I shouted, though the very vehemence of my denial proved what a liar I was. "I refuse to consider it."

Apparently, Andy had some wax buildup in his ears, since he went right on talking.

"When he comes in, I'll keep him contained," he said, patting the Taser that lay beside him on the couch. "Then you check out his aura, make sure he doesn't have company."

"Who died and made you king?" I asked, then grimaced at my choice of clichés.

"You're probably right, and Der Jäger probably hasn't gotten to him yet. But 'probably' isn't 'absolutely.' You know we have to make sure."

The problem was, I *did* know. And it didn't make a damn bit of difference whether I liked it or not.

Chapter **12**

I **was unhappy** with this plan on so many levels I couldn't even count them all. But I went along with it anyway.

As Andy and I waited for Brian to arrive, I pulled a single chair away from the dining room table, positioning it in the biggest open space I could find. I had to shove the coffee table and love seat to the side to make room. Then I dug into my supply of vanilla-scented candles, arranging them in a circle around the chair. When the security desk downstairs called, I told them to send Brian up, and I started lighting the candles, trying to pretend my hands weren't shaking as I did so. I moved one candle out of alignment to give Brian room to enter the circle. Then, I waited.

Andy, his strength slowly beginning to return, propped himself against the dining room wall, giving himself a clear shot at the doorway. The Taser was armed and ready to go, and Andy's face showed nothing but grim determination. I hoped he didn't have an itchy trigger finger, but it was too late to reverse our roles now.

The ding of the elevator gave me advance warning

of Brian's arrival. I gave up trying to sort out the clamor of emotions that warred within me, steadying my nerves as best I could. I still had no idea what I was going to tell him.

I opened the door before he had a chance to knock, and the sight of him stole my breath.

In the looks department, Brian can't compete with the perfection of Lugh or Adam, but he's still damn good-looking, in a sort of all-American-boy way that seemed so wrong for someone like me. My heart fluttered in my chest at the sight of him, even though he wasn't giving me the fabulous, warm smile that had melted away my cares so often.

He opened his mouth to say something, then caught sight of Andrew and the Taser. His whisky-brown eyes widened with shock and he gaped at me. Guilt gnawed at my guts, but I forced myself to meet his eyes.

"Step inside, please," I said, moving back a bit and holding the door open for him.

He just stood there, staring at me. "What's this all about?"

"Come in, and I'll explain. I'm really sorry about this. Andy and I are just being paranoid." When he still didn't move, I gave him my most beseeching look. I was pretty sure that if he didn't come in of his own free will, Andy was going to zap him, but if I could possibly avoid threatening him, I would.

Finally, Brian's shoulders slumped. "This ought to be an interesting explanation," he muttered.

Even though I didn't really believe Der Jäger had gotten to him yet, I kept my distance from him as he crossed the threshold and I closed the door behind him. It was then that he saw the chair and the circle of candles.

"You think I'm *possessed*?" he cried, giving me a look that said I was out of my mind.

I shook my head. "No. But I'd hate to be wrong. Please just take a seat. I'll take a quick look at your aura, and then we can talk."

He scowled at me. Before my bad influence had rubbed off on him, he'd been one of the most even-tempered individuals I'd ever met. I hated the thought that being with me had changed that.

"I should have known when you called me that it would be something like this." His face slightly flushed with his anger, he stomped over to the chair and plopped down on it, refusing to meet my eyes.

"I'm sorry," I said again, but he didn't look at me or acknowledge the apology.

Trying not to be hurt, because, after all, I'd be acting the same way in his shoes, I closed the circle. It wasn't really necessary for the candles to be arranged in a circle, and often I dispensed with the formality, but I was so miserable that I fell back on the more traditional ritual.

I sat cross-legged on the floor, facing the man I loved while my brother held him at Taser-point. Letting myself drift into the trance state might turn out to be something of an issue when I was such an emotional wreck.

I closed my eyes and breathed deeply, drawing the calming scent of vanilla into my lungs. It was a scent my body and mind associated with the peaceful, dreamy sensation of the trance state, and some of my tension fled with that first deep breath. I could do this. And when I'd explained, Brian would understand.

Even as I thought that to myself, I remembered Lugh's parting shot—*No, I would not expect you, of all people, to take anything on faith*. The memory almost dispelled the calm that had begun to settle, but after a quick spike of adrenaline, another breath of vanilla took me farther away from the physical world.

The trance descended on me like an altered state of consciousness. The real world fell away, and my mind opened to my otherworldly vision, the kind that did not rely on my eyes.

In the trance state, I can see nothing but living beings, the physical world around them nothing but a black, empty void. People show up as vaguely human-shaped patches of primary blue, their hue shaded by their emotions. Fear tends to tinge their auras with yellow, and though my focus was on Brian, I could see that Andy's aura was almost green. I wondered if he was afraid because he thought Brian might be hosting Der Jäger, or if he was just in a perpetual state of fear after what Raphael had done to him.

I forced my attention away from my brother and examined Brian's aura. There was no hint of demon-red in it, but it roiled with every shade of blue imaginable, his emotions raw and wild. I had a voyeur's temptation to linger in the trance, staring at his aura and picking out the emotions, finding out exactly what he felt about me at this moment. But then, did I really want to know?

I opened my eyes, and the real world reappeared. "You can relax," I told Andy. "His aura's clean."

Andy lowered the Taser, but I wouldn't exactly say he relaxed. I started blowing out candles, and the acrid smell of smoke blended with the vanilla.

"May I get up?" Brian asked acidly, "or are you planning to handcuff me to the chair for interrogation now?"

Guilt stabbed through me for a moment, but I fought against it. I hadn't done anything wrong. There would have been no other way to confirm that Der Jäger hadn't possessed him.

I blew out the last candle and spoke without looking at him. "I'm not going to apologize again. I've got a rogue demon after me, and I've got reason to believe he might try to get to me through people I care about. I had to make sure he hadn't gotten to you yet."

I was on my knees, gathering up the candles. I heard Brian stand up. I swallowed the lump in my throat and looked up at him, the still-warm candles clutched to my chest. The steely look in his eyes told me he hadn't forgiven me. I struggled to my feet.

"Please sit down," I said. "We really do need to talk."

His face closed and shuttered, he pulled the coffee table away from the couch so there was room for him to sit. It wasn't hard to read from his body language that he didn't want to hear what I had to say.

"I'll take those," Andy said, and I jumped a bit, not having noticed him approach. He reached for the candles, and I gratefully allowed him to take them from me. Then he mouthed "good luck" at me before he tactfully disappeared into the guest bedroom and closed the door.

I had a brief moment of worry, until I saw he'd left the Taser on the coffee table. Brian saw me looking at it, and before I could say anything, he grabbed it. At least he didn't point it at me.

Once upon a time, I'd have sat next to him on the couch and had a good snuggle—which would have led to a passionate bout of lovemaking. Now, I felt like I was with a stranger, maybe even a hostile one, so I sat on the love seat instead, my hands folded in my lap.

"Do you know how to fire that?" I asked him, and his eyes widened in surprise. I guess he hadn't been expecting the question. "If you don't, then I'd be more comfortable if you gave it to me. Just in case my new friend manages to get in the building and breaks down the door."

His mouth tightened into a grim line, but he put the Taser on the coffee table and slid it across to me. I was glad to have something to hold on to, even if my palm was clammy and my taped fingers made the grip awkward.

"So, what's the story?" he asked, and his voice was now carefully neutral. It was his lawyer-voice, and I'd always hated it.

A part of me wanted to spill my guts, tell him everything, lean on him so I wouldn't feel so alone anymore. And despite Andy, and Adam, and Lugh, I really was alone. I distrusted all three of them, to differing degrees and for different reasons. Brian had always been someone I trusted.

But I had done everything I could so far to keep the chaos of my life from dragging him down with me, and I wasn't going to let my selfish desire for comfort ruin everything.

"There's not a whole lot to tell," I lied. "I ran afoul of a rogue demon, and he's made it clear he's planning to come after me. I found out tonight that the host I met him in had been abandoned in an alley, and I realized his best chance of getting close to me was through someone I know. Do you have any vacation time coming to you? Is there any chance you could get out of town for a week or two?"

Brian laughed, but it was a bitter sound. "You don't learn, do you? I'm not the type to run and hide."

Heat flushed my face, and I had to pull back the reins on my temper. "I understand that. I really do. But this guy's a *demon*. And we have no idea what body he's in. There's no way you can protect yourself from that."

"Why is this demon after you?"

It was the question I'd been dreading, the question I had no good answer for. I did the best I could, though I'm a lousy liar. "I tried to exorcize him. I failed, and he got away. Now it's payback time."

Brian rolled his eyes. "That's bullshit. If a rogue demon had escaped confinement, it would be all over the news. I haven't heard a peep."

I did my best to improvise, but I knew my answer came too slowly, showing that I had to think a minute. "The police are trying to keep it quiet to prevent a panic."

He stood up, shaking his head. "Either tell me the truth, or I walk. In case you haven't noticed, I'm a grown, capable man. I don't need you to protect me."

I knew it was a stupid thing to do, but I couldn't help the snort of laughter. I tried to turn it into a cough, but failed. Brian glared at me, and I made a calming gesture with my hand.

"Sorry, but I'm an exorcist, and the bad guy's a demon. There's no one more qualified to protect you in this case than I am."

"Bye, Morgan," he said, spinning on his heel and striding for the door.

I surged to my feet, the Taser clutched in my hand. "Brian, please! We need to talk about this, come up with a plan, even if you're not willing to get out of town."

He held up his hand in a wave, not turning to look at me. Moving almost on autopilot, I armed the Taser and pointed it at his back.

"Brian, stop!" I said in my most commanding voice. When he ignored me and reached for the doorknob, I yelled even louder. "Stop, or I'll shoot!"

That gave him pause, and he glanced over his shoulder. When he saw the Taser, the blood drained from his face.

I felt a tear drip from the corner of my eye and crawl down my cheek. Words couldn't express how much I hated this. But how could I let him just walk away? He had absolutely no way to defend himself against a rogue demon. I doubted he could fire a Taser, even if he had one. I sniffled, but didn't relent.

"I'm sorry if I'm offending your macho, he-man sensibilities," I said with far more steel in my voice than I actually felt, "but if I have to save you in spite of yourself, I'll do it."

He blinked, hand still on the doorknob. "You dumped me, Morgan. I'm no longer your responsibility. Not that I ever was. If you're going to shoot, go ahead and do it."

He turned his back to me once more, turning the doorknob. My finger tightened on the trigger, and I braced my shaking hand as best I could with my other hand. The door swung open, and I willed myself to pull the trigger. Brian stepped over the threshold, and still I stood frozen in place, statue-still except for the tremors that ripped through me.

The door started to close behind him. It was my last chance. *Don't be such a baby,* I urged myself. *It's for his own good, and it doesn't matter if he hates you for it. Hell, that might even be a* good *thing.*

After what felt like about three years, I finally found the will to pull the trigger. Just in time for the Taser probes to thunk harmlessly into the closed door.

Chapter **13**

I could have gone after him. I could have ejected the spent cartridge from the Taser and probably gotten to him while he was waiting for the elevator. The Taser could also act as a stun gun at close range, and Brian was too much on the straight and narrow to be much of a fighter. Of course, it would be a tad inconvenient if any of my neighbors saw.

Yet despite my conviction that it was the right thing to do, I didn't follow him. Yeah, I'm a bit of a hard-ass, but let's face it, there was no way I could stand to hurt Brian.

Remembering that Brian wasn't the only person I needed the Taser for, I ejected the cartridge and reloaded. I tucked the Taser into the waistband of my jeans, even though that was very uncomfortable, then got out the vacuum cleaner to get rid of the cloud of confetti-like tags the cartridge ejects when it's fired. Andy emerged from his room, and I could feel his curious gaze on me, but he didn't say anything, even before the roar of the vacuum cleaner filled the air.

I was winding up the cord when I heard a knock on my door. My heart leapt into my throat, and I dropped the cord, reaching for the Taser. My nerves were completely shot, so when I yanked the Taser from my waistband, I fumbled and it dropped to the floor. I practically threw myself after it as the knock sounded again.

"Relax, kids," Adam's voice said from the hallway. "It's just me."

I grabbed the Taser anyway, my heartbeat still hammering wildly. I stayed on my knees for a moment, waiting for the adrenaline rush to calm. Meanwhile, Andy opened the door.

I looked up, expecting to see Adam, but instead Brian came flying through the doorway to land on his hands and knees. I blinked in confusion, finding the strength to stand up. Adam strode through the door behind Brian, his eyes narrowed.

"Look who I found trying to leave the building, completely unprotected and unarmed," Adam said.

Andy had started to close the door, but Dominic pushed it open again, entering the apartment less dramatically than Brian or Adam had. The whole tableau left me completely unbalanced, but I did my best not to show it.

"If I'd known we were having a party, I'd have baked a cake," I said.

Andy and Dom laughed, but neither Adam nor Brian seemed to think that was particularly funny. Adam glared at me.

"I thought you loved this guy," he growled. "And you were just going to let him walk out of here for Der Jäger to chew up and spit out?"

My throat tightened as Brian struggled to his feet. I could see the rug burn that reddened the heels of both his hands, and indignation surged through my veins, even as I realized Adam had probably done a good thing by preventing Brian from leaving.

"You didn't have to manhandle him like that, asshole!" I said, then hurried to put myself between Adam and Brian. I had more to say, but Dom interrupted.

"Time out, both of you. I know how much you love to fight, but we've got more important things to do right now." His voice was firm and authoritative, sure of himself. I kept thinking about him as a mildly submissive beta male—mainly because Adam was so dominant—but Dom had a steely backbone hidden beneath the nice-guy surface. And he didn't seem to be intimidated by Adam's death glare.

I stayed out of it as the two of them stared at each other as if they were having a silent conversation. And if I hadn't seen it happen before between the two of them, I'd have been shocked to see Adam actually back down. He held up both hands in a gesture of surrender. Meanwhile, Brian looked back and forth between Adam and Dominic and me. His gaze finally settled on me.

"You know these guys?" he asked.

I realized with a little shock that Brian had never met Adam and Dom. Not while conscious, at least. I cleared my throat.

"Uh, yeah. These are the guys who rescued you when you were kidnapped. Adam White," I said, pointing, "and Dominic Castello."

Brian took a moment to absorb that, turning his attention back to Adam and Dom. "Thanks, I guess." He looked more closely at Adam. "I've seen you on TV. You're the Director of Special Forces, aren't you?"

Adam nodded.

Brian held up his rug-burned hands. "So what's *this* all about?"

Adam ignored him and looked at me. "Didn't you tell him *anything*?"

Dom put a hand on his arm. "Take it down a notch."

Adam turned to him. "When did you get so goddamn pushy?" he complained. But I noticed he didn't make any attempt to shake off his lover's hand.

Dominic's eyes twinkled with mischief, and he grinned. "You can put me in my place later."

My cheeks went hot as I sorted out the nuances in Dominic's words. I wondered if everyone in the room heard them, or whether it was just because I had up-close-and-personal experience with them.

"I told him I had a rogue demon after me," I said a little too loudly, trying to cover my discomfort. "He made it clear he wasn't interested in my help, and I couldn't talk him into staying. What did you expect me to do?"

Adam flashed me a look that told me *exactly* what he'd expected me to do, but with Dominic's hand still on his arm, he managed to control his desire to tell me out loud.

Dominic smiled pleasantly at Brian. "Maybe it's better if I do the talking so we don't have to see any more of the snake-and-mongoose act." Adam and I snorted in unison. Dom ignored us. "Why don't we all sit down?"

Brian thought about that a minute, then went to sit on the couch without another word. Adam and Dom took the love seat, and Andy took the other end of the couch, leaving the middle seat for me. He refused to meet my narrowed eyes, but I couldn't help thinking he was doing a little matchmaking. Then again, maybe he just didn't like the idea of sitting right next to another guy on the sofa. My brain was conjuring up ulterior motives for everything.

I sat down and opened my mouth to say something— I'm not entirely sure what—but Dominic cut me off.

"Please let me do the talking. I find you and Adam entertaining, but I doubt Brian and Andrew are equally amused."

I made a zipping-my-lips gesture, and Dominic turned his attention to Brian.

"The demon that's after Morgan is known as Der Jäger. From what I understand, he's the demon equivalent of a sociopath, and we all believe the easiest way for him to get to Morgan is through someone she knows and trusts. Which means you and I and Andrew are all prime targets. He's already abandoned two hosts that we know of, which goes to show how little respect he has for human life. If he took one of us, he would destroy us and kill Morgan. I know you and Morgan aren't together anymore, but Der Jäger might not know that—and might not care even if he does."

Brian frowned at him. "And where do the two of you come into the picture?"

"Adam and I are Morgan's friends," Dominic answered, which made Adam snort with derision and Brian's eyes narrow in speculation. I supposed he hadn't caught the earlier innuendo that had made me so uncomfortable.

I gave Brian a little prod with my elbow. "Not *that* kind of friends," I said.

Adam chuckled and slung his arm around Dom's shoulders. "Definitely not."

I rolled my eyes. "Don't you two start."

Adam blinked at me innocently. "Start what?"

"Anyway," Dom said loudly before Adam and I could escalate, "with Der Jäger on the hunt, we really do need to take precautions. Andrew is staying here with Morgan, and I'm staying with Adam." He looked at Brian. "That leaves only you. It isn't safe for you to just go back to your apartment and act as if nothing's wrong."

Brian stared at Adam. "You're the Director of Special Forces. If you think I'm in danger from this demon, you can assign me some protection."

But Adam shook his head. "I'm not here in any official capacity. There are some facts about this case that I can't divulge."

"Like why this demon is after Morgan?"

Afraid I was about to be caught in a lie, I tried to keep Adam from commenting. "I told him—"

Brian spoke over me. "Don't tell him what you told me! I want to hear from Mr. White himself why he believes this demon is after you."

"Whatever Morgan told you is a lie," Adam said, and it was all I could do not to leap out of my chair and smack him. "She can't tell you the truth about this any more than I can. There are things you are better off not knowing. This is one of them."

Brian ignored me like I wasn't even there. "This doesn't have anything to do with why Andrew—that is, Andrew's demon—kidnapped me, does it?"

Adam grinned. "Would you believe me if I said no?"

We all knew the answer to that.

"If my life's in danger," Brian said, "I have a right to know why."

"I'm not at liberty to reveal that. And as I said, you're better off not knowing."

"That line of reasoning doesn't work for me. I don't buy into the whole ignorance is bliss thing."

Adam shrugged. "Doesn't matter. I've told you everything I can at the moment."

Brian stood up. "Then I guess I'm going home."

Adam arched an eyebrow. "And how, exactly, are you planning to get past me?"

"Are you threatening me?"

"In a manner of speaking. I'm not letting you leave this apartment on your own."

Brian rubbed his jaw. "And what would your superiors have to say if I reported that you threatened me?"

Okay, this was starting to get ugly. I reached for Brian's arm. "Don't mess with Adam. He's got the conscience of a tapeworm." Dominic swallowed a laugh as Adam's face reddened. "I don't agree with his methods, but he's right."

Brian stared down at me. "Considering you threatened to Taser me, I don't think you have any room to throw stones at his methods. And let me get this straight—am I being kidnapped again?"

Luckily for everyone involved, levelheaded Dominic intervened. "All we're trying to do is keep everyone safe. You can't have official police protection, but you need to take some kind of precautions. You don't want a hostile demon rampaging around in your head."

"I can tell you from personal experience that he's right," Andy said. He'd been so quiet, I'd almost forgotten he was in the room. His eyes were haunted and miserable as he stared into some inner distance.

Brian's jaw worked as he thought that over. Both Adam and I managed to keep our mouths shut, which was no doubt a very good thing. Finally, Brian let out a deep, frustrated breath and returned to the couch.

"What exactly do you suggest I do? Morgan suggested I take some vacation time, but I can't just take vacation on the spur of the moment."

Dominic shrugged. "Can you call in sick? The easiest way for Der Jäger to get to you is just to brush by you on the street. We have no idea who he's taken as a host, and as you know he can transfer to you in less than a second. You need to severely limit your contact with other people."

Brian is a goody-two-shoes through and through. I could tell from the look on his face that the idea of lying about being sick didn't sit well with him. A lawyer who's uncomfortable lying. You gotta love it. But though he was angry about the whole situation, he wasn't a dummy. With that first shot of indignation out of his system, he had to know how limited his choices were.

"Okay, so I call in sick. Then what? I lock myself in my apartment and hide there until someone tells me it's safe to come out?" He looked almost sullen, which was completely unlike him.

"Actually," Dominic said, "I don't think that would be a great idea, either. I doubt Der Jäger would have much trouble breaking into your apartment, and if you're there all by yourself, you'll be far too vulnerable."

Suddenly, I knew where he was going with this, and my emotions rioted. I would have blurted out some kind of incoherent protest, if only my brain were functioning well enough to muster one. Instead, I sat there at a loss for words, not even knowing how to label what I was feeling.

"I'm confident that I'm safe with Adam," Dominic said, "seeing as he's a demon. But I'm not so confident that Morgan and Andrew are safe together, being only human. If you would stay here, too, the three of you could guard the door in shifts."

Yup, that's what I thought he was going to say. It was a great way to try to salvage Brian's male ego, but I didn't know if I could bear it. It had taken more willpower than I'd thought I had to push Brian away in the first place. If he was right here in the apartment with me, would I be able to resist the temptation? If I gave him even the faintest hint that I still loved him, I'd *never* be able to shake him. Of course, Adam might have let the cat out of the bag when he shoved Brian through that doorway.

And in the deep recesses of my selfish heart, I wanted him back so desperately, I could taste it.

Out of the corner of my eye, I saw a quick smile flash across Brian's lips, gone in the blink of an eye. "Now *that's* an imprisonment I think I could bear," he said, and I saw a calculating gleam in his eye.

I groaned and lowered my head into my hands. One of the ways I had guarded my heart against Brian had been to keep him as far away from me as possible. That light in his eye told me he had hopes our forced proximity would let him break down my defenses. "Thanks a lot, Dom," I grumbled, once again wondering whether this was some kind of matchmaking scheme. But that was ridiculously self-centered of me. The fate of the world lay in the balance, and I suspected Dominic of matchmaking? Yeesh!

"Fine," I said, trying to sound annoyed, even while my heart leapt with hope I tried my damnedest to suppress. "Brian can stay here for a while. But we can't just sit around waiting for Der Jäger to attack. We've got to *do* something about him."

Adam raised an eyebrow at me. "Do you have something in mind?"

I gave him a narrow-eyed glare, but I was proud of myself for not making a smart-ass remark. We both knew I didn't have a plan. At least, not yet.

"Let's play defense first," Adam said. "We can't do much that's very useful until we've got some sense of security." He reached into his jacket pocket and pulled out a Taser. "I thought it might be a good idea if you had a backup piece," he said, putting the Taser on the coffee table. "Just in case. I'd like the three of you to sit tight for tonight. Dom and I are going to go interview some, uh, persons of interest."

I clenched my teeth. Hard. I had a sneaking suspicion these "persons of interest" were my parents. I shot a pleading look at Dom—I knew my protests would be useless with Adam. Dom gave me a reassuring smile, and I hoped that meant he wouldn't let Adam do anything drastic. Not that he had the power to stop Adam from doing whatever he damn well pleased.

"After that," Adam continued, "we can get together again and talk strategy. Maybe we'll figure out a way to trap Der Jäger."

I hoped so, but I knew our problems would be far from over even if we did. Der Jäger was an illegal and a rogue, which meant he would be executed by the state if caught. Unfortunately, the state thought exorcizing a demon would kill it. If an exorcist sent him back to the Demon Realm, that wouldn't do us a lick of good, because he'd be back in no time.

If I wanted to get Der Jäger off my tail, he, and whatever hapless human host he inhabited, would have to be burned.

If I could put off until tomorrow making a plan that called for burning someone alive, I was more than happy to do so. But I couldn't put off *thinking* about it, and the churning that had been eating away my stomach lining all day just kept getting worse.

Chapter **14**

After Adam and Dom left, my big brother once again abandoned me to the wolves by running off to his own room. I wanted to remind him how well it had worked out last time he'd left me alone with Brian, but I managed to refrain. When the door thunked closed behind him, silence, dense and oppressive, settled on the living room.

Brian was still sitting on the couch, but I was far too antsy to hold still, so I wandered around the living room pretending to tidy up while I tried to gather my wits about me. And convince myself that leaping into Brian's arms and kissing him senseless was a bad idea.

His quiet sigh made something clench in my gut.

"So, are you planning to look at me or speak to me?" he asked. "Or are you just going to ignore me and pretend I'm not here?"

I'd gathered a pile of magazines from the coffee table, but at Brian's gentle rebuke I dropped them onto the end table and forced myself to sit back down and face him.

"Sorry," I said. "This is kind of awkward, you know."

He crossed his arms and leaned back into the cushions of the couch. I realized neither one of us was being terribly watchful, so I picked up one of the Tasers and shifted position so I'd have a clear shot at the door if I needed it. That didn't save me from Brian's questioning glance.

"Your friend Adam seems to think you still love me."

I winced, remembering Adam bellowing something to that effect when he'd brought Brian back to the apartment. I'd hoped Brian was too distracted by all the rest of this mess to have noticed. I just couldn't seem to catch a break these days.

"If he's right," Brian continued mercilessly, "then why are you so determined to push me away?"

I swallowed a sudden lump in my throat. I could try to deny that I loved him, but who the hell would I be kidding? Certainly not Brian! "Because I didn't want you to get sucked into this shit."

He cocked his head, his lawyerly instincts perking up. "In other words, you knew you were still in trouble even after that demon abandoned your brother."

Reluctantly, I nodded. I stared at the Taser in my lap. "And I know it's not going to go away anytime soon." I forced myself to look up, to meet Brian's eyes. "You've gotten hurt because of me once before. I'm not going to let it happen again."

His jaw set grimly. "You're really a piece of work, you know? Did it ever occur to you that I'm a big boy and can make my own decisions about what risks I want to take?"

For someone who was supposedly trying to push her ex-boyfriend away, I sure was saying things better suited to the opposite purpose. I shook my head in frustration.

"You can't make an informed decision about this. There are too many things I can't tell you. All I can do is beg you to listen to me and keep away." I frowned. "Once it's safe for you to keep away."

"I'm not sure I can do that, Morgan."

As usual, my mouth started moving before my brain caught up. "You've been doing a pretty good job lately."

I felt the blood heating my cheeks, and even though I put a hand over my eyes—as if I could somehow hide from my own stupidity—I saw the spark of triumph in Brian's eyes. He didn't say anything, but I had begun to think his sudden disappearance from my life hadn't meant what I'd thought it had.

Indignation helped chase away my irritation with my runaway tongue. "You hadn't really given up on me," I said accusingly. "You were just playing with me!"

He shrugged, still looking smug. "You know what they say—absence makes the heart grow fonder. I thought I'd test the theory out."

And, damn him, his little experiment had worked. When he'd been pestering me relentlessly, sending me flowers and love letters, trying every romantic gesture known to mankind, it had been almost easy for me to be my normal, contrary self. Someone pushes me, I push right back. Harder, if possible.

"You're one manipulative son of a bitch," I told him, but there wasn't enough heat in my voice to make it the kind of slap-down it was meant to be.

"Honey, I'm a lawyer. I'm paid—and paid well, I might add—to be a manipulative son of a bitch. So now that we have all that out of the way, can we go to bed and have wild monkey sex? I've been missing you in more ways than one." He waggled his eyebrows at me.

The temptation was enough to make me squirm. I doubted he'd forgiven me, doubted even a bout of wild monkey sex would make things right between us after all I'd done to sabotage the relationship. But it would feel *so* good to lose myself in him, if only for a little while.

I tried not to think about what Brian's body felt like pressed up against mine. Tried not to think about the physical chemistry between us that practically lit the bed on fire when we were together. Tried not to think about everything I was giving up by giving up on him.

"Sorry," I said. "I don't do wild monkey sex when a sociopathic demon might come crashing through my front door any moment." I thought it made a damn good excuse.

He grinned at me. "So we ask Andrew to keep watch, and *then* we go have wild monkey sex."

I suppressed my sudden urge to grin right back at him. "I am *not* having sex of any kind when my brother's in the next room. That's just . . . eww." I crinkled up my nose in disgust, and Brian laughed.

"I'm sure your brother knows you're not a virgin," Brian started, but I made a slashing gesture across my throat.

"Cut it out. Now! I'm not having sex with you, and I'm not getting back together with you. That's final. Now, can we talk about something else? Or, better yet, maybe there's something good on TV."

I grabbed the remote and turned the TV on, desperate for any escape from the quicksand I was trying to pick my way through. Obviously, I was a lot safer if I just kept my mouth shut.

I expected Brian to protest, but he merely sat back in the cushions and made himself comfortable. He knew he'd pushed as far as he dared, and like any predator worth his salt, he knew when to back off and wait for his prey to make a fatal mistake.

I was beginning to feel like a gazelle with a pride of lions on its ass. Somehow, I needed to figure out how to run faster.

Brian, Andy, and I took turns keeping watch in two-hour shifts. Whoever got the short end of the stick for a shift got to hang out in the living room watching the door while the other two slept. Brian, of course, wanted to sleep in my bed. I told him he could sleep in it when it was my turn to watch, and dared him to keep pushing me. Wisely, he backed off.

After a quick Taser 101 course I let Andy take the first watch and retreated to my bedroom. My entire body felt heavy with exhaustion, not all of it physical. Even so, I had a hard time falling asleep. I wasn't sure how much I trusted either of my roommates to guard the door. And my treacherous mind kept conjuring images of Brian, nude and eager, lying in bed beside me.

Somehow, I managed to drift off, and once again I dreamed of Lugh. In retrospect, I think I knew he would have something to say to me that night, and perhaps that's part of why I had such a hard time falling asleep. For a demon, he's a really great guy, and I actually *like* him. But his ability to see inside the dark corners of my soul—and his insistence on sharing what he sees—scares the crap out of me. There's a reason I keep the metaphorical lights out in those corners.

At least we were back in his living room, not his bedroom. Brian's arrival had put my hormones in overdrive, and I wasn't sure I'd be able to resist Lugh's charms if we were in that bedroom.

He looked different today. No black leather. Instead, he wore a pair of close-fitting jeans and a plain white button-down shirt, and he sported a pair of pristine white sneakers. I knew exactly what he was up to. When I had any impure thoughts about Adam, Lugh would appear in my dreams as the S&M poster boy. Now that it was Brian who'd cranked up my hormones, he was going for the all-American-guy look. Only he was far too dangerous-looking to pull that off.

"I like the outfit," I commented as casually as possible, dropping into the love seat across from him. I myself was wearing comfy knit pajama bottoms with a wispy camisole top. It was better than being naked, but not by much.

Lugh smiled. "I thought you might."

I scrubbed at my eyes. "Can't you just let me get a good night's sleep?"

"You've only got two hours coming to you," he said, knowing I had taken the second watch shift, "and you wasted more than an hour of that tossing and turning. I'm not depriving you of much."

"But I'm too tired to deal with you right now." Even to my own ears, I sounded like I was whining.

Not surprisingly, Lugh didn't care about my desire to escape serious conversations. "I'll make this brief, then."

I gave him a dirty look, but he ignored it. "I understand your need to protect Brian," he said. "And ordinarily, I would do anything possible to keep a defenseless human out of the line of fire. But it's clear to me—as it is to you, in your heart of hearts—that even if you aren't actively dating him, he'll always be vulnerable because of your past history."

"Thanks!" I snapped. "I needed to feel a little more guilty about dragging him into the middle of a demon civil war."

"What this means is that there's no reason for you to keep pushing him away for his own safety. Doing so is hurting both of you, and it's obviously *not* keeping him safe."

But the reasons I was pushing Brian away were so much more complicated than that, and Lugh knew it. Yes, keeping him safe from Dougal's minions was my primary motivation. But I was also trying to keep him safe from my own majorly fucked-up life.

"And," Lugh continued, "I think if he's going to remain in the line of fire, he deserves to know the truth."

I blinked, not sure I'd heard him correctly. "The truth?"

Lugh nodded, his dark amber eyes seeming to peer into my soul as he stared at me. "You have my permission to tell him about me. And about Dougal."

"Since when do I need your permission?" I asked, hackles rising for no good reason except that I was uncomfortable.

He smiled. "All right then, my blessing. Does that sound better?"

"Not really," I muttered, my mind going in circles. If I told Brian everything, then I'd *never* get rid of him.

And I'd lose the excuse I'd been giving myself for why he couldn't make an informed decision to stay by my side.

I stared at my hands, my jaw clenched as I imagined tearing down the wall I'd built between myself and the man I loved. How could I bear to do that? I remembered how I'd felt when I'd discovered Raphael had kidnapped him, when I'd seen the terrible, terrifying videotape of the man I loved being tortured on my account. It had been the worst moment of my life, worse even than when I'd been tied to the stake with piles of kindling at my feet.

Tears burned my eyes, and my hands clenched so tightly my fingernails left bloodless crescents in my own skin. "I can't go through that again," I whispered.

I wasn't surprised when Lugh appeared on the love seat beside me and drew me into his arms. And I was too overwhelmed to object when he tucked my head into the crook of his neck and rubbed one strong hand up and down my back. My own arms slipped around his waist, and I squeezed tight, absorbing the warmth and comfort of his body, inhaling his unique scent.

There was nothing sexual about that embrace. Even though I can't deny I was attracted to him, nor could I fool myself into thinking he wasn't attracted to me. It was nothing but a glorious, comforting hug, at a time I badly needed one.

"He'll be safer if he knows," Lugh said, his voice a barely audible rumble.

Before I could muster another argument, I woke up to the sensation of Andrew tapping my shoulder.

"Wake up, little sister," he said. "It's your turn to keep watch."

I had the feeling I was in for a very long two hours.

I was right about that being one of the longest nights of my life. Even after Andrew had gotten me up and I'd taken my place on the couch, guarding the door, Lugh's words echoed through my brain. Was I, as usual, being a chickenshit and making excuses for why I was pushing Brian away?

Of course I was. I might not be thrilled to admit it to myself, but I knew truth when I heard it. But, I told myself, I'd had legitimate reasons as well. Reasons that had nothing to do with my hang-ups and insecurities, and everything to do with the danger that clung to me like the stench of cigarette smoke after a night at a bar.

When it was time to wake Brian up to take the next watch, I could have stayed up with him and told him my whole crazy story. I could have opened my heart to him, and eased some of the pain in my own soul. Instead, I merely climbed into bed and fell into a deep and blessedly dreamless sleep.

I woke up the next morning to discover that I'd been the victim of a male conspiracy to let me sleep. I was supposed to have been on watch for one more shift over the course of the night, but Brian and Andy had neglected to wake me, and for once, Lugh hadn't entered my dreams. I won't say I was exactly fresh as a daisy, but I didn't feel like I'd been run over by a truck, either, which was a nice change.

I followed the scent of brewing coffee into the kitchen, and discovered that I had even more company. Dominic was making himself at home in my kitchen, while Adam sat at the table sipping coffee from my favorite mug.

Before my caffeine-deprived brain could come up with an appropriately snarky comment, Brian shoved a mug in my face. The scent of coffee temporarily derailed me, and I took the mug and cupped it in both hands. Of course, after many mornings-after together, Brian knew exactly how I liked my coffee. Gulping down the heavenly brew, burning my tongue more than once, I retreated to the living room, trying my best to ignore the testosterone brigade that had invaded my tiny apartment. Sizzling sounds from the kitchen told me Dominic was cooking. Like Pavlov's dog, I started drooling at the thought, even before the enticing scents reached my nose.

Adam didn't take my not-so-subtle hint that I wanted to be left alone. Why was I not surprised? He sat beside me on the sofa, resting his elbow on the back and staring at me.

"What?" I asked, when I couldn't stand the scrutiny any longer.

"I'm just waiting for the caffeine to hit your system. I know how grumpy you are before your morning coffee."

I narrowed my eyes at him, then checked over my shoulder. Yup, Brian was standing right there. Heat flooded my cheeks. Brian's face was studiously neutral, but I knew him too well not to see the suspicion in his eyes. I figured my overactive blush reflex was just making me look even more guilty. And then I remembered the dream of watching Adam and Dominic together, remembered how incredibly hot it had made me, and my cheeks burned even brighter.

"Adam's just trying to make trouble," I said tightly. "We're not even *friends*, much less lovers."

"Adam, behave," Dominic called from the kitchen.

"Yes, Mother," Adam answered with a wicked grin.

I don't know if Brian believed me, but he didn't say anything. I slurped more coffee, feeling the pressure of his eyes on me. Then he shrugged and dismissed the whole thing.

"Whatever," he said. "I'm going to grab a quick shower."

I hated that the tension eased out of my shoulders when Brian disappeared into the guest room. I shouldn't let Adam get to me the way he did, but I just couldn't help it. And I couldn't help that Brian's presence gave Adam so much more fuel to torture me with.

"So what are you two doing here this morning, anyway?" I asked. "And help yourself to my coffee, by the way." I glanced at Dominic, slaving over my stove. "And help yourself to my kitchen."

"Thanks," Dom called cheerfully, frying up something that involved peppers and onions and filled the air with the most enticing aromas imaginable. Short of coffee. He must have been shopping before he'd come over—no way he'd gotten anything that smelled that good out of *my* fridge.

"I thought you might want to know that your parents have flown the coop," Adam said, and I almost choked on my coffee.

"What?"

"When I went to interview them last night, they were gone."

I figured I must not have had enough coffee yet. Surely he wasn't saying what I thought he was saying. "What do you mean 'gone'?"

"I mean packed up everything they own and disappeared."

"That's impossible."

Adam shook his head. "Oh, I assure you, it's quite possible. Aside from packing up everything they own, they also cleared out their bank accounts."

Andy came over and joined us, looking as shocked as I felt. "But Morgan was just over there yesterday!" he protested.

"Yes, I know," Adam said with exaggerated patience. "I was there, too, remember? But I assure you, when we went there last night, they were gone. Naturally, I'm trying to find out where they disappeared to, but no one can disappear this thoroughly and this suddenly without some kind of outside help."

"Bradley Cooper," I said, knowing the slimy little weasel had to have contacts all over the place. And that he wouldn't hesitate to use illegal means to cover up whatever the hell it was he—and the Spirit Society—was hiding.

"His name did spring to mind," Adam agreed.

"Have you had a chance to talk to him yet?"

"He claimed to know nothing. He said he was given the name of the demon to summon by his superiors, and he didn't ask any questions."

"Yeah, and cows grow on trees."

"Of course, since we know what demon he summoned now, I don't suppose his knowledge or lack thereof matters too much. I think we're pretty much on our own with Der Jäger. But I'd definitely like to have another chat with him."

So would I, not that I'd spoken to him anytime recently. I hadn't been able to entirely cut my parents out of my life, but Cooper had been a different story.

The problem was, Cooper was in this up to his ass, and that meant the likelihood of us getting any straight answers out of him was approximately zilch. I shuddered as I took another sip of coffee, wondering if Adam would now use his special interrogation techniques on Cooper. Better than on my parents—at least, from my point of view—but still dangerous. If Adam resorted to violence, then he'd have to kill Cooper when he was done. Otherwise, he'd be declared rogue and his life would be forfeit.

I couldn't stand Cooper, but I didn't want his death on my conscience.

"Let's hold off on talking to Cooper for now," I suggested. "I'd say he's about the *last* person we're likely to get info out of."

Adam gave me a penetrating look, telling me he'd followed my thought process easily. "And who would you suggest we talk to instead?"

Luckily, I had an idea. "Maybe my pediatrician. We have more than one mystery to solve, remember. I know he retired right around when I went to college, but we can probably track him down."

Adam arched an eyebrow skeptically. "And what exactly do you expect him to tell us?"

"He might be able to tell me what happened to me at The Healing Circle when I was thirteen."

"And the reason you expect to get a straight answer out of him is . . ."

I shrugged. "I probably won't. But I might be able to tell if he's hiding something or not."

I remembered Dr. Williams as a kindly old man, who was nice to me even when I was my usual difficult self. I had a hard time believing he'd have been involved with any kind of evil plan to harm me. But he'd been my doctor at the time of what I now was convinced was a suspicious hospitalization, and he had to know *something*.

I'd have to deal with the Adam problem no matter who I approached with questions, but with kindly old Dr. Williams, I thought I was more likely to get cooperation—and less likely to trigger Adam's dark side.

"So you've become a master interrogator?" Adam asked.

I kept my temper firmly in check. "I just plan to ask him a couple of questions, not interrogate him. And you're going to stay here and keep the people I care about safe while I do."

He laughed, as I'd figured he would. Brian, freshly scrubbed, his hair slicked back with water, emerged from the guest bedroom. He looked back and forth between me and Adam like he was trying to figure out the joke.

"Dominic?" I asked, raising my voice to something just under a shout to be heard over Adam's laughter.

Dom seemed to have finished cooking and was now opening random cabinets in the kitchen, probably looking for dishes. He stopped with his hand still on a cabinet door.

"Yes?"

"Can you talk your boyfriend into staying here on guard duty while I go do a little investigating?" I tried not to emphasize the word "boyfriend," and I also tried not to glance at Brian to see his reaction. I failed on both counts. When I accidentally caught his eye, he flashed me a rueful smile that could have meant anything.

"Do you really think that's a good idea?" Dom asked from the kitchen. He'd located the plates, and was now scooping something out of the pan.

"As long as I stay out in the open where people can see me, Der Jäger wouldn't dare come after me. Not unless he wants a date with the state of Pennsylvania's cremation ovens!"

"That's true, I suppose," Dominic said, carrying a pair of plates out to the table, which was barely big enough to seat four average-sized people. None of my unwanted visitors was average-sized—not that I was, either—and I didn't know how we were all supposed to fit at the table.

Since I was asking for a favor, I decided to make myself useful and help serve. I saw the plates were laden with extra-fluffy omelets and home fries, and I was tempted to take two of them for myself.

I set the plates in my hand down on the table, then turned to go get the last one. I almost ran smack into Adam, who'd come up behind me like a sudden summer storm.

"Leave Dom out of this," he said. "If you have to argue, argue with me."

"All right, fine. I do not want your company when I go talk to Dr. Williams. I don't want you—" I almost said *exactly* what I didn't want him to do, then remembered

just in time that Brian didn't have the faintest idea what
was going on. And despite the fact that Lugh had given
me "permission" to tell him everything, I knew I wasn't
going to.

I glanced over at him and saw him watching—and
listening—with silent curiosity. Damn it! We'd already
said *way* too much for my comfort. That's what I got
for talking before being fully fueled up on coffee.

"Look," I said more quietly, feeling almost de-
feated. "I need to do this my way. Let me at least try.
I'll be careful. I'll take a Taser. I'll stay in public places
where Der Jäger won't dare attack me. And I need to
know these guys are safe." I made a sweeping gesture
to encompass Brian and Andy and Dom.

Dom grabbed the last plate from the kitchen.
"Everyone sit down and eat," he said, leaning a hip
against the kitchen counter as he dug into his own
breakfast.

I tried not to hold my breath as the rest of us sat at
the table and I awaited Adam's verdict. He, of course,
had to stuff his face full of eggs and savor them before
he spoke.

"All right," he finally said, and I let out the breath
I'd been trying not to hold. "But if you don't get anything out of him, we're going to have to do it my
way."

I grimaced in what I hoped he'd take for agreement, then took a page from his book and ate like a
pig so I wouldn't have to talk anymore.

Chapter **15**

Finding Dr. Williams turned out not to be as easy as I'd hoped. His first name was Ned, but I didn't find anyone in the phone book under that name. I then looked under Edward, and found a depressingly large number of names. I went through the list and called each one. No luck, though there were a few who hadn't answered the phone. I realized my methods were going to take forever—and we didn't have forever. Reluctantly, I called Adam, who'd gone back to his house with Dom. I was under strict orders to call before I left my apartment, and much though I hated being given orders, I couldn't help agreeing with these.

Adam didn't pick up until after his answering machine had started its spiel. I was just starting to get worried when his real live voice came over the line and the machine cut off.

"You ready to go?" Adam asked, never one to waste time with greetings.

Even in four words, I could hear that he was out of breath. I didn't think it was from running to get the phone. When he'd left my apartment, he'd made up some lame story about how he had some paperwork to do at home, but the sly, secretive look he'd shared with Dom told me more than I'd wanted to know about what he was really up to. So to speak.

A shiver passed down my spine as I wondered whether Adam was breathless from pleasuring his lover or from hurting him. Not that I actually wanted to know. That uncomfortable train of thought made me slow to respond.

"Anything wrong?" Adam asked.

I snorted softly. "Is anything *right*?"

"You know what I mean."

"Yeah. Nothing's wrong. Except that with my brilliant investigation techniques, it's going to take me three weeks to locate Dr. Williams. I don't suppose you'd be able to help me with that, would you?"

His breathing steadied, and I could almost see the ironic lift of his brow. "You're willing to risk letting me know this paragon of virtue's address?"

"It's not like you couldn't find it anyway," I retorted. "Besides, you've already agreed that we're going to try it my way first. Right?"

"Sure. I've got some, uh, loose ends to take care of first, but I'll get back to you this afternoon at the latest."

I suspected it was a *tight* end he planned to take care of, but I tried not to think about it. "Thanks," was all I said before I let him get back to his regularly scheduled activities.

I didn't want to be alone with Brian, so I asked him to keep watch while I had a private word with my brother. It was something I needed to do anyway, and if it would save me some awkwardness to boot, I was all for it.

I think both the boys recognized what I was doing, but they didn't call me on it. I dragged Andy into the spare bedroom, which he had already branded with

his testosterone-fueled decorating tastes. Meaning un-
made bed, chair buried under discarded clothing, and
dirty socks on the floor.

I leaned against a wall—I wasn't touching his dirty
clothes to make room for myself on the chair—and
crossed my arms over my chest. "You do know you'll
be fumigating this room before you move out, right?"

He smiled at me, then grabbed the clothes off the
chair and dumped them on the floor. "Have a seat."

I wrinkled my nose. "I think I'll stand, thanks very
much." I'm not what you'd call a girly-girl, but I've always been tidy.

Andy shrugged, then sat on the edge of his bed.
"So, what did you want to talk to me about? Or was
that just an excuse to run away from Brian?"

I grimaced. "A little of both, actually." I took a
deep breath. "I've been very good so far about not
pushing you to tell me your secrets."

"Uh-oh."

"But there are some things I have to know."

I could almost see his mental doors slamming shut.
Every muscle in his body seemed to tighten up, and he
watched me with the wary caution of a tabby cat facing down a ferocious pit bull.

"Oh, relax!" I snapped. I hated having my own
brother look at me that way, like I was the enemy. "I
don't need you to tell me everything you know. But I'm
going to go question my doctor this afternoon, and if
Adam doesn't like the answers I get, he'll take matters
into his own hands. You haven't seen Adam at work
before. I have. He is *not* a nice guy." Understatement
of the century. "You *are* a nice guy." At least, he was
back when I knew him ten years ago. "And I'm really
hoping you won't let some poor old man get tortured
just because you don't want to talk about what you
know."

Andy didn't look at me, instead staring at the carpet. "I don't know anything about what happened to you at The Healing Circle."

"Then why the fuck won't you look me in the eye when you say that?"

He winced, like my harsh tone had hurt his feelings. Maybe it had, but under the circumstances, I felt I had a right to be angry with him. He kept his gaze pinned firmly on the rug.

"I'm sure Adam is a real badass," he said. "But Raphael is, too. And Raphael has been inside my head for ten years." He finally found the courage to look up, and the terror I saw in his eyes banished my anger. Andy had been through a kind of hell I couldn't even imagine. What a judgmental bitch I was for getting angry at him!

He visibly swallowed hard, then sucked in a deep breath. He looked away once more. "Imagine what a skilled torturer who knows every one of your hidden fears and nightmares can do. Then tell me you'd be willing to risk pissing him off."

"What does Raphael have to do with The Healing Circle?" I asked.

He gave a snort of bitter laughter. "You don't quit, do you?"

I finally forced myself to sit down. "I'm sorry, Andy. I get that you're scared of Raphael, and I know you have every reason to be. But despite all that, he's supposed to be one of the good guys. Sort of."

Andy shook his head. "Take my word for it, little sister. He's not one of the good guys."

"But he saved my life. And Lugh's life."

Andy met my gaze again, and I could practically see the gears turning in his mind as he carefully considered what to say to me. His words came slowly, each one chosen with meticulous care. "He's . . .

loyal to Lugh. He doesn't *like* Lugh, but he loves him, if that makes sense. He'll protect his brother at any cost. But that's the extent of his commitment to the cause."

I thought about that for a long moment and decided I knew what Andy was trying so hard not to say. "Meaning that whatever the hell's going on, he's in it up to his ears?"

Andy wouldn't answer, not even with a nod or shake of his head. His body language screamed "leave me alone," and though I wished I could get him to open up and trust me, I knew it wasn't happening.

With an aching lump in my throat, I gave him a hug, which he returned only halfheartedly. Not knowing what else I could say or do, I slipped out of the room.

My confidence in Adam's ability to locate Dr. Williams was well justified. By mid-afternoon, I had an address and phone number, delivered to me personally by Adam. With Dominic as a potential victim for Der Jäger, Adam wasn't about to let him out of his sight.

I was embarrassingly glad to get out of the apartment and away from the guys. All of them. It was a major testosterone overload in there, even though two of the guys were gay. Or at least bi. I was pretty sure Adam liked women just fine, based on some of the wolfish looks he'd given me, but I had no idea about Dominic. He wasn't your stereotypically campy gay man, but then he *was* with Adam, and he didn't seem to care who knew it.

I shook my head at myself as I walked the eight blocks between my apartment and Dr. Williams's condo. Why was I even speculating on their sexual orientation? Yes, they were both good-looking, majorly sexy men. However, they were obviously devoted to one another, so even if I'd been in the market for a new man in my life, neither of them was a candidate.

I dismissed them from my mind as I entered the lobby of the exclusive condo building on Rittenhouse Square. I had called Dr. Williams in advance, so the guy at the security desk was expecting me. I signed in while he called Dr. Williams to let him know his guest had arrived. There was a mirror behind the desk, and I caught a glimpse of the doorman giving my ass the once-over. He was a wizened little old man, but he still seemed to appreciate the view, and I couldn't help a little smile. I was wearing low-rise jeans and a clingy top that was almost long enough to tuck in. If he'd gotten a look at me in my leather pants, he'd probably have swallowed his dentures.

Dr. Williams had obviously retired wealthy, for his condo took up the entire top floor of the building. I needed a special key-card just to make the elevator go up that high.

He met me in the doorway, looking almost exactly as I remembered him from the last time I'd seen him, which had to be at least ten years ago. His hair was a gorgeous, snowy white, and the big, droopy mustache that had always fascinated me as a kid still adorned his upper lip.

His smile produced a dazzling collection of crow's-feet at the corners of his eyes, and he held out a hand for me to shake. "How nice it is to see you again," he said as I obediently shook his hand. His grip was firm and sure. He looked me up and down, then nodded approvingly. "You've grown up a bit since I last saw you."

"And you look exactly the same," I said, because it seemed like the right thing to say at the time.

Dr. Williams patted my hand, then let go and led

me into his condo. "All an illusion, I'm afraid. You just remember me as an ancient geezer, and I look the part."

If his eyes hadn't been sparkling with humor, I might have been embarrassed, because I suspected he was right. I followed him out into a small but cozy sunroom with a breathtaking view of the square. The room teemed with greenery, plants hanging from hooks in the glass ceiling, sitting on the floor, and adorning the many shelves set into the single brick wall. I sat in the wicker chair Dr. Williams pulled out for me, and he sat in its twin, across a glass-topped wicker coffee table.

Pride glowed in his eyes as I took in the abundance of healthy plant life that gave this room an almost junglelike feel. "I'm impressed," I told him. "If I so much as touch a plant, it generally dies within a couple of days."

He laughed. "Then may I request that you don't touch mine?"

I laughed with him, though in truth it was hard to move in that room without brushing a leaf or tendril. Luckily, my assessment of my effect on plants was a slight exaggeration—but only slight.

"Would you like some tea?" Dr. Williams asked, and I belatedly noticed that the coffee table was set with a delicate china tea set, complete with a plate of lemon wedges.

I'm a coffee person myself, but he seemed eager for me to accept, so I did. He poured me an aromatic cup, then poured one for himself, flavoring it only with a wedge of lemon. I creamed and sugared mine half to death, but he didn't seem insulted by my abuse of his offering.

The china was clearly feminine, and he wore a wedding band on his left hand. However, he made no mention of his wife, and I was left with the impression that he was probably a widower. And, based on his eagerness to make this interview into a social occasion, a lonely one at that.

My impressions could have been dead wrong, but I didn't think so. Despite the urgency of my mission, I sipped at my tea and made small talk for a good fifteen minutes, exclaiming some more over his plants and over the beauty of the view.

I was running out of friendly chatter when he finally smiled at me and put his teacup down.

"It's very kind of you to spend time entertaining an old man," he said, "but I'm sure you didn't come here solely for the pleasure of my company."

I squirmed a bit, suddenly uncomfortable with the idea that I'd thrown any suspicion onto his shoulders. No way was this sweet little old guy part of some evil conspiracy to . . . Well, I didn't actually know what the goal of the evil conspiracy was, if it even existed.

Dr. Williams leaned back in his chair, folding his hands over his stomach and regarding me with polite curiosity. "Is something wrong?"

I forced a smile and shook my head. "No. I just . . . have some questions for you."

He thought about that one for a moment, and I thought I saw a hint of unease flicker in his eyes. "Ah." He cast an almost longing look at the teapot, then seemed to decide against another cup. "What would you like to ask me about?"

I had the sinking feeling he already knew, but I tried my best to give him the benefit of the doubt. "I wanted to ask you about my bout with encephalitis."

The corners of his eyes tightened ever so slightly, and he nodded. "What would you like to know?"

Everything. Or perhaps nothing. I swallowed hard.

"I don't remember anything about my stay at the hospital. Literally. Is that . . . normal?"

"Based on the medications you would have been on at the time, I'd say that's perfectly normal."

On the one hand, he was clearly telling me my memory loss was expected. On the other hand, he'd used an awful lot of words to say what amounted to "yes," and that's the way people talk when they're lying.

"What medications were those, exactly?" I wished I'd thought to bring a pad of paper with me so I could write down his answers.

He met my eyes steadily. "I don't know."

I blinked at the unexpected answer, then frowned. "What do you mean?"

"As your primary care physician, I was the one who admitted you into the hospital. However, I wasn't the one who treated you."

My stomach felt suddenly queasy, though I wasn't entirely sure why. "Why wouldn't you have treated me?" I asked. One of the things that made The Healing Circle different from other hospitals was its emphasis on personal, consistent patient care, which meant keeping patients with the same physician as much as possible. They might have brought in a specialist or three to work with Dr. Williams, but he still should have been the director for my treatment.

He twisted his wedding ring around his finger absently, though aside from that one nervous gesture, he seemed mostly at ease. "On the night you were admitted, I was mugged on my way home from work."

My stomach gave another unhappy lurch.

"I was badly beaten," Dr. Williams continued. "I was in the hospital myself for the duration of your stay." He patted his knee. "I've got enough metal in this leg to set off the metal detectors at the airport."

If our doctor determines that she is, in fact, intractable, then other, more desperate measures may be needed.

I remembered that damning line from Bradley Cooper's letter verbatim.

"So who was the doctor who treated me while you were in the hospital?" I asked, but a strange, uneasy premonition had settled over me.

"He's one of The Healing Circle's top physicians," Dr. Williams said. "His name is Dr. Frederick Neely."

Chapter 16

After Dr. Williams dropped his bombshell, I got out of there as fast as I could. I had way too much to think about to concentrate on pleasantries and small talk.

What were the chances it was just a coincidence that Raphael had chosen Dr. Neely as his host? Personally, I'd put them at approximately zero. What the hell was he trying so hard to hide? I'd assumed it had something to do with the plot to overthrow Lugh, but now it seemed it had something to do with *me*, and with what had happened to me as a teenager.

I walked home slowly, considering my options and not liking what I came up with. Because all the evidence pointed to my brother knowing more than he should about whatever Raphael was up to.

Much as I wanted to respect his privacy, and as bad as I felt for him in his fear of Raphael, I knew now that I *had* to convince him to talk to me. I had a stomach-curdling suspicion I'd need to threaten him to open him up, but honestly, what choice did I have? It wasn't just my own life I was trying to protect. According to Lugh, Dougal couldn't be king until Lugh was dead, even if he was sitting on the throne as regent. As long as he was only regent, his powers were severely limited. But if he should become king, he'd rescind any protections his predecessors had established for humans. Demons were powerful enough to practically enslave the human race if they wanted to. And Dougal wanted to.

Maybe whatever Raphael was hiding had nothing to do with the palace coup. But my every instinct screamed it was something I—and Lugh—needed to know.

It was dinnertime when I got back to my apartment, and the guys had ordered about twelve servings of Chinese food from the nearby take-out joint. It looked like, between the four of them, they'd gone through the food like a school of piranhas. If I were even remotely hungry, I might have been annoyed. As it was, I ignored their requests for information—and Dominic's offer to put together a plate of leftovers for me—and pointed at Andy.

"I need to talk to you," I said.

My tone of voice must have been pretty brittle, because Andy paled. "Why don't you have something to eat first?" he suggested.

"Now!" I jerked my thumb toward the guest bedroom. Out of the corner of my eye, I saw Adam and Dom share a significant look, but I ignored them.

Doing his best condemned-prisoner impersonation, Andy slowly rose from the table and trudged toward the bedroom. I gave everyone else my most quelling glare.

"You three stay here and stay out of it."

One corner of Adam's mouth lifted in a hint of grin. "I wouldn't dream of interfering."

Neither Dom nor Brian seemed to think it necessary to make similar declarations. But then, I wasn't worried about them so much.

I followed Andy into the guest bedroom and closed the door behind us. The dirty clothes were back on his chair, and he didn't bother to move them off. Instead, he stood with his hands clasped behind his back and his gaze fixed on the carpet.

"I suppose you already knew Dr. Neely treated me when I was in the hospital," I said.

He didn't raise his eyes, but his chin dipped slightly in what I took for a nod.

"And you didn't think this was something important that you should tell me?"

He shrugged. "I figured it would lead to a conversation I didn't want to have."

I tried to control my temper, but I didn't have much success. I wanted to cross the space between us and slap him so hard his teeth rattled.

"It's been pointed out to me more than once that there's way more than my own life at stake here," I growled between clenched teeth. "That's true for you, too. So I'm sorry you don't want to talk about it, and I'm sorry you're scared of Raphael, but you're just going to have to get over it."

Now he did meet my eyes, and for the first time, I saw a flash of fire in his gaze. "You have no idea what you're talking about! You don't know what I've been through. It's not something I can just 'get over.' "

That was true, but at this point it didn't matter anymore. "Tough shit, Andy. You may have been through hell, but so have I. And *I* didn't volunteer for it." He winced, but I pressed on. "You volunteered to host because you wanted to be a hero. So be a hero. Tell me what you know."

He crossed his arms over his chest. "I can't do that."

Internally, I let out a sigh of regret, even as I continued to give him my hardest glare. I'd hoped to shame him into talking, but I could see that wasn't going to work. That left only one option. "You either talk to *me,* or you talk to Adam," I said, figuring I'd hate myself for this later. "Adam won't ask nicely."

Andy's eyes widened in shock. "You went out of your way to protect Cooper from your buddy the demon, but you'd turn your own brother in to him?"

My heart ached at the hurt in his eyes, and at the knowledge that I was capable of doing something so cruel. But I couldn't afford to let sentimentality stop me from doing the right thing—especially when I knew Adam was going to come up with this idea on his own the moment he heard what I'd learned. I was pretty sure this wasn't going to be any more than a scare tactic. I couldn't imagine Andy standing up to Adam's threats, no matter how much he feared Raphael. I refused to think about what would happen if I was wrong.

I was preparing as diplomatic an answer as possible, but before any words made it out of my mouth, the bedroom door swung open. I hadn't heard anyone approaching, so I jumped a bit.

"Actually," Adam said from the doorway, "she's just bluffing to scare you into talking. However, since I decided to eavesdrop, it becomes a moot point."

"You bastard!" I said as Adam stepped into the room and closed the door behind him. "I told you to stay at the table!"

He gave a little snort of laughter. "And what made you think I'd do what you told me to?"

He had a point there. And as my mind scrambled to adjust to the changed situation, I realized he'd done me a huge favor by bursting in at this moment. Because I *hadn't* been bluffing. I was pretty sure Adam knew that, and I was pretty sure his decision to interrupt at that moment had been deliberate.

Adam's eyes had an eerie, demonic glow to them as he stared Andy down. "As Morgan has no doubt told you, I find inflicting pain to be quite an enjoyable pastime. Ordinarily, I would only play with consenting adults, but I'm perfectly willing to make an exception for you. Believe me, I have a good deal of experience, and I can make you talk."

Andy was white and trembling. I wanted to cry.

"If I tell you anything, Raphael will—"

"Raphael isn't here at the moment," Adam insisted. "*I* am. We can keep him away from you. But right now, there's nothing that can keep *me* away from you. Understand?"

Andy's knees seemed to give out, and he sank down onto the edge of his bed. His eyes haunted, he nodded. A single tear escaped from the corner of my eye, and I wiped it away angrily. We didn't have a choice here. We *had* to make Andy talk.

But God, how I hated this. How I hated the look on my brother's face, the misery in his eyes. How I hated the realization that I had put it there, even if it was with a little help from my friends.

Adam shoved Andy's clothes off the chair and sat down, making himself comfortable while still keeping an eye on my brother. I just stood there and brooded.

"I don't know the full story," Andy said, staring at his feet, his voice barely audible. "I only know the bits and pieces Raphael let me hear, and that only happened when he first possessed me and got careless every once in a while."

"So tell us what you *do* know," Adam prompted when it seemed like Andy was about to clam up again.

Andy's hands gripped the side of the bed, his knuckles white. "Morgan's real father wasn't human, at least not exactly."

"Huh?" I said intelligently.

"Like I said, I don't know the whole story. I don't know who or what he was, only that he was impervious to demons. And that the demons were very, very interested in him."

I gave that a moment to sink in, but there wasn't enough information for me to make much sense out of anything. I knew there had to be more to it. "Keep talking," I said.

"When they found out Mom was pregnant by your father, they were really excited. They had high hopes that, because you were some sort of hybrid, you'd be able to host."

I shared a puzzled look with Adam, but he didn't seem to be making any more sense out of this than I was. "I don't get it," I said.

Andy shook his head. "I don't, either. At least, not really. I don't know what they wanted, other than that they wanted you possessed."

I couldn't suppress my shudder. "What happened to me at The Healing Circle?"

"I swear to God, I don't know. I wasn't allowed to visit more than once or twice, and you were out of it when I did. But I do know you didn't have encephalitis."

Not that big a shock, I suppose, but it made my heart skip a beat anyway. I found myself holding my breath as I waited for Andy to continue.

"Cooper gave Mom and Dad some kind of drug, and they put it in your orange juice so you'd have symptoms and they could take you to the hospital."

My knees felt shaky, so I leaned my back against the wall for support. I didn't know what was worse: the realization that Mom and Dad had drugged me, or my brand-new suspicions about what had happened at the hospital.

"They were trying to give me to the demons,

weren't they?" I asked in a scratchy whisper. Andy nodded, looking miserable.

They had tried to force a demon into my body, into the body of an unwilling, thirteen-year-old host. Something hovered on the edge of my memory. I knew if I concentrated, I might be able to bring it to the surface, but I couldn't bear to try. I didn't want to remember. If it was my own mental defenses that had locked up that memory and thrown away the key, then it was for a damn good reason.

"It didn't work," Andy said. "And they figured that like your biological father, you were incapable of hosting. That's how Raphael knew you'd be a very different sort of host for Lugh."

I frowned. "But if I'm so resistant to possession, how'd Lugh manage to get in?"

"Because he's not just any demon," Adam answered. "We aren't all created equal. There's a reason Lugh's line is the royal one. So he was powerful enough to get in, but not powerful enough to take over."

That certainly seemed to make sense, but something still eluded me. "I know once this all sinks in I'm going to have a nervous breakdown about it. But why is it some kind of deep, dark secret? Why does Raphael care if you tell us?" I directed the question to Andy, but once again it was Adam who answered, his voice grim.

"Because he knows exactly what happened at The Healing Circle. Hell, he might even be the one who gave the orders. And it's something he knows damn well Lugh won't like."

Andy nodded. "Like I told you before, he's got some personal loyalty to Lugh and doesn't want him killed. But that doesn't mean he feels compelled to uphold Lugh's ideals and protect the human race."

A long, uncomfortable silence filled the room as we thought about that. Then Adam said what I suspect we were all thinking.

"I guess it's time to have a long talk with 'Dr. Neely.' "

Andy closed his eyes, and his hands clenched even more tightly around the edge of the bed. I finally found the will to go to him, to put a hand on his shoulder and squeeze.

"We won't let him hurt you," I promised, hoping I was up to keeping that promise.

Andy jerked away from me. "Coming from a woman who'd have let her demon friend torture me, that isn't very comforting."

"I told you she was bluffing," Adam scoffed. "Why do you think I felt the need to listen at the door?"

"She wasn't bluffing," Andy said in a flat voice.

I wished like hell I could contradict him.

Chapter 17

Keeping Brian in the dark about what was going on was getting harder. He'd managed to keep his questions to a bare minimum so far, but I knew if he sensed an opening, he'd take full advantage. He wasn't a trial lawyer, but I suspect he has the skill set for one. When he starts asking questions, he tends to learn far more than you mean to reveal.

Which meant I really didn't want to meet with "Dr. Neely" in my apartment. I couldn't imagine any explanation I could give Brian that would satisfy his curiosity. Nor could I imagine how we'd keep him from overhearing things he didn't need to hear. Not unless we tied him up in the closet. I'd threatened both Andy and Brian with violence. I wasn't going to do it again. *Ever.*

After my conversation with Andy and Adam, I went to my own room and locked the door behind me. Then I dragged my cell phone into the closet—call me paranoid—and closed that door after me, too. I didn't exactly have Dr. Neely on speed-dial, but I called The Healing Circle and got semi-lucky. He was actually in his office to take my call.

"Why, Morgan!" he said when I'd identified myself. "What a pleasant surprise."

"I'll bet," I muttered. "You and I need to have a conversation."

"I'm always delighted to talk to you. You're like a sister to me, you know."

"Why don't you shove it up your—" I shut myself up at the last moment. Like Adam, Raphael really got a kick out of getting a rise out of me. The last thing I wanted to do was give him what he wanted.

He chuckled. "You and Lugh are well suited. I can usually get *him* cursing me within a couple of sentences, too."

"And that's your goal in life?"

"Let's just say I'm much more successful that way than if I try to win his approval."

I felt an unaccustomed tug of pity. I knew what it was like to abandon all hope of winning approval from your family. Was he such a bastard because he couldn't win approval, or was it the other way around?

I shook the pity off. Yeah, my whole dysfunctional family thing made me bitchy; it didn't make me into the kind of person who tortured innocent bystanders. "Do you feel even slightly bad for what you did to Andy and Brian?"

I expected a glib answer, but instead he seemed to think the question over. "Not really," he said finally. "If I were human, I probably would, but I'm a demon. I did what I had to do under the circumstances. I may not be as noble as my sainted brother, but I'm not a monster, either. It was never anything personal."

"Just like your desire to kill Andy now isn't personal?"

"Don't tell him this, but I have no desire to kill him. I'm under orders to do it, but there are advantages to being the king's brother. No one's going to ride me too hard if I don't get around to it. I have nothing to gain by killing him, and I'm quite secure in the knowledge that he won't tell you anything I don't want you to know."

Only because he didn't know I'd sic Adam on my own brother. Perhaps I should examine my own moral compass a little more closely before I started taking potshots at Raphael's.

"So what is it you'd like to talk about?" Raphael asked.

"It's not something we can do on the phone."

"All right. I'll come to your apartment later."

"No. It doesn't matter what you say—I don't trust you around Andy."

"You cut me to the quick."

"I wish." We definitely needed privacy for this conversation. And I knew the perfect place, even though I wasn't overly anxious to set foot in it again myself. "Adam White is kind of acting like my bodyguard while Der Jäger is after me."

"That's hardly a permanent solution. You and Lugh are going to have to do something about him. I can't help you without blowing my cover."

I knew exactly what he meant, but it wasn't something I wanted to think about right now. If I could lure Der Jäger into some kind of a trap and then let Lugh take over, we probably stood a chance against him if only because of the element of surprise. But there were too many holes in the plan.

"Let me worry about Der Jäger for the moment. That's not what I want to talk to you about."

"Uh-oh."

"Meet me at Adam's house at"—I looked at my watch—"nine tonight."

"And speaking of blowing my cover . . . Adam and I are on different sides of this little conflict, in case you've forgotten. I can't just go drop in on him for a chat."

"You'll find an excuse."

"I'd have an excuse if Andy were there. In all honesty, I can't take a legitimate shot at him in your apartment. I'd have to get by the security guard, and I believe there are security cameras in the elevator. Not to mention killing him might be noisy and attract a lot of attention. If I attacked him at Adam's place, the only significant witness would be Adam himself, and I can handle him. It would make a damn good excuse."

Yeah, and it would give him a damn good chance of getting to Andy if that's what he really wanted. "I guess you didn't get my subtle hint—I don't want you anywhere near Andy. That's why I didn't want you to come to the apartment."

"Yes, I got the hint. I'm just ignoring it. I give you my word I will not harm your brother. We'll figure out a good way to make my fake plan fail."

Did I trust Raphael's word? Hell no! But as long as we were prepared for him, we should be able to keep Andy safe. I hoped. I wasn't looking forward to hearing what Andy thought of me for volunteering him as bait.

"All right, then," I said. "I'll see you at Adam's at nine."

"I look forward to it."

"That makes one of us."

I wasn't about to leave Brian alone in my apartment, so that meant we had to drag him with us despite my desire to keep him as far from Raphael as possible. I told him we were going to interview what Adam would call a "person of interest." I also told him he would not be privy to said interview, even though we were bringing him along. I watched him debate internally whether to start pushing for answers. And I saw him decide to bide his time just a little longer. His eyes told me that the day of reckoning would soon be upon me.

Getting to Adam's house was harrowing, not because of anything that happened, but because of all the bad things that *could* have happened. All it would take was the most casual of touches of skin on skin for Der Jäger to transfer from his current host into Brian, Andy, or Dominic. Which meant Adam and I had to make sure no one got within touching distance.

Adam left the apartment first, retrieving his unmarked and parking right in front of the elevators in the garage to wait for us. We gave him a five-minute head start, then the boys and I piled into the elevator. I made them all stand behind me, and I clutched an armed Taser in one hand, keeping it concealed by tucking my hand into my jacket. The grip was still damned awkward with my fingers taped together, but I figured I could fire if my life depended on it. Dominic had the other Taser, and he made only the most halfhearted attempt to hide it behind his back. The tension in that elevator was palpable, and I thanked God we didn't have to stop for anyone else on the way down.

When the elevator doors opened in the garage, I let out a breath I hadn't realized I was holding. As promised, Adam was waiting for us, the car idling with its doors open.

"Coast is clear," he said, barely looking at us as he kept his eyes peeled for any suspicious pedestrians.

I ended up in the backseat, sandwiched between Andy and Brian. It was a good-sized car, but none of us was exactly petite. Andy was still giving me the cold shoulder, but Brian slipped his arm around me.

Pretending that he was just making more room, but I don't think he expected me to believe it. Just like I don't think he believed *me* when I pretended not to notice.

It occurred to me that Andy and Brian might be in for something of a shock when they got a look at Adam's house. Even if they were completely dense, they had to know by now that Adam and Dom were a couple. What they couldn't know about was the evil black room that loomed at the top of the steps on the second floor of Adam's house. The black room that held Adam's impressive collection of whips. The black room that would have had a starring role in my nightmares, if I didn't have Lugh to keep said nightmares at bay.

I would have liked to have warned them in advance, but it wasn't exactly something I could bring up in casual conversation. I would just have to hope the door to that damn room was closed or that we would all stay on the first floor.

We got to the house without incident, parking in the tiny private lot across the street. Adam and I shepherded the others inside, covering them like soldiers in a war zone. I'd have laughed at us for being so melodramatic if I weren't wound so tight myself.

Once we got there, we still had more than a half hour to wait before Raphael was due to arrive. So we talked strategy. Adam showed a rare hint of sensitivity and suggested that both Dominic and Brian hang out upstairs for the duration. I think if we'd tried to single Brian out, we'd have had a fight on our hands.

Of course, it might not have been sensitivity. It might have been that Adam expected his lover to keep Brian from eavesdropping. But for once in my life, I decided to give him the benefit of the doubt.

We couldn't be sure that Raphael wouldn't show up early, so Adam sent them upstairs as soon as we had our roles figured out. I wanted to ask about the black room, but I still couldn't imagine bringing it up in front of so many people. I prayed the door was closed.

I must have been wearing my thoughts on my face, because Adam took one look at me and started laughing. My face went red.

"What?" Andy asked, raising his eyebrows.

"Nothing," I mumbled.

But of course Adam couldn't resist the temptation to make me miserable.

"Morgan's worried what her boyfriend will think when he sees my collection of BDSM paraphernalia at the top of the stairs."

"Oh," Andy said, and looked almost as uncomfortable as I felt.

"There's no such thing as TMI with you, is there?" I asked Adam.

He laughed again. "I'd be happy to provide more details if you'd like."

I was saved from having to come up with a good retort by a knock on the door. Adam went to let our guest in, and I moved to stand beside Andy. His cell phone rang, startling us both, and he frowned.

"Who could that be?" he mused.

As far as I could tell, he hadn't talked to a single soul outside my apartment since he'd gotten out of the hospital. He pulled out the phone and stared at it. After looking at the number, he shrugged and stuck the phone back in his pocket.

I double-checked my Taser and pointed it as Adam guided Raphael inside.

"Stay behind me, Andy," I said.

Raphael smiled and put his hands up. Behind him, I saw that Adam had drawn his gun. Not the optimal weapon to use against a demon, but I supposed a gunshot wound to the leg might slow Raphael down if necessary.

"It's so nice to feel welcome," Raphael said, stopping when Adam ordered him to.

Andy's cell phone rang again. I was tempted to tell him to turn it off, but then I had a disturbing thought—what if it was Mom and Dad, calling from wherever they'd disappeared to? Without looking away from Raphael, I said, "Answer it, just in case it's important."

"May I put my hands down now?" Raphael asked.

"No," Adam and I said in concert.

Behind me, I heard Andy answer the phone. A voice buzzed on the other end of the line, but it was too faint for me to recognize or make out words. Andy said "yeah" and "uh-huh" a couple of times, then hung up.

"Who was it?" I asked.

"Just The Healing Circle, checking up on me. They must not realize Dr. Neely is paying me a house call."

I thought I heard a little something off about his voice, but I figured this wasn't a good time to pry.

"What was it you wanted to talk to me about?" Raphael asked.

"I told them everything I know," Andy said, shocking the hell out of me. That *so* was not part of the script.

I turned my head partway. "Andy? What are you doing?"

"I'm tired of being scared," he said, sounding scared shitless. "I want everything out in the open."

Raphael shrugged, which looked kind of funny with his hands still up. He didn't look particularly surprised by Andy's admission. Considering how certain he'd sounded that Andy would keep his mouth shut, that kind of surprised *me*.

"Water under the bridge now," Raphael said with a bland smile.

"Morgan," Andy said, and his voice was shaking. "Shoot him. That's not Raphael."

Chapter **18**

I was too slow on the uptake. Andy's words hadn't even begun to sink in yet when Dr. Neely lunged at me. I tried to fire my Taser, but Andy tackled me.

It was a heroic gesture, trying to get me out of the way of Neely's charge, but I could have done without it. I cursed him as we both fell down and the Taser was knocked out of my hand.

"Get off!" I screamed at Andy, and jabbed him with my elbow to punctuate the point.

Neely grabbed my arm in a brutal, crushing grip, dragging me up to my feet.

A gunshot nearly deafened me, and something hot and sticky splashed my face. Neely grunted in pain, but he didn't let go of me. He spun around, putting me between him and Adam and wrapping an arm around my neck.

"Shoot, and I'll take her head off before I die," Neely said.

I reached up to grab the forearm he had pressed against my neck, prying at it uselessly. It wasn't that I expected to be able to make him let go, especially with my taped fingers. I was just playing the helpless human female in hopes he'd underestimate me.

Adam's gun was still pointed straight at us, but he didn't fire. Footsteps pounded down the stairs.

"Stay away!" Adam bellowed, but Brian and Dom both ignored him and came charging into the room.

I felt Neely turn to look at them, and in that moment of distraction, I stomped down on his instep as hard as I could.

I already knew pain didn't bother this particular demon much, but it did startle him. I let myself become a dead weight in his arms, and he had to readjust his grip to keep me from falling.

Everything else seemed to happen pretty much in a split second, and it wasn't until afterward that I was able to piece together the sequence of events. At the time, all I noticed were the sounds.

Gunshot.

Scream of pain, but it wasn't from Neely.

Another gunshot.

Utter silence.

Time resumed moving normally, and my other senses caught up with me, when I collapsed to the floor with a limp body on top of me. I shoved Neely away and got to my knees.

Brian and Andy were standing around in shock. Adam was on the floor on his knees, bent over. A trickle of blood obscured my vision, and I had to wipe it away before my mind could finish figuring out what I saw.

Adam was bent over on the floor, clutching someone to his chest. Andy and Brian were still standing, and Neely was dead as a doornail. That left . . .

"No!" I choked, stumbling to my feet and crossing the short distance between me and Adam.

Dominic lay in Adam's arms, a huge bloodstain spreading across his chest.

"No!" I said again, eyes filming with tears as I dropped to my knees beside them.

Dom's eyes were squinched shut with pain, and his face was way too pale. Blood continued to pour from the wound.

"Do something!" I shouted at Adam.

He was a policeman. He had to know some rudimentary first aid! But when I took another look at the wound, I knew that rudimentary first aid wasn't going to cut it.

"Adam!" Dom gasped, terror and pain in his voice.

"Shh," Adam said, wrapping one of his hands around Dom's fingers. His face looked strangely serene, no sign of grief or horror or fear. I wanted to scream at him, curse him, hit him. *Make* him look like he was supposed to look when his lover lay dying in his arms.

"I'll take good care of you," Adam said, his voice a low croon, and the bastard had the nerve to smile.

Dom's eyes widened, as if he, too, were shocked by that smile. Then he made a pained sound. His back arched briefly; then he went limp and his eyes closed. Adam released the hand he'd been holding.

I put both my hands over my mouth to stifle the sob that was rising in my throat. Adam sighed, then turned to me and held out his hand.

"Nice to meet you," he said, with a little grin, "though I'd have preferred to do it under better circumstances."

I just sat there and gaped, not understanding. He lowered his hand.

"I'm Adam," he said, and I wondered if it was possible for demons to go into shock. I'd never heard of it before, but then his lover had just died in his arms. He blinked. "I mean I'm *Adam*," he said more forcefully. "My demon's taking care of Dom at the moment."

I shook my head, wondering if that would rattle the pieces of my brain back into place. Then I figured out what he meant and my eyes went saucer-wide.

"You mean he transferred to Dominic?" I cried, and I heard the shrillness of my own voice.

Adam nodded. "It's only temporary. He'll probably need about twenty-four hours to get Dominic fully healed, then he'll come back to me."

I stared at him, so full of questions I couldn't even figure out which one to spit out first. "Eighty percent of demon hosts are nonfunctional when their demons leave. And you and Dom are both in the lucky twenty percent?"

"It's not luck," Adam said. His voice sounded the same, and obviously he looked exactly the same, but though it might have been my imagination, I could have sworn there was something visibly different about him. Maybe it was just body language.

"Most of the time when you see a host without its demon, it's because the demon was illegal and was exorcized. Illegal demons generally don't give a damn about their hosts, so they don't take good care of them. That's why the hosts are such a wreck when they're gone."

I remembered that we weren't alone in the room, and I looked around. Brian had sagged down into a chair, his face green. Andy was still standing, hugging himself as if he were cold. I looked more closely at my brother while I continued to talk to Adam.

"So Andy was catatonic because Raphael abused him?"

"That would be my guess." He smiled. "And Adam's going to be extremely pissed off at me for telling you this. Humans aren't supposed to know this deep, dark secret, because then they'd know that even the legal demons aren't always so pure. He only told *me* so I wouldn't worry about Dom."

I shook my head in confusion. "*Adam's* going to be pissed? Don't you mean your demon?"

"Adam *is* my demon. As he informed me when he first possessed me, Adam is a very common name among male demons."

Dominic moaned softly, but his eyes were still closed. I bit my lip. "Is he going to be okay?"

Adam brushed a stray lock of hair off Dominic's face, an undeniably tender gesture. I wondered whether he intended it for Adam, or for Dominic.

"He'll be fine." His eyes swept over Dom's body, and he actually laughed.

Like a moron, I followed his gaze and saw that even out cold, bleeding from a gaping chest wound, Dominic had a very enthusiastic boner.

"I'd say Adam's making sure they both enjoy the healing process to its fullest."

Adam's strong, even without his demon, so he had no trouble picking Dom up and carrying him upstairs to the bedroom. Andy, Brian, and I hung out in the living room with Dr. Neely's body.

"What the hell happened?" I asked no one in particular.

"The phone call I got," Andy said. "It was from Raphael. He was ordered to take a new host so that Der Jäger could ride Dr. Neely to this meeting."

"Why did you tell Neely you'd told me everything?"

"That's what Raphael told me to tell him. He said Der Jäger wouldn't give a damn, and I could use that as an excuse to 'realize' it wasn't Raphael—while still letting Raphael keep his cover."

Frighteningly enough, that made sense to me. "And how did Dominic end up getting shot?"

"When you stomped on Neely, Adam took a shot and missed. I was trying to keep Dominic and Brian out of the line of fire, but I'm still not up to full strength. Dom got in the way."

And then Adam fired a second shot, killing Neely. I remembered how close together those two gunshots had come, and I felt a little queasy. I guess I was glad Adam was a demon, because a human might have had at least a moment or two of shock after accidentally shooting his lover, and that might have been enough to let Der Jäger recover.

We had lapsed into silence by the time Adam came back downstairs.

"How is he?" I asked.

"Resting comfortably," Adam assured me.

I looked at Dr. Neely's body. "And what are we going to do about him?"

"I'll take care of him." He looked grim. "I know where Adam hides the bodies, as it were."

I shook my head. "Do me a favor and just call him your demon. It's too weird to hear you talking about 'Adam.' "

"Have you never known two people with the same name before?" he asked with a very Adam-esque grin.

I decided to let the subject drop, seeing as it wasn't even remotely important. Of course, considering that what *was* of top importance right now was disposing of a dead body, I kinda wished we could stick to the unimportant stuff.

The only remotely good news was that for the moment, Der Jäger wasn't on the Mortal Plain anymore. But I sure wished I knew how long that would last.

Chapter **19**

Not surprisingly, the police paid us a visit before long. There'd been a rumor of gunshots in the neighborhood, but when Adam explained it had been a car backfiring, the cops believed him. After all, he was a cop himself. Convenient at times.

Adam hauled the body down into the basement while Andy and I did our best to clean up the blood on the floor. Brian was still sitting in a chair, looking sick and shell-shocked. He hadn't looked up or even blinked—as far as I could tell—when the police had come to the door. I wished I had some idea what to say to him. All that came to mind was something like "Welcome to my world," but I figured that probably was insensitive.

I noticed with a chill that my hands weren't shaking and I didn't feel an urgent need to puke. I was cleaning up blood from the floor while Adam hid the body of a man he'd just killed, and I was taking it all in stride. How scary was that? I should have been as freaked out as Brian.

For a while, there was no sound except the sloshing of water and the rub of a scrub brush against the carpet. I didn't think the carpet was salvageable. Yeah, we could get the worst of the blood out, but there would have to be a significant stain when we were done. And calling in a professional carpet cleaner wasn't exactly an option. I kept scrubbing anyway.

"Why aren't we calling the police?" Brian asked eventually.

I looked up from my scrubbing and saw that some color had returned to his face, and there was a spark of intelligence in his eyes again. At the moment, I wasn't sure that was an improvement. Brian is very much a law-abiding citizen, and I worried we'd have a battle on our hands if we wanted to keep him from blabbing to the cops.

"Adam *is* the police," I said, stalling while I tried to think of what to say.

Brian nodded. "And if I understand things correctly, he's even now hiding the body of a man he just shot to death. What the hell is going on?"

I sighed. Beside me, Andy was studiously ignoring us, scrubbing away as if he couldn't hear a word we said.

"There's a reason I've been trying to keep you out of this," I told him. "It's . . . complicated. And we can't afford to have the police involved." I was having a hard enough time figuring out how to answer *Brian's* questions. I couldn't imagine how we could explain all this to the police. Not without drawing way too much attention to ourselves and making our lives even harder. Based on all the violence that had happened around me when Lugh had first taken over, I was probably already on some kind of secret police watch list.

"That's not enough of an explanation," Brian said sharply. "Stop putting me off and tell me what's going on! I've done a pretty good job of keeping my mouth shut so far, but I'm not going to sit quietly by and watch a man get killed and do nothing!" Yeah, the color was coming back to his face, all right. He was turning an unattractive shade of red. "Not to mention that Dominic is now possessed by an illegal demon! Do you realize how many laws that demon just broke?"

I'd been so relieved that Dominic wasn't going to die that I hadn't even thought about that. Aside from the fact that Dom hadn't signed all the appropriate consent forms, transferring via skin-to-skin contact was strictly forbidden, no matter what the reason. The general public found that comforting, though several advocacy groups for the sick and dying continually fought the law in court. I didn't think that was a battle they'd win anytime soon. I was far from the only person who wasn't as a general rule overly fond of demons.

"I'd rather he break laws than let Dominic die," I said, my voice rising. I'd been doing pretty well at holding myself together up until then, but now something inside me snapped. "And he wouldn't have been hurt in the first place if you two hadn't come charging down the stairs like macho morons! What the hell were you thinking?"

Brian stood up, shoving the chair away from him. I wasn't about to argue with him on my knees while holding a scrub brush, so I scrambled to my feet as well.

"We heard fucking gunshots!" Brian screamed at me, towering over me and leaning into my personal space. I flinched, because Brian almost never uses curse words. "What were we supposed to do?" he continued. "Cower upstairs like little girls?"

"Yes!" I answered, poking him in the chest for no

good reason. "You should have stayed upstairs like we told you. You could have both gotten killed."

"So could the three of *you*."

"At least two of us had demons who could heal us, unlike—" I didn't even realize what I was saying until Brian's eyes widened with shock. I replayed my own words in my head, then felt the blood drain from my face.

Brian looked at Andy, who'd quit pretending to scrub the floor. "I thought . . ." Brian shook his head. "Your demon is gone! Or were you actually faking catatonia all that time?"

"No, my demon is gone," Andy said, ignoring my pleading look.

I swallowed hard, my heart throbbing in my throat, as Brian stared at me in horror. I could see him struggling for words, failing to find them. And I knew that no matter how badly I wanted to protect him from the truth, there was no way I could hide anymore. Three cheers for my fucking subconscious!

"Yes, Brian," I said. "I'm possessed. But it's all very weird. My demon is kind of . . . hidden. He can't seem to get control of me except when I'm sleeping. He's one of the good guys, but there are a lot of people who want him dead." I let out a long, slow breath. "I didn't want to tell you. I didn't want you caught in the middle of this. My life isn't my own right now."

I watched Brian trying to absorb what I'd just told him. And failing. I'd left a hell of a lot out, but based on the almost glassy look in his eyes, I figured that was just as well.

Silly me. When I'd thought about—and then rejected—the idea of telling him the truth before, my rationalization had always been that telling him would drag him into the middle of the demon civil war. It hadn't occurred to me that he might hear what I had to say and decide he wanted nothing more to do with me. But that's what the look on his face suggested at the moment.

"It's a lot to take in, I know," I said as gently as I knew how. "You could probably use a little time to figure out what you think and feel about it. You should be safe, at least for the time being. Maybe you should go home and sleep on it. We can talk again tomorrow, and I can answer any questions you have." Of course, I'd be very picky about which questions I'd answer and how. "The only thing I'd ask of you tonight is that you don't call the police. And don't tell anyone about any of this."

"The *only* thing you ask," he said, laughing bitterly. "You're asking me to be an accessory to murder."

"I'm asking you to trust me. You know how I feel about demons. But this one," I said, patting my chest, "I need to protect. Please."

He thought it over for what felt like twelve hours, then nodded. He fixed me with the coldest, most implacable stare I'd ever seen. "I won't call the police. And I won't tell anyone you're possessed. At least not yet. You're right that I need a little time to think. So I'm going to go home, and I'm going to think. Then tomorrow, we're going to talk. And Morgan, I'd better like your answers."

I hated having him look at me like that. I hated the hurt that pounded in my chest, and the tears that stung my eyes.

We all jumped when Adam cleared his throat from the basement doorway. He was standing between Brian and the front door, and though he was trying to look casual, his hand was hovering near his gun.

"Um, do you really think that's a good idea?" he asked, looking back and forth between me and Brian.

The hair on the back of my neck prickled with unease. I didn't much like Adam the demon, but I didn't know *anything* about Adam the human. Was he as much of a badass as his demon? He didn't have the hard, scary look on his face that Adam often had . . . but then his hand *was* near his gun.

Trying to look casual, I edged forward to put myself in the line of fire. The slight raise of Adam's eyebrows showed me I hadn't been as subtle as I'd thought.

"If Brian says he'll keep this to himself, he will," I said. "He's not one to break promises."

Adam chewed that one over for a bit. "A— My demon wouldn't let him leave. You know that."

I nodded slowly, because there was no question what Adam the demon would have done. "But he's busy right now, and you're in charge. Brian's an innocent bystander, and he's given his word. I have more to lose than anyone. I could be burned alive if I'm wrong. I'm that confident he's not going to break his word."

Adam grimaced. "Well. My demon's going to have some choice words for me about this, I'm sure." His hand moved away from the gun, and he stepped out of the way so Brian could move past him.

Brian didn't say a word to anyone. After one last look at the bloodstains on the carpet, he made a beeline for the door. He slammed it when he left.

We finished cleaning up the carpet with as little conversation as possible. Adam had some enzymatic cleanser he poured onto the remaining stain, and he swore that after it sat and worked for a while, we could soak it up and the carpet would look as good as new. I didn't want to know how he knew that.

"Well," Adam said when we were as done as we

could be for the time being. "I don't know about the two of you, but I could use a stiff drink after all that."

"Thanks," Andy said, "but if it's all the same to you, I'd like to go home for a while. I've had about all I can take."

I noticed that his hands were shaking, and I had to fight off a ridiculous urge to throw my arms around him and assure him that everything would be all right. I glanced nervously at the ceiling, then back at Adam.

"Do you think Dom will be all right alone while you drive us back to the apartment?"

Andy interrupted before Adam could answer. "I'll call a cab. And I'm going back to *my* apartment. Der Jäger's out of the way, at least for now, and I want to take advantage of the reprieve."

I frowned. "Yeah, but you were staying with me because of Raphael, not Der Jäger."

Andy's face took on a grim set. "I'm not going to spend the rest of my life in hiding. I'm a lot stronger now and I can take care of myself."

"Andy—"

"Are you forgetting our conversation earlier today?"

The words hit me like a slap in the face. I guess I sort of *had* allowed myself to forget. If our positions had been reversed, I don't think I'd have much wanted to go home with me, either.

"I understand why you did it," Andy said, "but that doesn't mean I forgive you."

And then he, too, left in anger. Once again, my eyes started burning. I *hate* crying, and I do it as little as possible. But right now, I wanted nothing so much as to bury my head against someone's shoulder and bawl my eyes out.

I jumped when Adam gave me a pat on the back.

"Come on," he said. "Have a seat and I'll get you that drink."

"I should get home," I said hoarsely, but when he gave me a little push toward the couch, I went.

Adam disappeared into the kitchen. Moments later, I heard the distinctive whine of an espresso machine. Not the kind of drink I'd been expecting, but probably better in the long run. I like some of the fruity, froo-froo drinks where you can't taste the alcohol, and I can choke down a rum and Coke in an emergency, but I'd expected him to give me some kind of manly-man drink like Scotch on the rocks. I felt miserable enough that I'd have forced it down, but I wouldn't have liked it.

He returned shortly with two steaming mugs. The aromatic, slightly bitter scent of espresso blended with the sweet scent of hazelnut. He put the two mugs down, and I saw that mine was heavily creamed while his was black. I wrapped both hands around the mug and inhaled deeply.

"Hazelnut espresso, eh?" I said. "I didn't know there was such a thing."

He smiled as he picked up his own mug. "There isn't. Your cup's heavily spiked with Frangelico. I know you're not really fond of hard liquor, but that stuff ought to be sweet enough to be drinkable."

I blinked at him. "You know my taste in drinks?"

He took a sip of his coffee. "I know just about everything Adam . . . er, my demon knows about you. He almost never shuts me out."

I sipped my own coffee. He was right—the liqueur was so sweet, and the espresso so strong, that I barely tasted the alcohol. "This is really good."

"Thanks. But drink it slow. It'll sneak up on you if you let it."

For maybe five minutes, we sat together on the

couch in companionable silence, sipping our coffees. I might not taste the alcohol much, but I definitely felt its mellowing effects. I wondered just how much Frangelico he'd put in my cup, then decided I didn't want to know.

"Don't you have some questions you'd like to ask me while my demon's not around?" Adam asked.

Usually, I managed to squelch my curiosity about Adam and anything demon. But either I was desperately in need of the illusion of friendship, or the liqueur had mellowed me more than I realized, because just this once, I gave in to temptation.

"Yeah. I guess I do, if you don't mind talking."

He settled more comfortably into the couch. "Not at all. I've got about a twenty-four-hour sabbatical. I'd like to take advantage of it."

"Do you want him back?" I blurted before I could think better of it.

Adam smiled. "Yeah, I want him back. We make a pretty good team."

"So you actually *like* him?" I sounded incredulous, even to my own ears.

Adam stared into his cup, swirling the remains around absently. "I've known him a lot longer, and I know him a lot better, than you. I don't always agree with his methods, and I know his people skills could use work at times, but he's a really good guy. So yeah, I like him."

"Even though he *almost never* shuts you out? Which, by the way, is not the same thing as *never*."

He shrugged. "He can be a horse's ass sometimes. But then, so can I. The only time he's shut me out for any significant length of time was when you told Dominic that Saul wasn't dead."

I winced. That had not been one of my most diplomatic moments. As far as most humans knew, demons died when they were exorcized. So when I performed the exorcism on Dominic—whose demon, Saul, had gotten a really bum rap—Dominic had mourned him as dead. Because it was against demon law to tell him the truth, neither Adam nor Saul had told him that exorcism would merely send Saul back to the Demon Realm, not kill him. I'd blurted it out at an inopportune moment, and had caused terrible strife in their relationship.

Adam had made Dom take the whip to him that night in penance, and it hadn't been for anything like pleasure. Worse, Adam had refused to heal the wounds.

"I told him he was being a dickhead," Adam continued, "and that he should just heal." I must have looked horrified, because he hastened to reassure me. "I didn't feel a thing. He was punishing himself, not me. Anyway, he wanted to wallow and he didn't want to hear my opinion, so he shut me out until you brought him to his senses."

There wasn't much left in my cup, and what was there was lukewarm at best, but I took a sip anyway.

"Did *you* know Saul wasn't dead?"

The corner of Adam's mouth tightened just a fraction. "No. Adam's let slip a few details here and there that I'm not supposed to know, but that wasn't one of them. I probably would have been angry at him myself if he weren't feeling so bad about Dom already." He ran his thumb around the rim of his cup and sighed. "Maybe I *was* mad at him, and that's why he shut me out. But he's too loyal to Lugh to break demon law, and I understand that about him and accept it."

"What was it like? Being shut out?"

He leaned forward to put his cup on the coffee table, but I think it was more to avoid meeting my gaze than anything. "It wasn't fun." He rubbed his hands together. "It was kind of like sitting at the bottom of a very dark, very deep oubliette. If he hadn't popped in every once in a while to reassure me he hadn't forgotten I was there . . ." He shivered. "I can see how your brother might have had trouble returning to himself if Raphael did that to him for long stretches of time."

I shook my head. "And yet you still want him back?"

He banished the troubled look on his face. "He shut me out for maybe twelve hours, tops. And even when I was shut out, he made sure I knew it was temporary. In the grand scheme of things, it wasn't really a big deal."

Not to him, maybe. To me, it sounded like hell on earth. I sighed. "I don't suppose I'll ever understand." To be so completely under someone else's control . . . I had a hard time dealing with Lugh's control over my dreams. I couldn't imagine what it would be like to be so helpless twenty-four hours a day, knowing it was for the rest of my life. I couldn't imagine being *willing* to submit to that.

Adam shrugged. "Maybe not. But then, I knew for almost my entire life that I was going to host a demon one day, and Adam and I are extremely compatible. It all feels very . . . comfortable to me."

I suppressed a shudder. "So you don't mind when he uses your body to torture people? Or to kill them? Or, hell, to hurt Dominic?"

"He doesn't do anything to Dom that Dom doesn't want him to do. Dom was into that stuff even before he became a host."

He was evading the important part of my question, but I thought that was answer enough in itself. He might put up a protest about his demon's methods occasionally, but the protest was only skin deep. "What about you?" I asked him.

Damn, did I just ask what amounted to a complete stranger whether he was into S&M? Time for more blushing and avoidance of eye contact.

Adam chuckled. "I'll plead the Fifth on that. Anything else you'd like to ask me?"

I meant to say no. Really I did. What came out instead was, "Does he hate me?"

Note to self: never have deep conversations after drinking unknown quantities of Frangelico in the wake of a traumatic event and not enough sleep.

Adam didn't answer right away, which gave me a brief moment of hope that he'd ignore the question. No such luck.

"Do *you* hate *him*?" he countered.

I met his curious gaze and couldn't find the voice to answer. I didn't *like* Adam the demon. I thought he was a world-class asshole, and I found his morals questionable at best. But in moments of weakness, I sometimes caught myself lusting after him. I was pretty sure that meant I didn't hate him.

"I think it's time for me to go home and crash," I said instead of answering the question.

Chapter **20**

I went home, slightly buzzed on caffeine, adrenaline, and alcohol, and wanted nothing more than to collapse into bed and sleep peacefully for a week or two. But I wasn't in the least surprised that I didn't get my wish.

Despite the caffeine and adrenaline, I think I must have fallen asleep within minutes of my head hitting the pillow, but I "awoke" almost instantly in Lugh's living room. He'd added a massive stone fireplace to one wall, complete with merrily crackling fire, and the furniture was rearranged to make that fire the focal point. A deliciously soft afghan was draped over my shoulders, and my bare feet were propped on an ottoman, the better to drink in the warmth of the fire. I breathed deeply, taking in the scents of wood smoke, leather, and Lugh.

He was sitting beside me on the couch, his body a second source of warmth that soaked into my pores and relaxed clenched muscles. My lips curled up in a goofy smile, and I reveled in the gentle sensory overload of my dream. Some feeble, paranoid corner of my brain whispered that I was *too* relaxed, that I shouldn't feel this at ease with Lugh by my side. I never had before. But I told that part of my brain to shut the hell up. This felt good, and, damn it, I deserved to feel good, if only for a little while.

I let my eyes slide shut, still smiling faintly. Lugh's fingers traced over my face, caressing from forehead to chin and back again. The leather of his jacket creaked with his movement, and even that sound was soothing. I sighed and turned my face into the caress, my body relaxing even more.

"That's it," Lugh murmured in my ear, his breath warming my skin. "Let everything go. Don't think. Just feel."

That annoying voice in my brain said, "He's up to something." Once again, I ignored it. If he was up to something, I didn't want to know.

Strong, warm fingers slid around to the back of my neck, digging into the tense muscles there and untying knots I didn't know I had. I hummed in appreciation, so comfortable I didn't even think to protest when he planted a soft kiss on my temple.

"How does that feel?" he asked.

I didn't think I had enough brain cells firing to form words, so I settled for another incoherent hum of pleasure.

"Here with me, you are always safe," he crooned. "Always protected. Always cherished."

My body felt heavy, my limbs so limp it seemed like moving even a fraction of an inch would be just too much damn trouble. If it was possible to fall asleep while I was already asleep, I thought I might be on the verge of doing so.

"No one and nothing can harm you here," he continued. "Not even your past. Do you believe me?"

I couldn't summon the energy to say anything, but he must have sensed my agreement.

"Earlier today," he said, and his voice was now so low it was positively hypnotic, "you started to remember something. Something about your stay at The Healing Circle."

A chill shivered through me, and my muscles tensed. Lugh moved closer to me on the couch, his arm around my shoulders, his body pressed up against mine from shoulder to hip as he cupped my cheek in his palm.

"You're safe with me," he reminded me. "The memories can't hurt you. I won't let them."

I shivered again, that annoying little corner of my mind trying to fight free of the glow of warmth that surrounded me. But I was too far gone, too deeply under his spell, to muster the energy to fight. Once again, I breathed in his scent, and the chill left me.

"Let yourself remember," Lugh urged. "Let yourself see."

My new doctor sat down beside me as I lay in the hospital bed, shivering and nauseated. Scared out of my wits, because I felt so awful, and I didn't know what was wrong. I'd never been in the hospital before, and I wanted out. *Now.* But I was so sick, I knew I wasn't leaving.

My parents stood in the far corner of the room, holding each other's hands. My father looked grim. My mother looked . . . guilty. I hadn't known what to make of the expression on her face back then, but as I watched my own memory from a curiously removed distance, I knew exactly what I was seeing.

Dr. Neely told me I was very sick and that if I didn't get the proper treatment, I would die. He injected something into the IV tube that dripped into my vein, and my vision went fuzzy around the edges. I heard my mom telling me not to be scared, that everything was going to be all right.

The next thing I knew, I wasn't in my room anymore. The new room was cold and sterile, with hospital-white walls and lots of stainless steel. I think it was an operating room. I was strapped to the table, restraints holding me so tightly I could barely move. I tried to struggle against them, but I was still too drugged up to make a credible effort.

Two men stood by the table. One of them was Dr. Neely. One of them was Bradley Cooper. They were both wearing surgical masks, and I might not have recognized Cooper from just his eyes if he hadn't spoken.

"Morgan," he said, hovering over me. "I'd like you to repeat these words after me." He said something that sounded like nonsense syllables to me at the time. I think it was Latin, though I couldn't remember the sounds well enough to be sure.

I didn't know what he was asking me to say, or why. But I was a rebel even then, and I wasn't about to just do what I was told.

"Why?" I gasped, my mouth dry and bitter-tasting.

"Just repeat them," Cooper ordered, then said the words again.

"No," I said, when he was finished. I clamped my jaw shut and looked beseechingly at Dr. Neely. "What's going on? Why am I tied up?"

"They're just words," he said soothingly. "It can't hurt you to repeat them."

I was only thirteen years old, but I was no dummy. Even with unknown drugs fogging my brain, I knew this wasn't anything like a normal treatment for a sick patient. I wasn't about to do what they demanded, even as those demands grew more strident. By now, I was beginning to suspect I knew what the words were.

I'd never witnessed a possession ceremony—only the inner circle of the Spirit Society ever did—but I knew it had something to do with repeating a ritual incantation.

I started to spiral down into the memory, feeling the terror that had filled me when I realized what they were trying to do, but something—Lugh, probably—pulled me back and kept me on the surface, watching without feeling. I remembered that when I'd stubbornly refused to repeat the incantation, they'd tried electric shock therapy. I'd borne it as long as I could, but I was a thirteen-year-old girl. Tough as I was, even back then, I wasn't tough enough to withstand torture. Sobbing in pain and defeat, I'd repeated the words they'd given me three times in a row, as required for the ritual. And nothing had happened.

They made me try again. And again. And again. Still, it didn't work.

They'd sent me back to my room, and more time passed in a drugged haze. My mind cleared again when I was once more in that sterile operating room. Cooper and Neely were there, along with an unidentified third man.

Once more, I was thoroughly restrained. When the third man reached out and grabbed my wrist with his bare hand, there was nothing I could do to avoid the grip. He just stood there beside me, holding my wrist and glaring at me.

And then I felt it. A tingling sensation where his hand gripped me. Tingling that turned to burning. Burning that turned to agony. I screamed, but he didn't let go, and the pain kept getting worse. Even worse than the pain was the awful, creeping, slimy sensation that accompanied it. It wasn't a physical sensation, but it was just as visceral. It was as if something dirty—no, *filthy*—was sinking into my skin, penetrating my flesh and oozing into my bloodstream.

I screamed until I had no voice left, as that creeping crud crawled through my system, thick and unclean and smothering. It surrounded me, clinging to my skin like liquid cobwebs, then trying to force its way inside me. It slithered into my mouth, choking me. It oozed into my ears, deafening me to my own screams. It penetrated other places, too, but my mind jerked away when that memory tried to surface.

The demon tried every trick he could imagine to break through my defenses, to find a crack in my armor. But no matter how hard he tried, he couldn't get a firm hold, and he finally had to give up.

I was gasping for breath, my heart banging against my breastbone as if it were trying to escape my chest. I wanted to vomit, but I couldn't turn my head far enough and I was afraid these bastards would let me choke on it. I swallowed convulsively to keep my gorge down.

The demon who'd tried to possess me shook his head and turned to Cooper. "I can't do it," he admitted. "But maybe a royal could. We should have Raphael try."

"I don't think Raphael wants to be a thirteen-year-old girl," Cooper responded.

The demon shrugged. "He doesn't have to *stay* in her. Just find out if he can get in."

But Cooper shook his head. "She doesn't have enough of her father's advantages to make it worthwhile if only a royal can take her. I'm afraid this strain is a dead end."

I lay on the table, shivering and sweating, fighting the nausea, barely conscious. Feeling like I would never be clean again in a million years.

The demon turned to me with an unpleasant smile.

"What a shame," he said. Then he reached out and pinched my nose with one hand while covering my mouth with the other.

"Don't," Cooper said calmly as panic seized me and I struggled with what little strength I had left.

"Why not?" the demon asked, showing no sign that the idea of suffocating a child to death was in any way bothersome. "We can't afford to have her spreading stories."

I was already seeing spots in front of my eyes.

"She won't," Dr. Neely said. "With all these drugs, she's unlikely to remember anything. And even if she remembers, we can say they were nightmares. It's not like anyone can prove anything."

"I'd rather not take chances," the demon said.

Darkness crept in at the edges of my vision.

"Killing her is taking a huge risk," Cooper argued. "I promised her parents she wouldn't be hurt. If she dies, they could raise a stink. And they know enough to make a hell of a lot of trouble."

The demon looked indecisive.

"Why don't we ask Raphael what he wants us to do with her?" Cooper suggested. "If he wants her dead, we can still take care of it later."

With a sigh of what sounded like disappointment, the demon released my nose and mouth. I sucked in several glorious gasps of air before I passed out.

Chapter **21**

I came back to myself still in Lugh's living room, the afghan tucked comfortably under my chin as the fire did its best to dispel the lingering chill. I shivered and clutched the blanket around me, wondering if I would ever get warm again.

Anger usually warms me up great, so I tried to summon a healthy dose of indignation to throw at Lugh. I didn't know exactly what he'd done to me to break the walls around those memories, but it had been a dirty trick. I turned to look at him, ready to let loose with some choice words, but none would come to me. My skin still crawled with the remembered sensation of the demon trying to get inside me, and I shuddered. No wonder demonic possession had been my worst nightmare after that little episode! And how ironic to discover I apparently owed my life to Raphael's mercy. If you'd have asked me before, I'd have sworn he wouldn't hesitate to kill someone so potentially dangerous, even if I was only a child. And if my parents made trouble, he could have killed them, too.

Lugh drew me into his arms, and I was too miserable and shaken to object. His body was a solid, protective wall of warmth, and he smelled delicious. I closed my eyes and buried my head against his shoulder. His hair tickled my cheek as he rubbed his chin on the top of my head.

"You bastard," I mumbled into his shoulder, and his arms tightened around me.

"I'm sorry. But your defenses were weakened. I had to find out what happened before you shored them up again."

"You shouldn't have made me remember that." My words probably would have had more conviction if I weren't cuddled in his arms at the moment, but I needed the comfort too much to pull away.

His fingers caressed my hair, my neck, my back. "I did what I had to do. And whatever you might think, keeping that memory locked away and not dealing with it is not the best way to heal."

I shook my head. "So you did it to heal me? Is that what you're saying?"

His regretful sigh made me feel childish. "You know why I did it." His hand cupped my cheek, and he pushed me away a bit so he could look into my eyes. "You'll be all right," he assured me, giving me a gentle smile that warmed me in ways the fire couldn't. "You're stronger than you give yourself credit for."

I closed my eyes. It was so easy to fall under his spell, to let myself relax and open up in his presence. Something deep inside me longed to let go completely, to entrust myself entirely to his care—to stop always being so vigilant and guarded. But while the idea tempted me, it also scared the shit out of me. My experiences in life had taught me that you trusted people at your own peril, and I was determined not to endanger myself.

I started to pull away from him, trying to disentangle my body from his while searching out the familiar anger that had always served as my most effective shield. But he just held me tighter, until I could barely move. My eyes popped open.

"What are you doing?" I asked, and my voice was little more than a squeak.

His sensuous lips curved into a smile, but he didn't say anything. Holding the back of my head, he bent his own head toward me. With a shock, I realized he was planning to kiss me.

Once again, I tried to pull away, a little harder this time. But his grip was like iron. If he didn't want me to move, I wasn't moving. The thought sent a chill of fear down my spine. If there was anything I hated, it was feeling helpless.

He hovered in front of me, lips maybe an inch from mine, his unique, spicy scent flooding my senses as he draped one leg over me to hold me even more securely, intensifying my feeling of being trapped. My heart thudded awkwardly in my chest, and my breaths came quick and short. Goose bumps prickled my skin, and I think I was even trembling.

But as he closed that final distance between us, as his lips touched mine, I felt a fire burning low in my belly. I made an incoherent sound, half protest, half pleasure, as he feathered kisses over my lips. I wanted to tell him to get the hell off me, but when I opened my mouth to say the words, nothing came out. I tried once more to squirm out of his grip, but I couldn't. And though it seemed completely out of place in this context, a bolt of arousal shot through me. He took advantage of what he must have considered an invitation and slid his tongue into my mouth.

I continued to struggle as he tasted the inside of my mouth with gentle, delicate licks. A moan rose from my throat, and even *I* could hear the longing in that sound. If I really wanted him to stop, all I had to do was close my mouth. Hell, a tough broad like me should feel no compunction about biting his tongue to give him the message. It wasn't like his was a real body anyway.

That wasn't what I did.

When Lugh's tongue stroked mine, I felt like my body might melt with the pleasure of it. He tasted so damn good I thought I'd never get enough, a bouquet of flavors I'd never get tired of sampling. His lips were soft and moist, his body a reassuring cocoon of warmth surrounding me. I abandoned myself to his kiss, my tongue tangling with his, my teeth nibbling at his lips.

My brain took a vacation. I forgot all the hell that he'd brought into my life. I forgot the childhood trauma he'd just forced me to dredge up. I forgot that he'd driven my body while I was asleep, and seduced me for his own purposes. All I could think of was how my body burned for him. I drowned in the pleasure of his kiss, abandoning a part of myself in the process.

I don't know how long it was before he broke the kiss. I think it was a long time. Although I couldn't miss his massive erection with his leg over mine, he hadn't even tried for second base, much less a home run—though I think I was far enough gone to let him do just about anything.

When he released me, my first reaction was a mew of protest. I was hot and wet and achy, and I wanted more.

He smiled gently at me. "Enough for now," he murmured. "You would hate me if I took further advantage."

It was on the tip of my tongue to assure him that I would do no such thing. I was ready to say whatever it would take to keep his lips on mine. But as he gave me space and freedom to move, my brain cells started firing again and I recoiled.

"You bastard!" I said, with more conviction than the last time.

He gave me a knowing look that reminded me how much I'd enjoyed that kiss, whether I'd wanted it or not.

"In the morning," he said, "I'd like you to arrange to speak with Raphael. Whatever it is he's hiding, it's time for it to come out in the open."

I let him distract me, because in truth I didn't want to talk about—or *think* about—how very easily I could lose myself to him.

"For all I know, you could be calling him right this moment," I muttered sourly.

"That would be difficult, as I don't know his new host's phone number. However, Andrew might have it on his cell phone."

"Oh."

"If there's any chance you could let *me* do the talking . . ." He took one look at my face, then shrugged. "I know you're still uncomfortable with the idea of ceding control to me, but—"

"Uncomfortable doesn't begin to describe it!" I remembered Adam's description of being dropped into an oubliette when his demon didn't want to hear from him. Lugh was a nice guy—for a demon—but I knew if he had cause, he wouldn't hesitate to do the same to me. Just one more reason why I could never again let him take control of me.

Lugh acted as if I hadn't spoken. "But he's more likely to talk to me than you."

I remembered Andy's description of the brothers' relationship, and I doubted Lugh was right on that count. From what I knew of Raphael, he wasn't likely to talk to either one of us.

"I'm not letting you take control," I said. "You know that already, so don't waste your breath arguing."

Lugh shook his head, looking disappointed in me. "Don't you think it would be better if you could let me take control sometimes? As long as you're hosting me, you'll be in danger. If Dougal's minions attack you, wouldn't you like to be able to let me take over and protect you?"

I crossed my arms over my chest. "Nice try, but I'm not buying. We've already established that I can find a way to let you in when there's a dire emergency." Such as having a mob of fanatics about to burn me at the stake. "That doesn't mean I have to let you in for a freakin' conversation."

"Do you remember how hard it was for me to take over?" he asked. "Do you know how close you came to burning? If Raphael hadn't goaded us both so much, it might not have happened. The next time you're in danger, you might not have that long."

And wasn't that just a cheery thought!

He had a point, and I knew it. He could protect me in ways I could never do for myself. But the price was just too steep.

"You still don't trust me," Lugh said, sounding hurt.

Instinct told me to rush in with reassurances, to soothe the hurt in his voice. But even if he couldn't read everything I felt, I would have squelched that instinct. He deserved honesty from me. He'd earned that, at least.

I met his gaze and raised my chin. "No, I don't trust you. Not that much. I'm *never* going to trust you that much. I'm sorry."

Something stirred in those dark amber eyes of his, but I couldn't have said what. Hurt, anger, exasperation, cunning? A combination of all, or maybe none of the above.

"It saddens me to hear that," he finally said.

I was still fumbling for the proper retort when the room faded to black and dreamless sleep overtook me.

Chapter **22**

I woke up the next morning feeling exhausted, even though I'd slept till nearly eleven. Lugh had left me alone after our chat, and I'd gotten plenty of sleep. But the emotional baggage was taking its toll. Everything about me felt heavy, from my eyelids to my heart, and I wondered how much more of this I could take.

I spent what little remained of the morning chugging coffee. When I'd drunk more cups than I wanted to count, I felt tired and jittery at the same time. Not an improvement.

Still, if I waited until I felt great to get in touch with Raphael, I doubted I'd get it done in this lifetime. I scarfed down a peanut butter and jelly sandwich in hopes that it might absorb some of the caffeine, then called Andy.

He was cool and aloof with me, still angry, but he checked his cell phone and was able to give me the number Raphael had called from. Naturally, I asked if he'd heard from his former demon again. He said no, but I wasn't sure I believed him. It didn't matter, because he was obviously anxious to get me off the phone, and I wasn't up to a round of twenty questions.

The food didn't seem to be helping the jitters, and I wished I'd shown a little more restraint when slurping cup after cup of coffee. I dialed the number Andy had given me. Of course I didn't recognize the voice that answered.

"Raphael?" I asked.

"Ah, Morgan," he said, confirming his identity. "So good to hear from you. Or am I speaking to Lugh, in which case it's even better?"

"It's Morgan, and I have some questions for you."

"Why am I not surprised?"

"How did Der Jäger get into Dr. Neely? And who's hosting you now?"

Raphael hesitated. I figured he was trying to decide what he was willing to tell me—which would be only what he thought I could figure out for myself.

"I made the mistake of admitting to my supposed coconspirators that I was going to meet you as Dr. Neely," he finally said. "The Powers That Be decided that was the perfect opportunity to get Der Jäger in past your defenses, so I moved into another host so that Der Jäger could have Neely."

I shuddered. "Dr. Neely was a human being. You're talking about him like he was a widget invented for your personal use. And why the hell did you let Der Jäger take him? Don't you outrank these mysterious Powers That Be?"

"If I'd refused, I'd have had to say why. No one would have believed me if I'd claimed to be defending poor Dr. Neely's rights. I did the best I could under the circumstances, which was to call and warn Andrew as soon as I had the privacy to do so."

"Yeah, that was really nice of you. You're a real prince." I regretted the choice of words—because, of course, he *was* a real prince.

He sighed. "One wonders why I bother helping

you and Lugh when all I get for my troubles is scorn and insults. I'm doing the best I can, but that's never good enough, is it?"

"Every time I start to feel sorry for you, I remember some of the terrible things you've done and the feeling goes away."

"Bitch," he said, but he sounded more resigned than angry. "If I had any sense, I'd give up on you and throw in with Dougal for real. It certainly would make my life easier."

"So why don't you?" I asked, genuinely curious.

He laughed. "That's the million-dollar question, isn't it? If I figure it out, I'll let you know, but right now I'm not in the mood for soul searching. I thought you should know that Der Jäger won't be bothering you again anytime soon. His orders were to kill Lugh and to be inconspicuous, and he's failed on both counts. Dougal has locked him up again, and I suspect this time he'll throw away the key. One less thing to worry about, though I'm sure Dougal will come up with something else unpleasant. He's nothing if not creative."

That should have been good news indeed, only it opened up a whole other line of questioning. "How the hell would you know that? There's no direct communication between the Demon Realm and the Mortal Plain." At least there wasn't as far as I knew.

"True, but there's plenty of *in*direct communication, and when you're the regent's brother, you get the best gossip. Perhaps this will remind you why it's a good thing to have a man on the inside, even if the things I do to keep my cover don't meet with your wholehearted approval."

I wisely let that one slide. "We still need to talk."

"So talk."

I shook my head, even though he couldn't see it.

"This isn't a conversation to have over the phone. Can you come to my apartment?"

"I *can*. But I won't."

"Excuse me?"

"How exactly am I supposed to explain that I'm popping in to visit with you? Andrew's no longer staying with you, and I'm no longer Dr. Neely."

"You can say you're coming to force me to tell you who's now hosting Lugh. Or who hosted him right after me."

Raphael chuckled. "So I should come over to torture you? Sounds like fun."

"It's not like it would be the first time," I said before thinking it through.

I hoped he would assume I was talking about the burning-at-the-stake incident, but the deafening silence on the other end of the line told me no such luck. I listened to the drumbeat of my heart as I tried to think of some way to explain away my words, but nothing came to mind. I sighed.

"I guess we'll do this on the phone after all," I said.

"I gather you've been doing some digging."

I couldn't tell from his tone of voice what he thought about my digging. Was he worried about what I'd learned? "Lugh helped me access some repressed memories. Your name came up."

"There are times when I fervently wish neither of my brothers had been born."

"I'm sure the feeling is mutual."

"I never tortured you, Morgan. I may not win any Humanitarian of the Year awards, but even *I* would not stoop so low as to torture a child. It hadn't occurred to me that a drugged thirteen-year-old would actually resist. I didn't know the methods Cooper and Neely used until afterward."

"Ignorance is bliss, huh?"

"For what little it's worth, I'm sorry. As you know, I have no qualms about necessary evils, but what they did to you was unnecessary. You did not have to summon a demon yourself for the purposes of the experiment."

That wasn't even worth "little." It was worth *nothing*. "Are you sorry you tried to have a child forcibly possessed? Or doesn't that count as torture in your book?" He didn't answer, but I didn't care. I had more important questions. "Why did you do it? Who or what was my father? Why was it so important to try to have me possessed?"

"This has nothing to do with the issue at hand. I'm not answering your questions, either on the phone or in person, so you might as well forget about it and move on with your life."

"Oh, no. You don't get off that easy!"

"Yes, I do," he said, then hung up on me. I don't think anyone has ever hung up on me as often as Raphael.

I tried calling back, but I wasn't exactly shocked when he didn't answer. I figured I could have Adam trace the number and find out who was hosting Raphael at the moment. But I knew Raphael had been telling nothing but the truth when he said he wouldn't answer my questions. I doubted even the demon Adam's most ruthless methods would persuade Raphael to talk if he didn't want to.

Of the people who I knew were directly involved in whatever had happened in that hospital, my parents were MIA, Dr. Neely was dead, the demon host was a mystery man and would probably stay that way, and Raphael wasn't talking. That left only Bradley Cooper.

With a shudder, I had to admit to myself that my kinder, gentler methods had failed to give us the information we needed. Which meant it was time to call in the big guns, no matter how badly my soul recoiled at the idea.

I spent a lot of time brooding, trying to come up with some alternative other than questioning Cooper with Adam at my side. No brilliant ideas leapt to mind. I considered going out to Cooper's place and interviewing him on my own. I even went so far as to call a cab to take me out there. Then I called back and cancelled. If I talked to Cooper, and he refused to tell me anything, he could vanish before I ever got a chance to sic Adam on him. After all, I'd already seen how fast the Spirit Society could make someone disappear.

Resolved to my course of action, I'd have loved nothing better than to rush to Cooper's house immediately and get it over with. Unfortunately, the demon Adam was currently inhabiting Dominic's body. If I was being honest with myself, I had to admit that the chances were frighteningly high that Cooper might not survive this interview. However, if Adam *did* let him live, it wouldn't do for Cooper to know Dominic was possessed, even temporarily. That would officially brand Adam as an illegal demon, and that would be . . . bad.

And so I had to bide my time, waiting until Adam had had the chance to heal Dominic's body. To keep myself from thinking too much, I spent the afternoon dealing with some of the endless hassles involved with trying to get my life back on track after having my house and all my earthly possessions burned to a crisp. It didn't do much for my temper, but at least it kept my mind off torture and death.

I had taken the tape off my fingers when Raphael told me Der Jäger was in prison once more, but paranoia had me putting it back on before I went out. I believed

Raphael was telling me the truth. Despite all his flaws, even Andy, who hated him the most, said he was loyal to Lugh. But I would feel like an idiot if Der Jäger had told his comrades all the little details of his interrupted interrogation.

It was slightly less than twenty-four hours since Dominic had been hurt when Adam opened the door of his house and let me in. At first, I wasn't sure which Adam it was. He ushered me into the living room, where Dominic lounged on a recliner. I never thought of myself as being particularly observant of body language, but it didn't take more than about fifteen seconds for me to know that the demon Adam was still in Dom. Something about the way he sat, or the facial expression . . .

"How's Dominic?" I asked, and Adam answered through Dom's mouth.

"Much better. We've been discussing when I should move back into Adam."

I had to suppress a shudder. It was just too weird hearing Adam's words coming from Dominic's mouth. "What have you decided?"

Dominic grinned one of Adam's grins. "I think Dom's ready to get rid of me. He tells me I'm a little too much of a good thing." He frowned. "I think there's a compliment in there, but I'm not sure."

"Only *you* would think that," his host grumbled, but he smiled when he said it.

Dominic sobered and met Adam's eyes. "Are you ready to take me back?"

Adam's brow furrowed, and he looked around the room as if searching for something. Then he shrugged. "I can't see any pressing reason why I should hang around." He turned to me and smiled, not looking in the least perturbed at the idea of once again being a passenger in his own body.

"It was nice talking to you," he told me, holding out his hand for me to shake.

Not knowing what else to do, I took it. "Uh, yeah. You, too." The awkward truth was, despite the many differences I had with Adam, I kind of wanted him back in his own . . . that is, his *original* body. Things were just too . . . weird this way.

Dominic heaved himself out of the recliner and came to stand near Adam. "Ready?" he asked, holding out his hand for a very different reason.

Adam let go of my hand, nodded briefly, then clasped Dominic's.

I held my breath for a moment as they stood there, holding hands and not speaking. I couldn't help worrying that Adam had been wrong, that somehow this time Dominic wouldn't be able to stand losing his demon.

Until Dom made a fist with the hand Adam wasn't holding and punched him in the shoulder.

"Ow!" Adam complained, letting go of Dom's hand to rub his shoulder. "What was that for?"

"For being a pain in the ass," Dom said, but he didn't look terribly pissed off, despite his words. And it was clearly *him* speaking, not Adam the demon.

"How was I a pain in the ass? I thought I took damn good care of you."

Dominic looked at me with a grimace. "I'll forgive him eventually, but I just had to listen to twenty-four straight hours of lectures about how I shouldn't have come charging down the stairs like an idiot. I'd hit him again if I didn't know he'd like it too much."

I grinned, feeling like at least one tiny corner of my world was back to normal. "Would you like to hear *my* version of the lecture now?"

He groaned theatrically, then covered his ears and started singing "La, la, la, I'm not listening."

Adam grunted. "And he says *I'm* a pain in the ass."

I pulled one of Dominic's hands away from his ear. "Welcome back," I said.

"Thanks. Now, since Adam was so busy lecturing me he didn't cook dinner, let's retire to the kitchen so I can remedy that situation."

I didn't think what I came to ask about would make good dinner conversation. Nor did I think I'd want to eat afterward, no matter how tempting Dominic's cooking was. Unfortunately, with his Italian upbringing, he would be mortally offended if I didn't stay.

"Is it okay if Adam and I have a little chat before we join you?" I asked.

A look that I couldn't interpret passed between them.

"Sure thing," Dominic said. "I could use a little time off for good behavior."

Adam cuffed him playfully on the side of the head, and for a moment I feared this was going to turn into a wrestling match. Or a make-out session. But then Dominic retreated to the kitchen, leaving me and Adam alone.

Adam gestured me toward the couch, and I sat reluctantly. My civilized self was horrified at what I was planning to say. And do. I licked my lips and tried to figure out how to get across what I meant without actually saying the words.

"I hope you don't play poker," Adam said.

I'd always had a habit of wearing my emotions where anyone could see them, and I didn't suppose that was going to change anytime soon.

"We have to question Bradley Cooper," I blurted, and we both knew what I meant by "question."

Adam nodded. "I have no problem with saying I told you so."

"Yeah, you're a fucking genius."

Each word coming with an effort, I told Adam what Lugh had made me remember. I also told him about Raphael's refusal to shed any light on the situation.

I concluded with "Maybe it's not that important . . ."

"You don't believe that any more than I do," Adam said. "If it weren't important, Raphael wouldn't give a damn if Lugh knew. Whatever it is, it's so important that he thinks Lugh will punish him for it, despite all the help he's been giving us."

That made me frown. "Punish him how?"

"We have our own system of laws," he answered vaguely. "Assuming we can ever get Lugh back on the throne, he's going to be exercising a lot of them."

"What's that supposed to mean?"

One corner of his mouth lifted in a lopsided smile. "It means 'ask Lugh.' I don't get to decide which state secrets to share with you."

I shook my head in disgust. "The way you guys act, what you had for breakfast is a fucking state secret!"

"Ask Lugh," he repeated, not perturbed by my pique.

I bit back any number of responses. I forced myself to change the subject back to that which I didn't want to talk about.

"So I guess it's important enough that we have to talk to Cooper."

"Yeah," Adam said, almost gently. "It may not be as bad as you think. You've met him. You know what a weasel he is. When you confront him with what you remember, he may break down and tell you everything."

It made a nice fantasy.

"Intimidation also makes for a very effective inter-rogation technique," Adam tried again. "One I'm very good at, I might add."

Why he was trying to soothe my conscience, I didn't know. I gave him a sad smile and patted him on the shoulder. "I appreciate the effort, but the damage is already done. Even if we don't have to lay a finger on him, even if all I have to do is tell him what I already know and he spews out everything, I know just how far I would go, and it's not a good feeling."

"When the idea starts to get to you, just remember what he was willing to do to you as a thirteen-year-old girl. And ask yourself if you could possibly be the only child he's ever hurt."

I winced. Was it terribly egocentric of me to think I was the only one? Or was it merely naive? "No one *deserves* to be tortured."

To that, Adam had no answer.

Chapter 23

Cooper lived in a charming Victorian house in the suburbs. When Adam and I pulled into the driveway, I felt a pang of longing for the house I had lost in the fire.

Of course, Cooper being a high muckety-muck in the Spirit Society, his house was on a different scale than mine had been. He was twice divorced, with no children, and I couldn't imagine what he did with all that extra space. Maybe he held Society meetings there.

His car was hidden in the garage, but there were lights on in the house, so we figured he was home. Adam turned to me when we brought the car to a stop.

"Are you ready for this, love?"

I grimaced. "No, I'm not ready. I'll never be ready."

He reached over and patted my leg in a way I would have objected to if I weren't so freaked out. "Then you're as ready as you'll ever be."

I grunted something he took for agreement, and we both got out of the car. My skin was clammy with sweat, and my mouth was dry. Thoughts collided and fought in my brain, and I wished I could think of some reason to stall. With Adam standing beside me as if to block my escape, I rang the bell. As we waited, I bit the inside of my cheek to try to moisten my mouth.

When I've described Cooper as a weasel, it hasn't been just because of his personality. He's tall and thin, with small beady eyes he makes even beadier-looking with his round-rimmed glasses, and buck teeth he should have had corrected when he was a child. His hair had been gray and thinning for as long as I'd known him, and no one had told him the comb-over didn't actually camouflage incipient baldness. It was no surprise that, despite his reverence for demons, he'd never had the "privilege" to host. Who the hell would want to spend a lifetime looking like *that*?

He blinked a couple of times when he saw me on the doorstep, his nose twitching in his most weasely manner. His eyes went wide when he looked past my shoulder and saw Adam standing there.

"May we come in?" I asked when it became clear he could stand there in silence for hours.

He frowned, causing his glasses to slide down his nose. "I'm very busy right now. If you'll call my office in the morning, I'm sure we can schedule you in sometime."

I put my foot in the door, just in case he was about to slam it in our faces. "This really can't wait until tomorrow," I said.

I thought I saw a flicker of unease in his eyes, but perhaps that was my wishful thinking. He looked back and forth between me and Adam and must have decided there wasn't a chance in hell he was getting rid of us. With a long-suffering sigh, he held the door open and gestured us in.

While his house was lovely on the outside, the inside screamed "single male occupant with no maid." There was clutter everywhere, stacks of books and papers, piles of junk mail, empty Diet Coke cans— though why a man as skinny as Cooper was drinking diet soda was anyone's guess.

Surprisingly, the sofa and chairs in the living room weren't serving as auxiliary tables, so Cooper didn't have to move anything aside to let Adam and me sit. I blew out a deep breath, hoping against hope that this interview would be easier than I was expecting. And I tried not to think about what would happen if Cooper refused to talk.

"I remember what you did to me at The Healing Circle," I said, and the words seemed to detonate like a land mine.

Cooper's already pale face lost all its color, and his eyes went wide. Tension screamed through his taut muscles, and he looked like he was poised to make a run for it.

"I don't know what you're talking about," he said.

Both Adam and I laughed. Cooper's back straightened, and his face took on an expression that was supposed to imply hurt feelings. No doubt he was about to say something scathing, but I cut him off.

"If you saw yourself in the mirror, you'd know why we were laughing. Why don't you save us all some time and cut the bullshit? You and Dr. Neely tortured me until I agreed to summon a demon, but it couldn't possess me. So you tried again with another demon that was already on the Mortal Plain, and he failed, too. When he tried to kill me, you told him that someone named Raphael wouldn't approve." Adam and I had agreed in advance that it wasn't in anyone's best interests for me to admit I knew who Raphael was. I think I managed to keep my lip from curling in distaste when I said his name.

Cooper sat there stuttering and stammering, not exactly cool under fire.

"I've got a number of questions for you, *Brad*," I continued, and saw him flinch at my use of his first name. I'd have been in big trouble growing up if I'd dared to call a man of his stature by first name, and I'd carried the habit well into adulthood. But after what he'd done to me, I'd be damned if I'd give him an ounce of respect.

"My first question is, who or what was my father?"

I could almost see him examining possible answers, then discarding them one by one. What finally came out of his mouth was "I think you should leave now." But he didn't say it like he thought we'd listen to him. I sat back on the couch and folded my arms, not saying anything. Beside me, Adam was also silent, but out of the corner of my eye I could see his malevolent stare.

Cooper might not be too worried about me, but I saw how his eyes kept darting in Adam's direction, then looking quickly away. He was still deathly pale, and there was a sheen of sweat on his upper lip. He clasped his hands together in his lap, his knuckles turning white.

"I can't answer that," he said, staring at his hands. "I'm very sorry, but I don't have the authority—"

"Mr. Cooper," Adam interrupted. "Ms. Kingsley has remembered more than enough to drop you in a kettle of very hot water. I'm willing to listen to your side of the story before I take any drastic actions."

Cooper raised his chin in what was supposed to look like defiance. It would have worked better if fear didn't radiate from his every pore. "I'll be happy to answer your questions. Just as soon as my lawyer is present."

Adam laughed, and the sound raised the hairs on the back of my neck. I can't imagine what it must have done to Cooper. I laid my hand on Adam's arm.

"Let's just stay calm and discuss this like civilized human beings," I said. Only with Adam was it possible for *me* to play the "good cop." Adam leaned forward in his seat, staring at Cooper once more with unblinking eyes, but he didn't say anything. That was probably creepier than any threat he could have uttered.

"The cat is well and truly out of the bag," I said. "There's no point in trying to hold on to your secrets."

Cooper took off his glasses and started polishing the lenses with his shirttail. "You don't know what you're talking about."

"No," I answered patiently, "I don't. That's why I'm asking you to explain."

He kept polishing. "I can't answer your questions."

"Yes, you can. You just don't want to. Unfortunately for you, you don't have a choice."

He didn't say anything, just shook his head and kept polishing those glasses as if his life depended on it.

"Are we going to have to resort to the same methods you used on me when I wouldn't do what you wanted?"

His hands jerked, and the glasses dropped to the floor. When he bent to retrieve them, I saw that he was shaking. If I didn't have the image in my mind of him ordering Dr. Neely to give me another jolt of electricity, I might have felt sorry for him.

"Are you threatening me?" he asked, his voice shaking as badly as his hands.

Well, duh! "If you have no memory of doing anything bad to me, then why should you be worried?"

He jammed the glasses back on his face. "I didn't say I didn't remember. I said I can't talk about it."

"You can and will," Adam said, his voice surprisingly mild. But to Cooper, that mild voice must have sounded as terrifying as a growl.

He shook his head, and white showed all around his pupils. "I *can't*!" he repeated. "Raphael would kill me. Or worse." He looked at Adam with pleading eyes. "*You* know who Raphael is!"

"Yeah, and I don't give a flying fuck." Cooper jumped at the sudden vulgarity.

Playing good cop again, I reached out to pat Adam's arm. "Take it down a notch." I gave Cooper my best sympathetic smile, though I didn't care if it was patently false. "I asked Adam to let me do the talking, but as I'm sure you know, he's got a bit of a temper on him." Beside me, Adam cracked his knuckles, and Cooper jumped. I gave Adam a dirty look out of the corner of my eye. If Cooper were any more terrified, he might faint dead away.

I put the smile back on. "It's not like we're going to go to Raphael and report everything you tell us. He never has to know how we got our information. For all he'll know, it *all* came back to me, and someone let slip your big secrets while they thought I was out cold."

Cooper's Adam's apple bobbed as he swallowed hard. "You don't know Raphael."

Actually, I probably knew him far better than Cooper, but that was beside the point. "And *you* don't know me and Adam. We're asking you *nicely*, but that could change."

This time, he didn't feel compelled to ask if that was a threat. He lowered his face into his hands, forgetting about the glasses until he inadvertently knocked them off. He didn't bother to retrieve them. His shoulders shook, and I realized with my first hint of genuine pity that he was crying. I had never liked Raphael, and after talking with Andy, I knew he was a bad dude. But I hadn't realized until now just *how* bad.

"Are you going to talk to us?" Adam asked, and he'd gone back to using his calm, gentle voice.

I prayed that Cooper would start talking, and I held my breath as I waited for his answer. When he shook his head, the air rushed out of my lungs, and I felt something very much like despair. It didn't matter what this bastard had done to me—I didn't know how I could stand to see Adam interrogate him.

I turned to Adam to beg him for more time, but he held up his hand for silence, his eyes meeting mine.

"There's another way we can do this," he said cryptically, then rose from the couch and crossed to Cooper. Cooper didn't raise his head, didn't acknowledge in any way that he noticed. Adam crouched in front of him, then reached out and touched Cooper's hand.

It was just a casual touch, a quick brush of skin on skin. But Cooper's whole body shuddered, and when Adam rose and came to sit beside me on the couch once more, I knew what he had done.

Cooper didn't move, and Adam didn't speak. I had to clear my throat before I could find my own voice.

"Is Cooper going to be a vegetable when this is over?" I asked.

Adam sighed. He promised he'd do his best not to do any damage, but he couldn't guarantee results.

Then I asked the important question. "And is Cooper going to live through this interview?"

Adam nodded. "He can't prove we did anything to him, so he's not really a threat to us."

I stared at Cooper, who still hadn't moved. "How long is this going to take?"

"Shouldn't be long. He can access Cooper's memories almost instantly. He'll just need to stay in there long enough to sort them out and make sure he knows all the important stuff."

In all the possible scenarios I had built in my mind, this one had never occurred to me, though now it seemed patently obvious. What better way to get the truth out of Cooper than to rummage through his mind? Even if we'd gotten answers out of him using Adam's more dubious interrogation techniques, we couldn't have been sure it was the truth.

A chill crawled down my spine as I absorbed all the implications. "Why didn't he do this when he interrogated Val?" In reality, he hadn't hurt my best friend and betrayer very much, but he could have avoided everything just by possessing her.

Cooper raised his head, but it was the demon Adam who looked out of his eyes. "Don't," he said, staring at his host intensely.

His host returned the stare, but spoke anyway. "Because Adam knew from the beginning he was going to kill her. She was a danger to both of you, even if he hadn't laid a hand on her."

Cooper made a disgusted face. "Thanks a lot. Now I'm going to have to listen to Morgan's opinion of me for the entire ride home."

"She would have figured it out on her own anyway. Are you ready to come back to me?"

Instead of answering, Cooper just held out his hand. While I was still struggling to process everything, Adam clasped Cooper's hand. A moment later, Cooper collapsed in a heap on the floor, and Adam was back to himself once more.

Chapter **24**

Cooper was conscious and sentient when we left him. Traumatized, angry, scared, but other than that he was okay. I know Adam expected me to light into him the moment we got into his car to drive back to my apartment, but I didn't. We drove for perhaps fifteen minutes in total silence before he looked at me out of the corner of his eye and asked, "Aren't you planning to tell me what you think of me?"

I let out a heavy sigh, hoping in vain that it would release some of the tension from my body. "Ordinarily, I would. But you know what they say about people in glass houses."

Once upon a time, I might have felt that Adam's premeditated murder of Valerie was somehow worse than if it had been spur of the moment. But hadn't I just gone to Cooper's house prepared to let Adam kill him if necessary? What had I become? I shuddered, wondering if I really wanted to know.

"At least we got what we needed to know out of Cooper without having to hurt him," Adam commented.

It was a cold comfort, but it would have to do.

"*You* got what we needed to know. Care to share your knowledge with the little people?"

He grunted in what may have been amusement—of course, it could have been gas for all I knew. He was silent for so long I was afraid he wasn't going to answer. Maybe he'd decided he didn't dare speak without Lugh's permission. But this was my heritage we were talking about. I had a right to know.

Apparently, Adam agreed.

"Dougal's been attempting to create a better host."

"*Create?*" I asked in astonishment.

Adam nodded. "We've understood about genes and heredity ever since the first demons walked the Mortal Plain. It's always been against our laws to muck with it, but apparently Dougal doesn't give a crap. He started centuries ago, abducting pregnant women and having demons possess their unborn children. They used the same skills we generally use to help us heal to manipulate the fetuses' genes."

Pain stabbed through my head, and I realized it was Lugh letting me know what he thought of Dougal's pet project. I don't think he did it intentionally, and he let up almost immediately.

"What, exactly, was he hoping to accomplish? And where does Raphael fit in?"

"Dougal hasn't set foot in the Mortal Plain since his project began. He's been running it through Raphael. As for what they've been trying to accomplish . . . They were trying to create a more powerful host. Stronger, faster, harder to hurt, longer lived—and easier to control."

"*Easier!*" I cried. "You guys have total control of our bodies when you possess us! What could possibly be easier?"

Even in the intermittent flashes of light from the streetlamps, I could see the grimness of Adam's expression. "It would be easier if the host didn't have the intelligence to object."

I think I might have turned green.

"To demons like Raphael," Adam continued, "having a native personality in his host is something of an inconvenience. To demons like me, part of the appeal of walking the Mortal Plain is the interaction with our hosts. If Adam were merely an empty vessel for me to fill, I'm not sure I would have chosen to return to the Mortal Plain after my first stint. I enjoy the pleasures of the flesh, to be sure. But it wouldn't be the same without Adam."

"So let me get this straight. Dougal and Raphael are hoping to create a race of superhuman vegetables?"

"That's it in a nutshell."

"And my father was one of their experimental rats?"

Adam nodded. "Apparently, there's much more to The Healing Circle than we know. Underneath the hospital, they have extensive labs—and holding cells. They bred various . . . strains, trying to isolate the traits they found most desirable. Your father's strain was bred specifically for increased healing capacity, and, they hoped, longer life span.

"When that 'batch'—and I'm using Cooper's word—reached maturity, it was time to summon demons for them. Can you guess what happened?"

I thought about it a moment, then nodded. "They found this batch were resistant to demonic possession."

"Not just resistant—impervious. Raphael himself tried to take one, just to see if it could be done. They still felt the batch was a step in the right direction, and if they could breed them with other strains, they could take another step closer to their ideal. Then they discovered that the batch was extremely hard to breed. They tried them with various other strains, and even with normal human beings, and weren't able to get any viable offspring. So Raphael decided they'd hit a dead end with that strain, and ordered them all destroyed."

Pain stabbed through my head so hard I gasped. It didn't let up as fast as it had last time, either.

"You all right?" Adam asked.

I pinched the bridge of my nose, though that didn't bring me any relief. "Calm down, Lugh!" I said. "Please!" The pain subsided, and I blew out a breath of relief. "Go on," I said to Adam.

"You pretty much know the rest. Your father escaped the purge. When Raphael found out your mother was pregnant, he thought to take advantage of what he considered a lucky break. Obviously, things didn't exactly pan out like he wanted."

I was doing my best to absorb everything Adam had told me, but it wasn't what you'd call easy. I mean, holy crap! I could chew on that for a week and not have it fully digested.

"And the Spirit Society is in on all this," I said, because there was no other way Cooper could have known so much.

"Hard to believe, huh?"

I leaned my head back against the headrest and closed my eyes. "Not really. They're fanatics. If their damned 'Higher Powers' want their help creating superhuman vegetables, they'll do it. Do you know what happened to my biological father?"

Adam shook his head. "Cooper had no idea. He was never found. And the reason Cooper was so terrified of Raphael is he saw what Raphael did to the director of the lab after your father escaped. Let's just say he made me look like a soft touch."

"Spare me the details," I said, and was glad Adam listened to me for once.

The rest of the car ride passed in silence. I'd like to say I was thinking deep thoughts about the nature of fanaticism and the sanctity of human life, but really I was just brooding—having one of those "why me" moments. I figured I was entitled. Of course, if I wasn't careful, the "why me" moment would turn into a "why me" week and then a "why me" month.

When he pulled up in front of my apartment building, Adam turned to me awkwardly. "Er, would you like me to come up? Do you need someone to talk to?"

The last thing I'd expected was a *nice* gesture from Adam. Strangely, his unaccustomed niceness brought a lump to my throat. I forced a smile, when usually I would have offered a snarky comment instead. "Thanks, but I think I need some time to myself just now."

He nodded his understanding, and I got out of the car. I had to fight the urge to watch longingly as he pulled away.

I thought I'd had my share of strife and trauma for the day. I should have known better.

I'd been so distracted by the idea of questioning Cooper—and about how that questioning would go down—that I'd somehow miraculously managed to forget about Brian. While I was riding the elevator up to my apartment, I remembered I was supposed to have a conversation with him. Internally, I groaned. He was going to be pissed at me for waiting this long to call him. Not that he wasn't pissed enough already, what with me having made him an accessory to murder and all. If there were a chance in hell I could have avoided our little chat, you can bet I would have. As it was, I spent the entire elevator ride chewing my lip, trying to anticipate what questions he was going to ask me. How would I answer them all? Did I dare give him complete honesty? Impossible to say, especially when I couldn't seem to figure out what I wanted from him just now.

Lost in thought, I opened the door to my apartment and stepped in. I tossed my keys on a side table and turned toward the coat closet to stash the Taser I'd been carrying in my purse all day.

That's when I noticed that the lights were on. I knew for a fact that I'd turned them off before I'd left. I reached for my Taser with a very different purpose, turning to face the living room.

It says something about how distracted I'd been that I hadn't noticed Brian sitting there on my living room sofa as soon as I'd walked in the door. A little yelp escaped me when I saw him, and I put my hand to my chest to feel the frantic hammering of my heart.

"Jesus, you scared me," I said, taking a deep breath to try to calm myself. And belatedly letting go of the Taser.

Brian leaned back into the cushions of the sofa and regarded me with an inscrutable lawyer look.

"How did you get in here?" I asked, still flustered beyond belief.

He shook his head at me, his usually warm eyes cold. "I kept waiting for you to call, and you didn't. I got tired of waiting, so I came over. Andrew was here moving his stuff out, and he kindly let me in to wait for you."

I would owe Andy a good kick in the ass for that. But thinking about giving my big brother hell wasn't my top priority at the moment. Letting out a silent—I hoped—sigh, I dropped my purse on the dining room table and sat on the other end of the sofa from Brian.

"I'm sorry," I told him, and I meant it. "My life is complete and utter chaos these days, and I can only handle one or two problems at a time. I was planning to call you as soon as I got home."

"Uh-huh." His voice dripped with skepticism.

"I was!" I insisted. No need to mention that I hadn't come up with that plan until the elevator ride up. He didn't look any less skeptical, and I guess I didn't blame him. I scrubbed a hand through my hair and wished with all my heart that Raphael had chosen some other human/superhost hybrid to host his brother the king. My life hadn't exactly been sugar and spice and everything nice beforehand, but I would happily trade the problems I had now for the ones I'd had then.

"What do you want from me?" I said, and I was almost whispering. "I'm possessed by the king of the demons, and there are all kinds of people out there who want to kill me. My love life can't be my first priority."

He snorted. "Like it ever was," he muttered. "But this isn't about your love life. This is about you owing me a lot of answers."

Brian was far too self-aware to be fooling himself that much, but if he wanted to focus on something other than our mixed-up relationship, that was okay with me.

"Fine," I said. "Ask me your questions."

So he did. And I answered him, as honestly as I dared.

The cross-examination went on for about half an hour, and Brian was in full lawyer mode, meaning he revealed as little as possible about what he was feeling. As for myself, I was too worn out to feel much of anything.

When he ran out of questions, we both fell silent,

lost in our own thoughts. I felt the rift that had opened between us like a physical pain, and I realized with a shock that my reasons for pushing him away might not have been as selfless as I'd told myself. Had I pushed him away for his own good? Or had it been because it was easier on me to push him away on my own terms than to have him leave me? As I watched him mull over everything I'd said, I couldn't be sure, and something ached deep inside me.

"Do you still love me?" he asked out of the blue, and I almost jumped because he'd been silent so long.

The ache rose from my core and lodged in my throat. I clasped my hands in my lap and stared at them, because I couldn't bear to meet his eyes. If I wanted to keep protecting him—and protecting my own heart—I should tell him no. He probably wouldn't believe me—after all, he hadn't believed me up until now, and I saw no reason why anything I'd said would change that. But the words might shore up the fortress I'd built around my heart.

I tried to force myself to deny him. But I couldn't.

"I never stopped loving you," I said softly, still staring at my clasped hands. "I wanted to, but I couldn't." My eyes burned as though I were on the verge of tears, but I blinked rapidly until the burn faded. "Love doesn't conquer all. There are just too many obstacles." He started to object, but I held up my hand for silence. "I've had some truly miserable moments in my life," I said, "but there's *nothing* that compares to what I felt when Raphael kidnapped you." I forced myself to look at him, making no attempt to hide my anguish. "Don't you understand that it's impossible for me to consider facing something like that again?"

To my dismay, he moved closer to me. If I could have moved away without falling over the arm of the couch, I would have done so. When I tried to turn my head to avoid his gaze, he put his hand on my face to hold me still. My whole body jolted in shock at the pleasure of that simple touch.

"Stop lying to yourself, Morgan," he chided gently. "I know that was awful for you—it wasn't exactly a bowl of cherries for *me,* either—but you were pushing me away long before that. I've managed to keep loving you anyway, even when you're being a horse's ass. What are you so afraid of?"

The easy answer, the answer I'd been giving myself ever since I realized my heart was in danger, was that I was a corrupting influence on him, that being with me was souring and changing him, destroying the man I once loved. But I knew now that wasn't the truth. The truth was I was afraid that one day he'd wise up and realize what a pathetic specimen of humanity I was. My self-esteem wasn't so hot to begin with. If I openly gave my heart to Brian, and he shoved it back in my face, I didn't think I could bear it.

There was no way in hell I was telling him that, though. So instead, in my typical emotional cowardice, I changed the subject. "Are you going to call the cops on us?"

He laughed, but there was no humor in the sound. "I must be insane to keep banging my head against this wall," he muttered, and I winced. "You are far more trouble than you're worth."

I was still reeling from the pain of those words when he grabbed me, hauled me up against his body, and kissed me. My resistance to that kiss lasted perhaps a total of ten seconds. When I gave in to it, I gave in with all my heart, wrapping my arms around his neck and clinging for all I was worth.

In the weeks I'd been without his kiss, I'd almost forgotten how good he tasted. Now I was forcefully reminded, and my senses reeled. When his tongue dipped into my mouth, I let out an uninhibited moan of pleasure. His hand cupped the side of my face, and the warmth of that touch melted some of the ice that had formed around my heart.

I never wanted him to stop. While his lips were on mine, my mind went on vacation. Instead of *thinking* all the time, I merely *felt*.

Unfortunately, Brian still had more to say to me, so he broke the kiss long before I was ready. I made an incoherent sound of protest and tried to capture his lips again, but he put his hands on my shoulders to hold me off. He was breathing hard, and his eyes were dark with desire, but somehow he found the willpower to stop.

"I love you, Morgan," he said as he stared intently into my eyes. "I think you're worth fighting for. But eventually, you'll have to start trying, too. I can't keep this up forever."

My heart constricted, but I knew he was right. I reached out and brushed the back of my hand over his cheek. "Believe it or not, I *am* trying. But we both know how screwed up I am. I was a mess even before I found myself a key player in a demon civil war. I don't know if I'm *capable* of having anything resembling a normal relationship."

He shook his head. "That's a cop-out. Lots of people have fucked-up family lives and still manage to have solid relationships."

I wasn't so sure I agreed with that. It seemed to me that those so-called solid relationships were probably illusions. But I didn't think I'd get Brian to agree with me, so I kept that opinion to myself.

"All I can do is my best," I said, "I know it's inadequate on a lot of levels, but—"

Once again, he interrupted me with a kiss. If he

had to interrupt me, this was definitely my preferred method. It didn't solve any of the issues between us, but it felt so damn good! Knowing I was probably making my life even more complicated, I nonetheless abandoned myself to his kiss, to the taste and smell and feel of him. Fire burned through my veins, and my heart hammered in my chest as I straddled him on the couch. With a moan, he shifted so I could feel his erection pressing firmly between my legs.

My hands moved with a will of their own, plucking open the buttons on his shirt. The tape on my fingers made me clumsy, and I lost patience with it. Still kissing him as if my life depended on it, I scraped at the tape with my fingernails until I found the edge, then ripped it off and tossed it aside.

My fingers now free, I hurried to open the last few buttons on Brian's shirt, then smoothed my hands over the skin of his chest. He had very little hair on his chest, and what there was felt smooth and silky under my caress. When I found his nipples and tweaked them, he moaned and jerked beneath me. He pushed my shirt and bra up until my breasts were bared, not bothering to unbutton or unclasp anything. I pinched his nipples again, and he surged forward, seizing one of my nipples between his clever lips.

It was my turn to moan, and my back arched without my conscious volition. His tongue rasped over the hardened bud, and he sucked just hard enough to be almost painful. Then he fastened his hands under my butt, pressing me against him as he rose to his feet. I wrapped my legs around him, clinging to his neck as he carried me to the bedroom.

He set me on my feet by the bed, then attacked my button-fly jeans. I took advantage of his moment of distraction to pull the shirt off over my head and lose the bra. I pushed his hands away before he'd finished with the buttons, but his cry of protest died when I slid his shirt off his shoulders. I reached for his belt as he tackled the remaining buttons on my jeans.

The fragment of my mind that still held a hint of intelligence noticed that Brian's belt held both a cell phone and another cell-phone-sized accessory. One that I'd have to ask him about—since I recognized it as a mini stun gun—but not until later. We had better things to do with our mouths right now than talk.

Brian toed off his shoes as I shoved his pants and briefs down his legs. I meant to go down on my knees and take him in my mouth, but apparently Brian was impatient to get to the main event. He pushed me onto the bed, dragging my jeans and panties down, then cursing when everything got tangled around my sneakers. He cursed some more as he pried the sneakers off and successfully freed my legs from the bundle of clothing.

Brian was usually a slow and gentle lover, loving the foreplay and the buildup as much or even more than the climax itself. Tonight, he was too desperate, too needy. But then, so was I. He fell on top of me, using his knee to shove my legs apart. We hadn't even managed to get all the way onto the bed, my legs dangling over the edge as he thrust home in one powerful, almost angry stroke. I wrapped my legs around him and tried to pull his head down for a kiss, but he pinned my wrists to the bed beside my head.

It was on the tip of my tongue to protest this sudden show of dominance. I wanted to touch him, wanted to feel the quivering of his muscles and the frantic beat of his pulse as he took me. And yet, once he started to move, the protest turned into a protracted groan of pleasure.

He thrust into me with such force I felt the bed moving beneath us. Sweat beaded his face, and his breath came in loud gasps. His hands squeezed my wrists brutally, holding me still so he could pound into me as hard as he wanted. My fingers curled into fists, nails biting into my palms, as I tried to control the flood of sensation that threatened to overwhelm me.

I didn't want to like this. Brian was being so rough with me I'd be bruised and sore when this was over. Probably what he was doing should be hurting me even now, but endorphins or adrenaline or just plain desperation had me feeling no pain. The pressure on my wrists, the sensation of being pinned down, should have angered me. There was no give-and-take to this lovemaking. And yet my body sang with the pleasure of it, my back arching, my heels digging into his ass, my mouth open on a silent scream.

Then the climax hit me, and the scream was no longer silent. The sound that escaped me was raw, and urgent, and so loud they might have heard me in the next building. My cry triggered Brian's release, and he pounded into me even harder, if that was possible.

When it was over, he went limp on top of me, his hands releasing their death grip on my wrists as his forehead dropped to touch mine. We were both gasping for breath, both drenched in sweat. I barely had the strength for it, but I wrapped my arms around him and held him to me, my hands stroking the sweat-slicked skin of his back.

As the sweat cooled, I became aware of a burning sensation between my legs and a fierce ache in both my wrists. Apparently, the adrenaline had worn off, but despite the discomfort, I couldn't regret what we'd done. Brian might not have been the sweet, sensitive lover I'd come to expect, but he was still the man I loved.

Still panting, he slipped out of me, then slid his arms under me and scooted me all the way onto the bed, climbing on after me and wrapping me in his arms. Our legs twined, and he tucked my head under his chin, my ear pressed against his chest so I could hear the pounding of his heart.

We didn't speak, instead lying quietly in each other's arms as we caught our breath. I closed my eyes and inhaled the musky, familiar scent of him, the scent I'd missed so desperately in the days since I'd turned him away. And I knew I was lost.

It didn't matter what danger being with me put Brian in, and it didn't matter that I was handing him the power to crush my heart. I *couldn't* keep pushing him away. I needed him too badly, needed to be with the man who loved me just the way I was, even if I wasn't sure that love could stand the test of time.

I raised my head to say something appropriately mushy, but before I opened my mouth, the phone rang. Brian and I grimaced at the same time.

"They can leave a message," he said, stroking my still-sweaty cheek with one hand.

I was severely tempted to ignore the goddamn phone. There was so much I still had to say to Brian, and I had to say it now or I might chicken out. But as Lugh had pointed out on more than one occasion, there was much more at stake here than my own life and happiness. I sat up with an unhappy moan, wincing slightly at the soreness between my legs. "With all the drama surrounding my life, I have to at least see who it is."

I felt his eyes on me as I reached for the phone and checked the caller ID. It was the front desk, which usually meant a visitor or a package. It was too late for a package.

I picked up the phone, then practically dropped it when Mr. Watkins, the front desk clerk, told me my father wanted to come up. My brain did a few jumping jacks as I tried to figure out (1) what the likelihood was that this was really my father, and (2) what the hell he could want to see me about if it was.

Mr. Watkins waited patiently while I thought about it for what felt like five minutes.

"Ms. Kingsley?" he finally prompted when my hesitation lasted too long.

If my father really had come out of hiding to talk to me, then I supposed I had no choice but to see him. Maybe the Spirit Society had sent him on Dougal's behalf to try to pry information out of me. Then again, maybe Cooper had called and told him what I now knew about my past, and my father had come to try to make amends. Hey, it made a nice fantasy! "Send him up."

Brian looked at me reprovingly as I slipped out of bed.

I gave him an apologetic smile as I pulled my jeans back on. "It's my father. I have to talk to him." There was so much I needed to say, but the thought of beating the crap out of him for what he'd allowed the Society to do to me was more tempting than I wanted to admit. "I'll try to make it quick." I dragged my shirt on over my head, not bothering with the bra. "Wait for me," I said, then bent to give Brian a quick kiss.

But he got up and reached for his clothes. "I'll wait," he assured me before I could protest. "I'm just not going to wait naked in bed with your father in the next room."

I laughed briefly, until I caught another glimpse of the stun gun clipped to his belt. "When did you get *that*?" I asked with a jerk of my chin.

"This morning. I was feeling a little skittish after everything that's happened."

I frowned. I didn't like the idea of Brian carrying a weapon. Yeah, I wanted him to have some defense in the event of a demon attack, but it seemed like another step down a path I wished I could keep him from walking. I glanced at the bruises that were forming around my wrists and realized he might already be farther down that path than I liked to admit.

My doorbell rang, and though I wanted to stay here with Brian, to talk to him and to work things out, I knew now was not the time. Leaving him to finish getting dressed, I slipped out into the living room as the bell rang a second time. I hesitated before I answered the door. My father had conspired with the Society and with Lugh's brothers to have me possessed by a demon against my will. He'd drugged me so he could take me to the hospital, then apparently left me to Cooper and Neely's mercy without a second thought. Had he known what those bastards had been planning to do to me? Had he condoned them torturing me?

My mind rebelled at the thought. No matter that he wasn't my biological father, no matter that we'd never gotten along, he had still raised me since I was a baby. My mind couldn't encompass the idea that he was evil. Yes, he'd tried to give me to the demons, but in his worldview being possessed was a *good* thing.

The bell rang a third time, but despite my bone-deep conviction that my father wouldn't harm me, I fished my Taser out of my handbag before answering. I checked through the peephole to be sure it really was my father on the doorstep, then swung the door open. As a concession to our close, personal relationship, I kept the Taser down by my side instead of pointing at him, although it was armed and ready to go.

His face as he stood there regarding me was studiously neutral, even when he saw the Taser. I had to resist the urge to punch him.

"Nice of you to drop by, Pops," I said. "Give me

one good reason I shouldn't slam the door in your face."

His expression didn't change. "You wouldn't have opened the door in the first place if you didn't want to talk to me."

"I want to talk to you about as much as I want to have my tonsils removed without anesthetic."

"Then by all means slam the door."

I almost did it. Almost convinced myself I'd had more than my quota of confrontations today. But I knew if I shut him out now, I might never hear from him again. And boy did I have a lot of questions for him!

With a grunt of frustration—I really hate having my bluff called—I flung the door all the way open and stepped back. Dad's expression finally changed, a hint of triumph sparking in his eyes. He stepped through the doorway then closed the door behind him and turned the dead bolt.

I didn't feel like offering him a seat, so I stood in front of him in my most aggressive posture, legs shoulder-width apart, head held high, finger on the trigger of my Taser. I probably looked like a body-guard wannabe, but I didn't give a damn.

"So where the hell did you and Mom disappear to?" I asked.

He regarded me steadily. "If we'd wanted you to know, we'd have left a forwarding address."

I blinked at that. *I* was the smart-ass of the family, and my dad usually stuck to "just the facts." I supposed he was under a lot of strain these days, though I had to admit he didn't look particularly stressed out. In fact, if I didn't know better, I'd think he was enjoying himself.

"I assume Cooper called and told you I remembered what you did to me."

For half a second, I thought he looked surprised, but that hint of expression was gone before I was sure. "I never did anything to you."

I waved his protest away. "You let Dr. Neely and Cooper have their way with me. They couldn't have done it without your permission. Even *you* can't deny your role in that."

He shrugged. "If you expect me to wring my hands in guilt, you've got another think coming. I could have insisted your mother abort you. All in all I think I've treated you rather decently."

I curled my lip in disgust. "If that's the case, you need to look up 'decently' in the dictionary. Don't you feel even a hint of remorse for what you did?"

I'd never been under the impression that my dad harbored any great love for me, but I'd always thought he'd felt at least *some* parental responsibility. Based on his total lack of remorse, I supposed that wasn't the case.

He waved off my complaint as if it meant nothing to him. "That's not what I came here to talk about."

I was seriously tempted to force the issue, but after he and my mom had made such a production of disappearing, I figured if he'd come out of the woodwork voluntarily, it must have been something really important. So I swallowed my questions and my emotions and let him put me off.

"So what *did* you come to talk about?"

He gave me a flinty, steely-eyed glare that chilled me to the marrow. "I came to talk about the host you transferred Lugh into. I believe you said his name was Peter Bishop?" The glare was followed by a triumphant smile.

I shook my head, clearing the cobwebs as any number of sickening revelations bloomed in my mind. Der Jäger was the only one who knew the name of the fictitious host who'd taken Lugh from me. He could have told his cohorts about it, but he didn't exactly strike me as a team player. Raphael had told me Der Jäger was safely imprisoned back in the Demon Realm. I had believed Raphael would never do anything to endanger Lugh.

But the man who'd raised me as his daughter was watching me now with a predatory gleam in his eyes. A gleam that I couldn't help recognizing as evil. Raphael had lied.

I swallowed hard. "Der Jäger, I presume?"

Chapter **25**

Der Jäger's smile broadened as he took a step closer to me. I took a corresponding step back as my Taser hand rose. My reflexes are pretty quick, but not as quick as a demon's. Before I had a chance to get off a shot, Der Jäger slapped the Taser out of my hand, sending it flying across the room. I backpedaled, but he didn't immediately pursue.

"We meet again," he said with a mocking bow. "I was disappointed we weren't able to finish our little . . . chat."

"Yeah, me, too," I said, edging toward the Taser, which lay on the floor by the couch. Der Jäger had destroyed the minds of his previous hosts. My stomach curdled as I realized that in all likelihood, my dad was now officially a vegetable.

Had Dad willingly taken Der Jäger, knowing what the demon was planning to do to me? I shook my head. I'd had a lot of bad thoughts about my dad, and I would never forgive him for handing me over to Cooper and Neely, but I refused to believe he would have given himself to a sociopathic demon. He was a fanatic, but he had at least a small streak of decency in him.

My throat tightened as grief tried to push tears out of my eyes. I fought them, hating to give Der Jäger even the faintest hint of satisfaction.

"Tell me," Der Jäger said, still smiling, "was that a real name you gave me, or did you just make it up?"

I took another step toward the Taser. Der Jäger allowed it, as if he didn't notice what I was up to. Every instinct in my body screamed that he was toying with me. However, I didn't see any more attractive options to fix my hopes on.

"I told you the truth," I said. "But since I don't know where Peter Bishop is these days, I don't have anything else I can tell you. Even if I wanted to."

The arrogant prick still didn't stop me from moving closer to the Taser. Hope speared through me. Maybe he was so arrogant I'd be able to make him pay for it.

"How's the finger?" he asked, and I stopped in my tracks.

Shit! I'd taken the tape off when I took Brian to bed, and it hadn't even occurred to me to put it back on to face my father. Der Jäger could see with his own eyes that my finger was uninjured. What were the chances he wouldn't be able to figure out what that meant? His smile told me they were nil.

Der Jäger cocked his head, a furrow appearing between his brows. "How very odd," he said. "All the evidence says you must still be hosting Lugh, and yet I can't sense him on you at all. Why is that?"

I leapt for the Taser, hoping his puzzlement would leave him momentarily distracted.

His body slammed into mine with the force of a Mack truck, and we both fell to the floor. Der Jäger's weight crushed the breath out of me, stealing my cry of pain, but we still made a mighty crash when we landed. I was facedown, so I jerked my head backward, my skull making solid contact with his nose. I heard the crunch of cartilage, and felt the hot, sticky gush of blood on the back of my neck.

Der Jäger didn't seem to much mind the pain, but I think I surprised him, because I was able to pitch him off me. I reached for the Taser, my fingers almost closing on it, but Der Jäger grabbed my ankle and yanked me back. The motion sent the Taser skidding across the floor, once again well out of reach.

The door to the bedroom opened, and my heart nearly stopped when Brian came charging through.

"No!" I screamed, unable to muster a more coherent protest in my sudden terror.

Why do men always feel the need to come riding to the rescue even when they know they're outgunned? I swore to myself that if we both lived through this, I was going to have a long, heartfelt talk with Brian about his misguided hero complex.

My own cry of distress was a mistake as well. Even through the blood that coated his face from his broken, misshapen nose, I could see the vicious smile that tugged at the corners of Der Jäger's mouth. He let go of my ankle, homing in on a new target. I threw myself at him, wrapping my arms around him even though I knew I hadn't the strength to hold him.

"Brian, run!" I screamed. "Get out of here!"

But the curse of testosterone poisoning wouldn't let him leave me there to fight Der Jäger alone. Instead of running, he was wading into the fight. All it would take was one touch of skin on skin, and Der Jäger could take possession of the man I loved. And destroy him.

No way I was letting that happen! I'd already lost my father to Der Jäger. I refused to lose Brian, too.

In desperation, I tried to open my mental doors to Lugh. After all, Der Jäger already knew I had him, so there was no longer any reason to hide. Pain stabbed through my head, but though I strained to let Lugh in, my body and mind stayed stubbornly linked.

Der Jäger easily broke my hold on him, lurching to his feet to meet Brian's charge. Despair strangled the scream in my throat.

Der Jäger sidestepped, like a matador evading an enraged bull. Brian's eyes widened in surprise, and he tried to pull up. I noticed his right hand reaching under the tails of his shirt, going for the stun gun. He should have drawn the stun gun immediately, but I guess reaching for a weapon isn't a corporate attorney's first instinct, especially when he'd just bought the damn thing this morning.

Before his hand found the stun gun, Der Jäger grabbed him, hauling Brian up against his chest while pinning his arms to his sides. Brian's shirt was long-sleeved, so there was no skin-to-skin contact at first. Not until Der Jäger wrapped a hand around his throat and squeezed.

Brian's eyes bugged out, and I could hear him struggle to drag air into his lungs. However, he *was* breathing, and since my dad hadn't collapsed to the floor in a heap, I knew Der Jäger hadn't taken Brian yet. Of course, why would he, when my own reactions had revealed what a stellar hostage Brian would make?

I hardly dared move or breathe. I sat frozen on the floor where I had fallen, one hand reaching out toward Brian as I cursed fate for putting me back in my worst nightmare. The Taser had come to rest near the legs of the dining room table, and there was no way I was getting my hands on it again. My head throbbed, but Lugh couldn't help me now, so I resisted his push. He knew how much Brian meant to me, and he would try his best to protect him. However, I knew that in the grand scheme of things, Lugh would consider Brian expendable. *I* could never think of Brian that way, and so it was best if I remained in control, even if I didn't know what I could do to help either of us.

"Shall I take a new host?" Der Jäger asked, his eyes dilated with excitement as Brian struggled helplessly.

I swallowed hard, trembling in every limb. "Please don't," I said in a quavering voice. "I'll do whatever you want. Tell you whatever you want to know. Just let Brian go." Like I thought there was a chance in hell that was going to happen!

Der Jäger's eyes lit with a gloating smile. "I knew you could be reasonable. Behave yourself, and I just *might* let your boyfriend go."

"Let him go *now*!"

He laughed. "Why should I?"

I wished I could think of a clever answer, but all my brain could focus on was the threat to the man I loved. Being in love sapped every ounce of logic from my mind, and I just sat on the floor and sputtered like an idiot. Lugh gave another push, and I mentally snarled at him to knock it off. I wasn't letting him in, and that was final.

The moment of pain seemed to refocus some of my brain cells, and I found the will to answer Der Jäger's question.

"Because if you don't let him go now, I'll know you never intend to let him go, and I won't have any incentive to answer you."

Der Jäger laughed. "And if I let him go, you have no incentive to answer me. I guess if it doesn't matter to you one way or another, I should go ahead and take him now."

I leapt to my feet. "Don't!" I held out my hand beseechingly.

"Are you going to answer my questions?"

What choice did I have? I nodded.

"Good. Now why don't we take this discussion somewhere more private?"

At the moment, my apartment was about as private as you could get, though Der Jäger didn't know that. I wished I felt more hopeful that someone had heard my screams and called the police. But my neighbors on one side were on vacation somewhere, and my neighbor on the other side refused to admit he needed a hearing aid. I was on my own.

"I'll do whatever you want," I said, holding my hands out to my sides. "Just don't hurt Brian. He has nothing to do with any of this."

I think Brian's manly instincts were offended by my attempts to protect him, but Der Jäger was putting enough pressure on his windpipe so that he could barely breathe, much less protest.

"Your concern is touching," Der Jäger said. "We're going to go down to the garage and get your car. You're going to drive, and your boyfriend and I will sit in the backseat. You aren't going to try any heroic moves, and you aren't going to talk to anyone. Is that all perfectly clear?"

I nodded, then started moving toward the table and my purse. The Taser beckoned from the floor, so tantalizing close and yet so far away.

"Stop right there!" Der Jäger barked.

I gave him my best innocent face. "I have to get my car keys," I told him.

Der Jäger scowled. "Move very, very slowly, and keep your hands in plain sight. Get the keys and leave everything else."

I did as he told me, moving practically in slow motion. I had to remind myself to breathe every once in a while. My fingers itched to reach for the Taser, but I knew if I did, Brian was dead. Lugh pounded at my head. He figured Brian was dead no matter what. But, damn it, I wasn't giving up until all hope was lost.

All hope is *lost,* a voice that sounded disturbingly like Lugh's whispered in my head. I shook it off.

I carefully unzipped the front compartment of my purse, then pulled it wide open so that Der Jäger could see that I wasn't reaching for a weapon. Heart pounding in my throat, I drew out my keys and let the purse drop back down to the table.

Der Jäger kept his hand wrapped around Brian's throat as he wiped blood away from his already-healing nose. "Lead the way," he ordered.

And I did.

Chapter 26

It was getting late, and we didn't run in to anyone on our way from my apartment to the car. Der Jäger gave up his choke hold on Brian, instead grabbing him by the back of the neck and jerking him around like a cop with a juvenile delinquent.

"Don't you dare try anything!" I growled at Brian when the three of us piled into the elevator. "You're not faster than a demon."

Der Jäger seemed to find that terribly amusing, and Brian gave me a mutinous look. My heart almost stopped in fear that he was going to try the heroics after all, but even testosterone poisoning didn't completely fry his intelligence. I knew he was just biding his time, that if Der Jäger let go of him for even an instant, he would try something and get himself killed.

Der Jäger's going to kill him anyway, Lugh's voice whispered in my mind. A chill shivered down my spine. Was I just imagining what he would say if he had a chance, or was he actually talking to me? I didn't want to know.

I drove out of the garage without incident, the attendant not even bothering to glance at me or my parking pass before hitting the button to raise the gate. What can I say, my building has great security.

It didn't take me long to figure out where Der Jäger was taking me. It isn't exactly easy to find privacy in the middle of a city the size of Philadelphia, but as the Art Museum loomed in front of me, I remembered that nearby Fairmount Park covered thousands of acres. Easily enough room for our little threesome to disappear into.

The lights of the boathouses along the Schuylkill River looked incongruously picturesque and cheerful as we drove by them and plunged into the depths of the park.

Once upon a time in the mid–nineteenth century, Philadelphia's water supply had been in jeopardy because of the rapid development of the city. The Fairmount Park system had been born when the great estate of Lemon Hill had been dedicated as a public park. As the years went by, more and more estates, particularly those situated by the Schuylkill, were absorbed by the park, until it became one of the largest urban parks in the country. Technically, all the parks throughout the city—and several beyond it— are part of the Fairmount Park system, but when Philadelphians think of Fairmount Park, they think of the grounds that had once been those old estates by the river.

Like the city, the park sprawls, some of it beautifully landscaped, with bike trails and horse trails and picnic areas, and some as close to natural forest as you can get in such a major metropolitan area. On a sunny spring day, the place would be teeming, but at this time of night, it was eerily deserted.

Eventually, we pulled into a closed parking lot. I had to drive through the chain over the driveway, but Der Jäger didn't seem too concerned about the damage to my car. I might have hoped a cop would drive by, see the broken chain and my illegally parked car, and call in the cavalry. However, Der Jäger had chosen this location carefully, and when I pulled into the farthest corner and killed the lights, I realized the chances of anyone seeing us from the road were slim and none.

Lugh pounded at my head again as I followed Der Jäger's orders and opened the door for him and Brian. If I'd been any less determined to keep him out, I probably would have crumbled under that assault. But I didn't care how much pain Lugh put me through—I was going to save Brian if it killed me.

You can't! Lugh protested, and I felt more sure this time that it was really him rather than my imagination.

Fuck off! was my pithy reply.

Apparently, the parking lot wasn't private enough for Der Jäger's taste, for he dragged Brian deeper into the park, until the feeble moonlight could barely penetrate the dense canopy of the trees. It felt for all the world like we were in the middle of some remote forest, rather than within the Philadelphia city limits.

Finally, Der Jäger was satisfied with our location and pushed Brian up against a tree, hand at his throat once more. In the thick gloom of the night, I could barely see either of them. Brian's dark shirt and jeans disappeared against the trunk of the tree, until he looked almost like a disembodied head floating in the air.

"Now," Der Jäger said, "I think it's time we have a chat, don't you?"

"He's going to kill me anyway," Brian started, but the sound choked off when Der Jäger's hand tightened on his throat.

"Only one thing is certain," Der Jäger said. "If you don't talk to me, I *will* kill him. I'm sure you know I'm not bluffing."

I nodded, though I wasn't sure he could see it in the dark.

"So," Der Jäger continued conversationally, "you are still hosting Lugh after all. How interesting. It would seem that Raphael has not been entirely honest with us."

I did a mental double take at that, though I hoped it didn't show on my face. I had assumed Raphael had betrayed us to Der Jäger. Why else would he have told me Der Jäger was imprisoned, if it wasn't to give me enough of a false sense of security to let him get close to me?

It was really easy to assume the worst of Raphael, especially after all I'd learned about his involvement in my life. But if there was one thing we good guys had on our side, it was that the bad guys didn't seem to play nice with each other all the time. I had no idea who was lying to whom about what, and they probably didn't, either. It was just as well it stayed that way.

I managed what I hoped was a sneer. "When has Raphael been completely honest with *anyone*?"

Der Jäger shrugged. "I suppose you have a point." My eyes were adjusting to the darkness, for I saw the sudden flare of his nostrils as he breathed in deeply, then frowned. "I still can't catch Lugh's scent on you. I've never experienced anything of the sort before."

I figured at least one of us was going to be dead before this was all over, so there was no harm if I did a little talking—and stalling. I didn't know if time was going to be on my side, exactly, but putting off whatever nastiness was to come seemed like as good a plan as any.

"He can't actually control me," I explained. "We've got sort of a role reversal going, where the demon gets to be the passenger and the host drives. I guess that's why you can't sense him."

Der Jäger looked appropriately fascinated. "I wonder why his dear brother would have neglected to mention that."

I shrugged. "If I understood Raphael worth a damn, I'd do my best to explain it."

Der Jäger's eyes seemed to glow in the dark. "Don't worry. I'll enjoy persuading him to explain it all in his own words. Unlike myself, he seems to find physical pain an unpleasant experience. A shameful weakness in a royal."

I had to suppress a shudder. No doubt Raphael deserved whatever Der Jäger would do to him—even if he *hadn't* betrayed us—but what about his poor host?

"Your situation leaves me in somewhat of a dilemma," Der Jäger continued. "It seems likely that you're telling the truth and you do indeed host Lugh. Obviously you have hosted a demon sometime since I last saw you. However, I have no proof whatsoever that you are currently possessed. Perhaps you are more clever than I've given you credit for. If I were to kill you and then find out you aren't hosting Lugh anymore, I will have lost my chance to learn who you transferred him to."

"Yeah, that's a tough situation all right. I'd hate to be you right now."

The spark in his eye said he didn't much appreciate my sarcasm, but he kept quiet about it. Still pinning Brian to the tree with one hand, he reached into his back pocket and pulled out a pair of handcuffs, flinging them to the ground just in front of my feet.

"Put those on."

I stared at the handcuffs and shivered. Call me a control freak, but I hate having my hands restrained. Of course, even with my hands free, I was essentially useless against my enemy as long as he had Brian as a hostage.

Apparently, Der Jäger got tired of my hesitation. He drove his fist into Brian's gut. I let out a choked scream as Brian tried to double over. Of course, Der Jäger's grip on his throat wouldn't allow it.

"Put the handcuffs on," Der Jäger repeated.

I bent and grabbed the cuffs, thinking furiously. No brilliant ideas leapt to mind.

I can break the handcuffs if you'll just let me in, Lugh said.

God, I hoped he was only able to talk to me like this because of the stress. He was invasive enough in my dreams. The last thing I needed was to be constantly reminded that he was inside me all day, every day.

Of course, if Der Jäger had his way, it wouldn't be a problem for much longer.

I didn't deign to answer Lugh as I fastened one cuff over my right wrist. I went to fasten the other one, but Der Jäger stopped me.

"Behind your back, please."

I bared my teeth at him, though it seemed only to amuse him. Brian's face was still a rictus of pain, and he'd wrapped both his arms around his stomach where Der Jäger had hit him. Wind rustled through the trees above us, and the movement of the branches opened the path for a pale beam of moonlight to illuminate the two of them.

I had to suppress a gasp when I saw that Brian wasn't just clutching his gut in pain—his hand had slipped under the tail of his shirt again. In that brief splash of moonlight, I saw the mini stun gun holstered on his belt. No bigger than a pack of cigarettes, it nonetheless had the power to drop a demon.

I forced myself not to stare. I didn't know what the hell Brian thought he was going to do, seeing as the damn demon still had skin-on-skin contact, but my calling attention to it wasn't going to help. The wind died down, and the branches overhead shaded the moonlight once more.

"I am losing my patience," Der Jäger said, smiling at me. "Perhaps I should show you just how much I can hurt lover-boy here without having to take him as my host."

A wail of protest was rising in my throat when suddenly all hell broke loose.

Der Jäger hauled Brian away from the tree, moving his hand away from his throat as he threw a brutal punch at his face. Brian jerked the stun gun from his waistband, but Der Jäger's fist caught his chin long before he had time to do anything useful with the weapon.

Blood fountained from Brian's mouth as the punch lifted him off his feet and threw him backward. The stun gun flew from his limp hand to land in the leaf litter about ten yards away.

Der Jäger had been advancing for another blow, but his head jerked to follow the trajectory of the stun gun. He said something that sounded very much like a curse, though I wasn't familiar with the language.

There was no way I was getting to that stun gun before Der Jäger got to Brian. There was also no way I could protect Brian unless I was armed, not unless I could let Lugh take over in the span of a heartbeat, which I'd already established I couldn't. And so I propelled myself toward the stun gun.

And, thank God, Der Jäger did, too, leaving Brian where he lay, bleeding, on the ground.

I dove the last few feet, hands fishing through the dead leaves for the stun gun. My fingers skimmed over something man-made in the midst of the leaf litter, but then Der Jäger's hand closed over my wrist and squeezed. Lugh flung himself at the barriers of my mind, and once again I tried to let him in. As long as Der Jäger didn't have a hand on Brian, I knew we were all better off with Lugh driving.

Even as I tried to let Lugh in, I flailed for the stun gun with my other hand. Der Jäger tried to jerk me to my feet, but I caught him in the kneecap with a wild kick. I heard something crack, and Der Jäger collapsed to the ground once more. However, he didn't let go of my wrist, and his grip became even more crushing. I was actually thankful for the handcuff, which was for the moment keeping my bones in one piece, though it was digging into my flesh. Pain forced tears from my eyes, but my free hand found the stun gun once more, and this time I was able to get a grip. I armed it by feel and prayed it was fully charged.

I rammed the stun gun into Der Jäger's stomach and gave him a healthy jolt.

He cried out in mingled pain and surprise, then collapsed on top of me in a nerveless heap. I took about half a second to suck in a few frantic gasps of air, then heaved him off me. His eyes glittered with hatred as he lay there in the darkness, but the electricity would keep him from being able to do anything about it for at least ten or fifteen minutes. I started to wonder what the hell I was going to do with him now, but I forcibly yanked my mind away from the subject.

Keeping a close watch on Der Jäger out of the corner of my eye, I hurried over to where Brian lay, still not moving. I knelt beside him and was so relieved I could have cried when I saw his chest rise and fall.

Blood coated his lips and chin, and I hoped to God nothing was broken.

"Brian?" I said, smoothing his hair back from his face. "Can you hear me?"

His lashes fluttered for a moment; then he opened his eyes. I swallowed convulsively to keep myself from bawling like a baby. Brian blinked and groaned, and I knew instinctively that he was going to try to get up, so I put a hand firmly in the center of his chest.

"Take it slow," I ordered him.

"The demon—"

I hushed him with a shake of my head. "He's out of commission for the moment," I assured him, jerking my chin in Der Jäger's direction. Brian turned his head to look, then winced. I bet he had one hell of a headache. "Are you all right?" I asked, because I couldn't *not* ask.

Brian pushed himself up on his elbows, and I allowed it. He then spit out a mouthful of blood. "Could have been worse," he mumbled. "*Much* worse."

I helped him sit up. "Still have all your teeth?"

He grimaced. "All still here, but one feels loose and one feels broken. Guess I'll be paying a call on the dentist tomorrow."

"I'm so sorry—"

"Not your fault." I opened my mouth to protest my guilt more vehemently, but he stared me into silence. "We've got more important things to think about right now," he said, and reluctantly I followed his gaze to where Der Jäger lay.

He was twitching now, but didn't seem to have enough control of his limbs even to sit up. I double-checked the charge on the stun gun anyway.

"What are we going to do with him?" Brian asked softly.

Nausea roiled in my stomach. I knew beyond a shadow of a doubt what had to be done. Der Jäger knew far too much, and was far too dangerous, to be allowed to return to the Demon Realm. He had to die.

But killing him meant killing my father, and I didn't know if I was capable of doing it.

Chapter **27**

I felt the pressure of Brian's eyes on me as his question hung unanswered. During the brief time I'd been under Lugh's control back when I'd almost been burned at the stake, he had used me to help Raphael burn another demon host alive. In that case, both the demon and his host had richly deserved it, and yet everything inside me had recoiled at the idea. I'm sure if Lugh weren't with me to keep me from dreaming anything he doesn't want me to dream, I'd have had nightmares about that. But bad as it had been, how much worse would it be when the host was the man who'd raised me since birth?

My head swam, and for a moment I thought I might faint.

I shook my head violently to clear it. Oh, no. I was *not* going to faint. That might be the easy way out—faint dead away and let Lugh take care of the ugly business—but I've never been one to do anything the easy way. And if I was going to condone burning a man alive, I had damn well better step up to the plate and admit it.

"Can you exorcize the demon?" Brian asked me,

and I realized I'd neglected to mention to him my hard-won revelation that exorcism merely sends demons back to the Demon Realm.

I swallowed the lump that was forming in my throat as I pushed myself to my feet. "Possibly. Unfortunately, I found out from Lugh that exorcism doesn't actually kill them. And Der Jäger has to die."

Der Jäger had been fixing me with a baleful, hostile glare the whole time. But when he heard my words, his eyes went wide, and an expression that looked a lot like fear crossed his face. He opened his mouth to say something, but I didn't want to hear it, so I gave him another jolt. His body convulsed with the new dose of electricity, and he couldn't control my father's mouth enough to form words.

"You can't be serious," Brian said quietly, and I realized he'd managed to drag himself to his feet beside me.

I didn't answer.

"Jesus, Morgan! That's your *father*!"

"No shit?" I retorted, in what was supposed to sound like an angry voice. I think it came out more like hysteria.

"Surely there has to be a better way," Brian said, but it sounded more like a question than a statement.

My heart was jackhammering again, and I swayed dizzily. How much easier it would be if I'd just let myself pass out! I could wash my hands of all responsibility. I wouldn't have to kill my dad, and I wouldn't have to see the horrified look in Brian's eyes.

I felt Lugh once again knocking on the doors of my mind, but I locked them up tight. If I could have thrown away the keys, I would have.

"If you've got a better idea how to neutralize him without killing him, I'm all ears," I heard myself saying. It was almost like I was having an out-of-body experience, my soul trying to retreat from the horrible reality of what I had to do. I kept reminding myself that my dad was long gone, buried in some deep, dark oubliette inside his own mind. Better for him to die than to live like that for the rest of his life.

But *would* he live like that the rest of his life? After all, Andy had made it back, and he'd had Raphael in his head for ten years. My father couldn't have had Der Jäger for even twenty-four hours yet. My heart thudded. It didn't matter *what* he'd allowed Cooper and Neely to do to me. It didn't matter that he'd never really loved me. It didn't matter that he was cold and unfeeling and could be downright nasty. It didn't even matter that he wasn't biologically my father. He was my *dad*.

Demons adhere to a strict code of morality wherein the ends justify the means. Even the nicest, kindest, gentlest of them would not hesitate to do the "right thing" in my position. But as I looked at my father sprawled on the ground with a sociopathic demon staring out of his eyes, I knew I didn't have what it takes.

I winced in pain as Lugh started pounding on my skull again. I wasn't hearing his voice in my head at the moment, but I knew what he was thinking.

"Are you all right?" Brian asked, putting his hand on my arm and peering into my face with obvious concern.

I couldn't imagine what expression I must have been wearing to make him look at me like that when he still thought I was about to commit patricide. I whimpered as Lugh kept up his assault.

"You're right," I gasped to Brian as I tried to remember how to breathe through the pain of keeping my mental doors shut. "I can't kill him." In reality, I wasn't really sure I could have done it even if the host *hadn't* been my dad. Shit, what kind of person has what it takes to burn another human being alive? Not the kind of person I want to be, that's for sure. And that was even if I could work out the logistics of how to do it without being arrested for murder.

"What's the matter with you?" Brian asked, and I would have been touched by the worry in his voice if I didn't hurt so damn much.

"Lugh is trying his best to take over. I can't let him or he'll take the decision out of both of our hands." I was glad for Brian's hands on my shoulders. I needed an anchor as the pain threatened to wash me away.

"What are you going to do?"

Another whimper crawled up my throat, and I wondered how long it would be before I passed out from the pain. "I'd exorcize him if Lugh would only let up, but I don't think he's going to. We need to get out of here before Lugh wins."

I twisted out of Brian's grip, hurting too much to talk anymore. He watched me with haunted eyes. "But even if you exorcized him, he could just come back in another host, right? And he'll come after you again."

I pinched the bridge of my nose, not that it helped. "It doesn't matter," I insisted, though I knew it did. "I can't kill my own father." I was disoriented in the darkened woods and had no idea which direction the parking lot was, but I knew I had to get out of here soon. I couldn't take much more.

Picking a direction at random, I started to run. I couldn't see worth a damn, and my head hurt so much I could barely keep my eyes open. I ran smack-dab into a tree, stumbling back a couple of steps before plunging forward again.

Distantly, I heard Brian yelling at me to stop, but I

was sure that if I stopped, I'd collapse to the ground and that would be all she wrote.

"Please, Lugh," I begged with the small amount of air I managed to drag into my lungs. "Please don't do this." But he didn't let up, and I didn't stop running.

Until something slammed into my legs and I fell flat on my face.

I kicked out blindly, and Brian cursed when my foot glanced off the side of his leg.

"Stop it!" he shouted at me. "You're going to hurt yourself."

"No!" I wailed as darkness seemed to be creeping into the edges of my vision. "I can't hold him off much longer." I tried to get up, but Brian held me down, practically sitting on me.

"Calm down!" he said, but he didn't exactly sound calm himself.

"Let me go."

"Not until you calm down."

There was still an edge of panic in his voice, but I also heard implacable will. I tried to slow down my breathing, tried to do as he ordered, but the pain wouldn't let me. I wanted to tell him exactly what was happening to me in a calm, logical manner, but my brain refused to cooperate. Instead of talking, I struggled helplessly until the effort became too much and my defenses crumpled.

The last time Lugh had taken over my body while I was conscious, I'd had the unsettling experience of riding around in my own body without being able to move a muscle. This time was different.

One moment, I was lying on the forest floor with Brian sitting on my ass to keep me down. The next, I was somewhere else, surrounded by inky, impenetrable darkness.

"Lugh!" I shouted. "Don't you dare do this!"

Naturally, there was no response. I couldn't see my hand in front of my face, so I stuck both hands out in front of me as I took a step.

It only took two steps before my hands encountered what felt like a stone wall. I tried to tell myself this was good news, that I'd found a way to orient myself in the darkness. I didn't even come close to convincing myself.

Hand over hand, I followed that stone wall for about three more paces until I found a corner. I skimmed over the corner and continued following the wall, but my heart now beat like a frightened rabbit's. I knew where I was, what Lugh had done to me.

My cell seemed to be maybe seven by seven, and completely barren. Cold, damp stone comprised the four walls, and cold, damp earth the floor. When I craned my neck upward, I saw a circular opening about two stories up. Pale blue moonlight filtered through the bars that blocked that opening, but it didn't reach even halfway down the walls before it was swallowed by the dark.

Shivering, I crossed my arms over my chest. "You bastard," I said, but I sounded as scared as I felt. I didn't believe Lugh would leave me down here indefinitely. He was no doubt pissed at me for not letting him in voluntarily, but he was a lot better at letting go of his anger than I was. But even knowing my imprisonment was bound to be short-term, dread pooled in my gut, and my nerves vibrated as if I'd drunk about fifteen cups of coffee.

Unable to hold still, I started pounding on one wall with the flat of my hand.

"Lugh! Let me out of here!" Even the sound of my

hand hitting the walls seemed to be swallowed by the darkness, and my voice sounded small and tinny. If this were a real place rather than a waking nightmare, the sound would have echoed.

My hand started to hurt from the abuse, so I kicked the wall instead, my voice rising and growing thinner as panic threatened to overwhelm me.

"Lugh!"

But there was no answer, and the walls stayed firm and solid. I flung myself across the cell to a different wall, pounding with my fist even though I knew I was bruising the hell out of my hand. The panic was taking on a life of its own, sucking the air from the depths of the oubliette, making my lungs work doubly hard.

The stone wall was rough and craggy, so I tried to climb it. Maybe if I were a seasoned rock climber, I would have been able to make it to the top. Probably not, though. And even if I had, the opening was barred.

As it was, all I managed to do was break my fingernails to the quick and throw more fuel onto the fire of my panic. Desperate to escape, I rammed my shoulder into the wall as if it were a door I was intent on breaking down. Of course, it didn't budge, and the force of my charge caused me to bang my head for good measure.

The blow stunned me, and I staggered. My head spun, my knees weakened, and I collapsed to the cold, earthen floor.

I lay there on my back, staring up at the faint hint of light from above, wishing I would pass out, knowing I wouldn't. Tears dripped from the corners of my eyes, sliding down my face into my ears. My whole body was drenched with sweat, and yet I shivered incessantly, my teeth chattering loudly in the otherwise oppressive silence.

How long would it take for me to go completely mad? Some hosts seemed to lose themselves within hours of taking on demons, but surely Lugh wouldn't do that to me, wouldn't destroy me so utterly in a fit of pique.

My heart seemed to stutter in my chest. What if Lugh had miscalculated? What if he thought I could stand this for a short period of time, but he was wrong? What if he tried to free me, but he couldn't get me out? I could spend the rest of my life down here, alone in the dark.

Terror drove me to my feet once more, and, screaming like a maniac, I battered myself against the walls, not caring how much it hurt or how little good it seemed to do. When battering them didn't work, I scrabbled at them with my jagged, broken fingernails, as if I could claw my way through solid stone.

Suddenly, my limbs went completely limp, and I crumpled to the ground once more.

Chapter 28

When I fell, I curled myself into fetal position, desperate to escape the reality of my situation. If I'd had a blanket to pull over my head, I'd have done it.

The first hint that I was no longer in the oubliette was the distinctive crackling sound of fire. Then I noticed the smell of smoke in the air.

I forced my eyes open and found myself looking up at an unmarked police car, its bubble light streaking the scene with flashes of red. Adam moved into my line of vision, standing beside me to peer at my face.

"I'll give you a hand up when you're ready," he said, and I could have sworn that was sympathy I saw on his face. "Take it slow."

I closed my eyes again and sucked in a deep breath, but the smoke smell made me wish I hadn't. From what I could tell, my real body was uninjured, despite all the damage I'd done to myself in the oubliette. I wasn't even sweating or shivering, though my stomach wasn't feeling too happy, and I felt like I could lie here for a week and be perfectly content not to move.

Letting out the deep breath, I opened my eyes and

held out my hand. One corner of Adam's mouth lifted in a lopsided grin.

"Never one to take it slow, are you, love?"

My only answer was a soft snort. He took my hand and hauled me to my feet, steadying me when I swayed. In the distance, I heard the sound of sirens.

We were standing by the side of the road. A few yards from us, the guardrail was twisted and broken, and at the bottom of the embankment, a burning car lay wrapped around an old oak tree. A little past the gap in the guardrail sat my own car, its bumper dragging on the ground amidst a smattering of broken glass and streaks of burned rubber. Brian stood by the car, staring down at the fire below.

My stomach threatened to revolt, but I swallowed hard. "I gather my dad was 'driving' that car?" I said, jerking my chin toward the fire.

Adam nodded. "He must have fallen asleep at the wheel. He was in the wrong lane, and when Brian honked at him, he swerved and lost control of his car." He looked at me out of the corner of his eye. "You were asleep in the passenger seat when it happened, so you didn't see a thing."

"Uh-huh." The sirens were getting closer. "The fire trucks will be too late to save him?"

Adam put a hand on my shoulder and squeezed, and I was so desperate for comfort that I didn't object.

I watched Brian watch the flames below. He didn't turn to look at me, though he must have known I was myself again. I couldn't interpret the look on his face, though it most definitely wasn't a happy one.

Had Lugh overpowered him and forced him to participate in my father's murder? Or had Brian held me down with the sole purpose of letting Lugh win our battle and take over? If it was the latter, I didn't know Brian as well as I thought I did.

The next hour or two passed in a blur. I could barely string two coherent thoughts together, so when I heard Brian describe the accident to the cops, all I could manage was to nod my agreement. When one of the cops started pushing me to tell him what *I* thought had happened, I kept repeating that I'd been asleep and hadn't seen anything until he was finally convinced he wasn't going to get anything out of me.

Brian came to stand beside me as we waited for permission to get the hell out of there. Neither of us looked at the other as he reached for my hand and gave it a squeeze.

"I'm sorry," he said in a voice soft enough not to carry.

I didn't ask him for what. I extricated my hand from his. "You killed my father."

He didn't look at me. "No, I didn't."

"But you *helped*."

He let out a shuddering sigh and met my gaze. Horror and pain swam in his eyes, but his voice was firm and sure. "You would have gotten yourself killed if I hadn't. I had to choose between you and your father. I chose you."

Who was this man who stood beside me? Was he the same man who'd gone ape shit over the death of Dr. Neely? He was the law-abiding citizen, the goody-two-shoes who always did the right thing. For Christ's sake, he was the lawyer who hated lying!

I couldn't deal with the paradox that was the man I'd thought I'd known, so I put some distance between us and nagged the cops to let me go home. Eventually, they did, after Adam pulled off my bumper so it wouldn't drag. The car was driveable, and I promised I'd get it to the shop tomorrow. I didn't offer to give Brian a ride home.

I probably wasn't the safest driver on the road that night. Luckily, it was late and the streets nearly deserted, because I had barely a tenth of my concentration on the road. My brain was on betrayal overload, although both my betrayers tonight had no doubt thought they were doing the right thing.

I shook that thought off as soon as it crossed my mind. Killing Der Jäger might have been the right thing, and I could excuse Brian's methods even if I couldn't forgive them. But Lugh hadn't had to put me in that damned oubliette, no matter how pissed off he might have been!

I had to keep you from breaking my control, his voice whispered in my mind. *I didn't do it to hurt you.*

I almost rammed into a parked car. "Shut the fuck up!" I snarled. For once, he actually listened to me.

My intention had been to go home, crawl into bed, and sleep for as long as I could manage to stay unconscious. Usually, the more miserable I am, the more desperately I want to be alone. But just this once, I couldn't stand the idea of being alone with my thoughts. I knew Andy hadn't forgiven me for siccing Adam on him, but there was no one else I could go to for comfort just now.

It was almost three in the morning by the time I reached his apartment, but there was light shining under his door. I knocked softly, hoping not to wake any of the other residents.

He answered the door quickly enough to let me know he hadn't been asleep, though he was dressed in pajamas and had a bad case of bed-head. He ushered me into his apartment without a word, which was a good thing because I couldn't think of anything to say.

He disappeared into the kitchen, then returned carrying two glasses with a couple fingers of amber liquid apiece. I made a face because I hated the taste of hard liquor, but I took the glass when he handed it to me. We both drained the contents in a single gulp, though I coughed and sputtered for about ten minutes afterward.

When I finally had the air to speak again, I stared at the glass in my hands and asked, "Did Adam call you about . . . ?"

I heard the sound of his glass clinking on the coffee table, but I couldn't tear my gaze away from the single drop of liquid that remained in the bottom of mine.

"Yeah." Andy's voice sounded hoarse, either from sleep, from grief, or from hard liquor.

A tear rolled down my cheek and dripped into my glass. Andy gently pried the glass from my fingers, then put an arm around my shoulders. That was all the encouragement I needed to let down my guard, to let my grief and pain batter and buffet me. He held me and rocked me, the perfect big brother even though he must have been grief-stricken himself. After all, he'd never had the problems I'd had with our father, and had always been closer to him than I had.

"Tell me the whole story," he urged when the storm seemed close to subsiding.

And so I did, my voice stuttering along between hiccups and sobs. I told him how Raphael had betrayed me to Der Jäger. I told him how Brian had betrayed me to Lugh. And I told him how Lugh had given me firsthand experience in the oubliette that Adam had once described to me.

When I thought of the oubliette, a hint of anger stirred in my center, fighting its way up through the grief, then taking hold and growing. I seized it with the desperation of a drowning woman. Anger is so much easier, so much more comfortable for me than grief. I wanted to get good and pissed, so that at least for a few minutes, I wouldn't have to feel the pain.

"I will never forgive him for doing that to me," I declared, and was more thankful than I could say that Lugh didn't interject any commentary in my brain.

Andy met my eyes, his expression both grave and guarded. "He was doing what he thought was best."

Outrage swelled in my chest. "Don't you dare defend him! You're supposed to be on *my* side."

A faint smile curled his lips. "I *am* on your side. I'm just trying to point out—"

"No! I don't care why he did it. I don't care if it's some kind of abstract 'right thing.' He used me, just like any other demon uses and abuses its host. He pretends he's better than the rest of them, that he cares about human rights, and it's all bullshit!" I heard my voice rising and forced myself to quiet down for the sake of the neighbors. "I used to think he was different. I was wrong."

Andy shook his head. "Lugh *is* different. He's one of the good guys, and I think you know it, even if you're angry with him."

Now I was beginning to be as pissed at Andy as I was at Lugh. "Last time I talked about Lugh, you were warning me to be careful of him and telling me he was just like all the rest. What's gotten into you?"

He shrugged. "I just have a little more perspective now." He fixed me with a pointed stare. "If I offered to take Lugh from you, would you do it?"

The question sucked all the air out of my lungs, and it took a moment for me to find my voice. "Are you offering?"

"Let's say I am. Would you give him to me?"

My head felt about two sizes too big, and I

couldn't make sense of what was happening. Was he offering to take Lugh, or wasn't he?

Andy smiled. "If you hated him as much as you claim, that wouldn't be a hard question."

I grunted. "I'm just trying to figure out if you mean it or not."

He rolled his eyes. "You are such a hard case, Morgan." He reached out and grabbed my hand. "Yes, I mean it. Will you give him to me?"

Lugh had to be in control to transfer to a different host, but all I'd have to do is take a little nap and Lugh could surface and move out of my life. "He might not leave me even if I tried to give him to you," I said.

"Are you fooling yourself? Because you're not fooling me. Will you give him to me?"

I swallowed hard. Andy had always wanted to be a hero. That's why he'd chosen to be a demon host in the first place. After his experiences with Raphael, he'd seemed to have soured on the idea, but perhaps the desire was too deeply ingrained in him to disappear entirely. If he was determined to be a hero, he'd be a hell of a lot safer with a demon to protect his fragile human body.

And hell, after living with Raphael for ten years, living with Lugh would be a piece of cake. Yeah, I was mad at Lugh, but I had to admit that between him and Raphael, he was very much the lesser of two evils. I could let Andy be the hero he'd always wanted to be, and I could let my life return to a semblance of normalcy. Had it been only a week ago that Andy had awakened from his catatonia and I had dreamed of doing just that?

It was on the tip of my tongue to agree, to take the unbearably heavy burden on my shoulders and shrug it off onto someone else.

But as Lugh had reminded me more than once,

there was so much more at stake than just my own life. Lugh might find it inconvenient that he couldn't control me as he could any other human host, but there were advantages to our partnership. As long as I was his host, no one would ever be able to find him, because no one can tell I'm possessed. That wouldn't be the case with Andy. I wasn't only Lugh's host, I was his refuge as well.

I shook my head at myself. Since Raphael had decided covering his ass was more important than saving his brother's life, that line of reasoning no longer worked. For all I knew, everyone in the Demon Realm now knew exactly who was hosting Lugh.

I imagined what my life would be like if I gave him up—assuming said life didn't get cut really, really short when the rebel demons burned me alive on the assumption that I still had him. I could go back to being nothing more than a simple exorcist. I could send predatory demons to the Demon Realm, where they could find their way back to the Mortal Plain at a moment's notice.

Was that really meant to be the sum total of my contribution to the human race? And how could I possibly find any hint of satisfaction in my futile endeavor, when I'd always know I'd taken the coward's way out and shoved my big brother into the line of fire in my place?

I let out a deep breath as something settled inside me and I felt almost calm for the first time in forever. "No," I said softly. "No, I wouldn't give him to you. He's my cross to bear now, so to speak."

Andy nodded sagely and let go of my hand. Luckily for both of us, he refrained from saying "I told you so."

It was time—past time, really—for me to go home.

But something about the expression on Andy's face made me hesitate.

"What is it?" I asked, though I was pretty sure I didn't want to know.

He ran a hand through his hair, scrubbing at his scalp and looking remarkably uncomfortable. "I have something I need to tell you, and you're not going to like it. I was going to wait until a better time, but it occurs to me that the longer I put it off, the more you're not going to like it."

I groaned. Nope, definitely not something I wanted to hear. But of course, now that he'd dangled that little delicacy in front of my nose, I wouldn't be able to stop thinking about it until I'd gotten the full story.

"Spill it," I said.

He stood up and moved away from me as if in fear of physical violence. He even made sure there was a solid, bulky chair between us. I wasn't sure I was going to be able to hear what he had to say over the alarm bells that were blaring in my head. I sat up straighter and waited for him to drop his bombshell.

Finally, he sighed and squared his shoulders like he was going into battle. "I didn't betray you," he said, and I frowned at the words.

"I never said you did."

He met my eyes steadily. "It appears my cover is blown," he continued. "They lied to me about Der Jäger. I swear to God I thought he was imprisoned."

My jaw dropped, and I wished like hell I could come up with another way to explain the words that were coming out of Andy's mouth. "Raphael?" I gasped.

His gaze dropped to the floor and he gave a quick, jerky nod. "I knew you'd think I betrayed you. So I returned to a host I knew you wouldn't be willing to destroy."

Tears blurred my vision yet again. I should have been furious, but I was just too beaten down, so I sat there shaking my head and crying, unable to encompass the idea that I'd lost both my father and my brother in the span of just a few hours.

"I swear to you it will be different this time," Raphael said. "I will take very good care of Andrew. I *am* capable of it, despite what you think."

"You tried to breed a race of empty vessels so you wouldn't have to be inconvenienced by dealing with host personalities. You don't give a damn about human beings. Never have, never will."

He seemed to think he was safe from physical violence, for he moved out from behind the chair and took a seat. "I wanted empty vessels so I could walk the Mortal Plain without having to deal with a fragile human psyche in the process. Taking care of one's host is hard work. *Unrelenting* hard work, and that's not why I like being here."

"Adam seems to think it's worth the effort!"

Raphael shrugged. "I'm not Adam. As Lugh has kindly pointed out any number of times during my life, I am a selfish bastard." He didn't look particularly torn up about the fact, although I couldn't help seeing the bitterness in his expression. "I wanted to enjoy the pleasures of life on the Mortal Plain without the responsibilities."

"And so you headed up a project to treat people like prize breeding stock, mucking with their genes and destroying the rejects."

"If the project had worked, demons would be able to walk the Mortal Plain without taking sentient hosts. People like Andrew would never have to give up their identities for us again."

I snorted. "You expect me to believe your motives

were pure? Not that it would matter if they were. Good intentions can only excuse so much."

Raphael closed his eyes. "It would be nice if just once you or Lugh could cut me some slack. Maybe I'm not the nicest guy in the world, but I've risked—and now *lost*—everything to keep you safe. And do you know how my dear brother will reward me for my efforts if I ever manage to put him back on the throne? He will no doubt imprison me the moment I set foot in the Demon Realm again.

"But no matter how much the two of you may despise me, I *am* loyal. I will do as much as you let me to help you both, even when I know it's not in my own best interests. And I will protect Andrew to the best of my ability—not for *his* sake, because as you can obviously tell we don't much like each other, but for Lugh's."

"I could exorcize you right now," I said, though without my Taser handy I somehow doubted I could convince him to hold still for it.

"No, you couldn't," he replied calmly. "As I suspect Lugh told you the last time Andrew was my host, as a royal, I'm too powerful for you to cast out. Lugh *might* be able to do it, but you'd have to let him take control first."

I was too exhausted and traumatized to muster the kind of reply that would have felt morally satisfying. "Words can't describe how much I loathe you," I said instead, my voice flat and dull.

If I didn't know better, I would have said a hint of hurt flashed across his face before he schooled his expression.

"Go home, Morgan. Get some rest. And try to forgive Lugh for what he did. I'll be the first one to admit he has his faults, but he always does what he thinks is right, no matter how much it costs him. Or anyone else, for that matter."

I couldn't think of a good parting shot, so I just gave him one last scathing look before I got the hell out of there.

I hate demons. Every last one of them.

Then why, you might ask, did I choose to keep hosting Lugh when I thought I had a chance to get rid of him?

Beats the hell out of me.

Epilogue

My mom came out of the woodwork for my father's funeral. I knew she was going to be there, though I hadn't spoken to her since the day Dad had kicked me out of the house.

Raphael was there, of course, playing the part of Andrew, but I refused to talk to him or even look at him. We sat together in the family waiting area in the funeral parlor, the silence between us dense and oppressive. It's saying something about the strain between us that my mother's arrival actually broke up the tension some.

I was shocked when I first caught sight of her. Mrs. Perfect's face was devoid of makeup, so there was no disguising the dark circles under her eyes, and her hair lay flat against her head, no evidence of having encountered a curling iron and a bottle of hairspray. Her simple black dress made her skin look almost paper white, except for the mottled color of her face. When she saw me, her eyes welled with tears, and she crossed the short distance between us and gathered me into a fierce hug.

Not knowing what else to do, I returned the embrace awkwardly. My own eyes were dry, although that didn't mean I wasn't grieving inside. For the loss of my father, for the loss of my brother, for the troubles that had arisen once again between myself and Brian. So far, I hadn't been able to bring myself to talk to him. It wasn't that I didn't understand what he'd done or why he'd done it. I could even admit to myself that it had been a noble gesture, doing something that was anathema to him to save me from myself. But I wasn't sure I could forgive him.

Mom pushed away from me and blotted her tears with an already sodden tissue. Guilt twisted in my gut as I looked into her grief-stricken eyes. Of course, she had no idea the role I'd played in her husband's death, and though I'd always found my father cold, there was no doubt in my mind that my mom had loved him. My throat tightened, and no words would come.

Raphael stood, drawing Mom's attention, then dutifully hugged her, eyes fixed on me the entire time. When he let go, Mom excused herself, drawing me with her to the far side of the room. Raphael took the hint and sat back down as far away from us as possible.

She visibly swallowed hard, then firmed her chin and met my eyes. "Mr. Cooper came to see your father and me the day of the accident," she said quietly, and the tears sprang back to life. She blinked them away. "He told us what happened to you at The Healing Circle. I want you to know neither your father nor I had any idea what they were planning to do to you. We never would have allowed them to take you if we had known they were going to hurt you."

I couldn't help a derisive snort. "You knew they were going to give me to the demons." I lowered my voice, since the engineer of my childhood trauma was sitting so close. "You drugged me and took me to the hospital so I could be mind-raped."

Her face paled and her chin quivered. "It was for the greater good," she whispered, but I saw the doubt that swam behind her eyes. She reached out to touch my face, and for some reason I let her do it. "Your father and I did what we thought was right. Maybe in hindsight I think we were wrong, but I can't change the past. What could we have done differently, when we believed with all our hearts that sacrificing our daughter was the right thing to do?" She shook her head. "How could we have faced ourselves if we had selfishly done as we preferred when we believed it was wrong?"

I remembered the terrible moment when I'd realized that to protect myself, to protect Lugh, I would have to kill my father. I'd faced the same kind of decision my parents had faced: do what I was convinced was right, or do what I'd prefer. I'd turned away from the "right" choice. If Brian hadn't tackled me, Der Jäger could even now be back in the Demon Realm, telling Dougal and all his minions exactly where Lugh was. Very possibly, that would have led to Lugh's death and the subjugation of the human race to the demons. How could I be so sure that my decision had been the correct one?

It was the most slippery of moral slopes, and nothing I could deal with in the midst of this maelstrom of grief. I couldn't force myself to speak words of forgiveness, but neither could I wholeheartedly condemn her.

The world is rarely painted in black and white, Lugh's voice whispered in my mind, reminding me to shore up my mental defenses. So far, it seemed that I could block his voice out with a concerted effort, but how long before he found a way around that obstacle as well?

"Are you officially coming out of hiding?" I asked my mom.

She looked momentarily taken aback by the change of subject, but she recovered quickly. "Yes. We—I'm in the process of moving back into the house." The tears returned, and before I knew what I was going to do, I had stepped forward and hugged her.

I could count on one hand the number of times I'd voluntarily hugged my mom as an adult. I had no idea where the impulse had come from, though I hoped it had been my own idea, not Lugh's. Inside, I shuddered. When Raphael had pretended to offer to take Lugh from me, I'd decided to keep him. But now I wondered if I'd been suffering from temporary insanity. It seemed like every day, he intruded further into my life, and I had no idea where it would all end.

The funeral director stepped into the room and quietly informed us that it was time for the service to begin. Turning away from me, my mom snatched another handful of tissues from the box beside the couch, then raised her chin like a soldier going into battle. Raphael stepped up beside her and put his arm around her shoulders. She leaned into him, taking comfort from the man she thought was her son.

Choking on an upswelling of rage, I watched them walk out into the chapel together. The fate of the world might very well rest on my shoulders, but at the moment, figuring out a way to kick Raphael out of Andy's body was my top priority. And if it turned out he was lying to me, abusing my brother like he had before, then I would find a way to make him pay.

Seizing my anger, nurturing it to drown out the lingering echoes of grief, I followed my remaining family out into the chapel.

About the Author

JENNA BLACK is your typical writer. Which means she's an "experience junkie." She got her BA in physical anthropology and French from Duke University.

Once upon a time, she dreamed she would be the next Jane Goodall, camping in the bush making fabulous discoveries about primate behavior. Then, during her senior year at Duke, she did some actual research in the field and made this shocking discovery: primates spend something like 80 percent of their time doing such exciting things as sleeping and eating.

Concluding that this discovery was her life's work in the field of primatology, she then moved on to such varied pastimes as grooming dogs and writing technical documentation. Visit her on the Web at www.JennaBlack.com.

*And if you can't wait for more of
Morgan and Lugh's kick-ass adventures,
be sure not to miss*

The Devil's Due

by
Jenna Black

the next book in the Morgan Kingsley series,
coming in fall 2008 from Dell Spectra.

Here's a special preview. . . .

The Devil's Due

On sale in 2008

It was my first time in the office in more than a week. Somehow, my actual paying job as an exorcist didn't seem so satisfying these days. Finding out that exorcizing demons doesn't actually kill them had robbed me of my joie de vivre. Of course, being possessed by the king of the demons myself had something to do with it, too.

Still, harboring the demon king and trying to protect him from his brother Dougal, the would-be usurper of the demon throne, didn't pay the bills, and I had a lot of them piling up. It had been less than two months since my house had burned to the ground with all my worldly possessions inside, and my insurance company had yet to begin showering me with largesse.

I was seriously behind in my paperwork, and was disappointed to discover that the Paperwork Fairy hadn't taken care of everything during my absence. With something between a sigh and a groan, I dropped into my chair and turned on my computer. While I waited for the dinosaur to muster the energy to boot up, I checked my phone messages. There were a bunch from the U.S. Exorcism Board reminding me that a) I was late paying my dues, and b) I was late filing the paperwork on my last three exorcisms. There were also the usual calls from telemarketers who were desperate for me to change long-distance phone companies, but I was much more interested in the three messages—each one more urgent than the last—from a woman who identified herself as Claudia Brewster. She didn't say what she wanted, but I made an educated guess that she had a loved one who'd been possessed by an illegal demon.

I frowned as I took down her number, because it was local. In Philadelphia and the surrounding area, I'm almost always contacted by the court system when there's an illegal or rogue demon in custody, and I hadn't heard anything. It wasn't unusual for me to be hired by distraught family members (not to brag or anything, but I have the best record of any exorcist in the United States), but those were usually out-of-state cases.

I called the daytime number Ms. Brewster left and got her secretary. Ms. Brewster was in a meeting, but the secretary took a message and said I should receive a call back within a couple of hours. I hung up, and my shoulders slumped. So much for my reprieve from the dreaded paperwork.

My computer had finally roused itself from its slumber, so I began slogging my way through my backlog. As you might have guessed by now, this wasn't my favorite part of my job, and I had to work hard to resist the lure of a rousing game of Spider Solitaire.

About an hour later, I was feeling conspicuously virtuous about my productivity—and about my willpower—when there came a tentative rap on my office door. I wasn't expecting anyone, and as far as I knew, no one knew I was here. I pulled my bag from my desk drawer and grabbed my Taser. Hey, better safe than sorry, right?

"Come in," I beckoned, now armed and ready, holding the Taser in my lap, where my desk would hide it from view.

The door opened, and a lovely forty-something woman walked in. Dressed in a dark blue pinstripe pantsuit that looked like it had been made exactly to her measurements, she screamed conservative corporate America. That image was enhanced by the blond hair fastened in a well-sprayed French twist and the makeup job that was supposed to make her look like she wasn't wearing any. She'd have fit right in as the token female in a boardroom full of old fogies.

I took a wild guess as to who my visitor might be. "Ms. Brewster?" I asked, wondering why she hadn't bothered to call first. Paranoia—which was my constant and very reasonable state of mind these days—brought any number of unpalatable suggestions to mind, so instead of standing up and offering to shake hands, I remained seated with my Taser at the ready.

"Please call me Claudia," she said with a brittle-looking smile as she closed the door behind her.

"Claudia," I agreed, taking an instant dislike to her for no good reason. "I usually meet with clients by appointment only, and I'm very busy at the moment." I idly tapped a couple keys on my keyboard, turning my face to the screen while keeping a watch on her out of the corner of my eye. "I can fit you in tomorrow at . . ." I pretended to scrutinize a calendar. "Three o'clock. Will that work for you?" I turned to face her once more, putting on my blandest smile.

Claudia licked her lips and shifted her grip on the designer pocketbook that hung from her shoulder. It was only then that I noticed how she clutched the strap of that bag as if it were a lifeline.

"Please, Ms. Kingsley," she said, and she sounded like she might be on the verge of tears. "I've been trying to reach you for a week, and I'm . . . well, I'm desperate."

My opinion of her softened, and I realized my initial dislike had been a result of her looking so much like she had her shit together—in deep contrast to myself. But no power suit and fancy makeup could camouflage her misery for long, and I felt a surge of kinship.

"You can call me Morgan," I said, and I let my curiosity get the better of me. "Please have a seat." I indicated the pair of chairs in front of my desk, and with a sigh of relief, she sat in the one on the right and put her bag on the one on the left. I folded my hands on the desk in front of me, leaving the Taser on my lap, where I could easily reach it if necessary.

"What can I do for you, Claudia?" I asked.

She took a deep breath as if steeling herself for a mighty effort. Strain showed in the tightness in the corners of her eyes, and she wet her lips again. "I don't know where else to turn," she said, giving me a pleading look.

"Okay," I said slowly, then gestured for her to continue when she seemed to stall out.

"I'm in desperate need of your . . . services."

People were often reluctant and uncomfortable

when they hired me. For reasons that escaped me, they often found having a loved one possessed to be a source of embarrassment. However, Claudia was taking it to the extreme with this strange hesitancy. I'd been sympathetic for about sixty seconds, which I think is a personal record. I decided it was high time to revert to my usual bluntness.

"Just spit it out already," I said, with more than a touch of impatience. "You want me to exorcize someone."

A hint of fire flared in her eyes, and it seemed like my prickly bedside manner had steadied her some. "Yes. But of course it's not quite that simple or I'd have gone through more traditional channels."

That made me frown. "You don't consider an exorcist the traditional channel for exorcizing demons?"

She crossed her legs, her foot jiggling restlessly as she ignored my question. "It's about my son, Tommy." She grimaced. "Tom," she corrected herself, and I had to suppress a smile.

"You think your son is possessed."

She shook her head. "I *know* he's possessed." She seemed to notice her jiggling foot and stopped herself with what looked like a concerted effort. "He was possessed while his father and I were on vacation."

I still didn't get why she was here. "It's a police matter at this point," I told her. "Once they take him into custody, I can come to the containment center and make an official diagnosis." I held up a hand to forestall her attempt to interrupt. "I'm not saying I don't believe you—it's just that we have to follow standard procedures. After I diagnose him—"

"Ms. Kingsley," she cut in, "let me get right to the crux of the matter. All the evidence except for common sense says that my son is a willing host."

"A willing host," I repeated stupidly. I'd pictured Tommy Brewster as a petulant teenager, but he had to be at least twenty-one to be a legal host. I nudged my estimation of Claudia's age up a few years.

She nodded. "They've got the signed forms and everything. But there is no way in hell my son volunteered to host a demon."

And to think I'd believed she had her shit together! I thought I was the queen of denial, but it looked like there was a new contender to the throne. "You do understand the process of registering to be a legal demon host, don't you?" I asked.

She made an impatient tsking sound. "Of course I do, but—"

I counted off the points on my fingers. "He had to sign the documents before witnesses. In a courtroom. On videotape. And after he'd been interviewed by a shrink to establish competency." I shook my head. "Are you seriously trying to tell me he did all that against his will? And that no one noticed?"

She pressed her lips tightly together. "I know how it looks. And I know you think I'm just the distraught mother who can't accept that her baby has grown up." She managed a rictus of a smile. "That last part's even true." The forced smile faded. "But volunteering to host is the last thing in the world Tommy would do. He *hates* demons. Hates them with a passion."

I wasn't so fond of them myself—hence my career choice—but I had to admit getting to know Lugh, the demon king, had lessened my hate by approximately one hair. "People change their minds."

"Not like this they don't. You see, when my husband and I left for the Bahamas, we'd finally given up hope that we could extricate Tommy . . . *Tom* . . . from God's Wrath."

I couldn't suppress a bit of a gasp. God's Wrath is the most militant of the anti-demon hate groups. They specialize in roasting people alive to destroy the Spawn of Satan, as they consider demons. They're so radical, they even hate exorcists, because when we kick a demon out of its host, its host gets to live. Of course, about eighty percent of them live the rest of their lives as vegetables, but God's Wrath didn't think that was a severe enough punishment for those sinners who'd invited demons into our world. So I had to admit the idea of a God's Wrath member volunteering to host a demon was a bit . . . out there.

"We were gone ten days," Claudia continued. "Do you really believe someone could be a card-carrying member of God's Wrath one day, and then ten days later be a willing demon host?"

There was no denying it sounded hinky. Hell, I didn't even see how a former God's Wrath member could get accepted into the Spirit Society in such a short time frame, much less get an appointment with a judge, get all the paperwork approved, and have a summoning ceremony.

"I presume you voiced your concerns to the police?" I asked.

She nodded. "Naturally. Everyone agrees it sounds like an unusual case, but there's no evidence of a crime having been committed." Her voice turned bitter. "Everyone tells me with great sympathy that there's nothing they can do to help me."

"What do *you* think happened?"

Claudia blinked away what might have been the start of tears. "I think he had to have been possessed already when he signed the papers."

I shook my head. "That con hasn't worked for at least thirty or forty years." There was a famous case back in the sixties of a young man who'd turned out to be possessed when he signed the consent forms. Ever since then, the applicant had to be examined by an exorcist first.

"I know the exorcist who was on duty claimed Tommy wasn't possessed, but he could have been paid off."

It sounded plausible, if hard to prove. "Who was the exorcist?"

"His name was Sammy Cho."

I think I managed to avoid making a face. Sammy was a second-rate exorcist—which explained why he was doing shit work like examining host wannabes. However, even the worst exorcist in existence can read auras well enough to spot a demon, and Sammy had such a big stick up his ass I half expected leaves to sprout from his ears in the spring.

"There's no way Sammy would take a bribe," I said.

"No one is incorruptible."

"Sammy's about as close as you can get. Believe me, I know him well." Only in a professional capacity, mind you, and being an inveterate rule-breaker myself, I tried to spend as little time in his presence as possible. But I'd stake my reputation on the fact that he'd rather die than take a bribe.

Claudia dismissed my assertion with a wave of her hand. "It doesn't really matter in the long run *how* it happened. The fact remains that my son has been possessed against his will." She swallowed hard. "I know it may already be too late, that he may never recover, but I *have* to get that demon out of him."

And I realized now exactly what she wanted me to do. "You want me to perform an illegal exorcism."

She held her chin up defiantly. "We—my husband and I—have money. We're willing to pay whatever it would take."

I wasn't sure whether to be offended that she thought I could be bought or sympathetic to her terrible situation. What I *did* know was that there was no way I would be performing an illegal exorcism.

"You could pay me a king's ransom, and it wouldn't matter to me one bit as I rotted in prison. Illegal exorcism is considered murder." Only because the authorities didn't know that the demons didn't die but were merely sent back to the Demon Realm, but no one was going to believe me if I declared that in my own defense. Besides, I'd been arrested for illegal exorcism once before, and I hadn't enjoyed the experience.

"I understand you'd be taking a great risk," she said, her voice soothing despite the desperation in her eyes. "But once we get Tommy back, he can confirm that he wasn't willing, and—"

"You said yourself it might be too late." If Tommy Brewster really *was* hosting an illegal demon, then there was considerably more than an eighty percent chance of him becoming a vegetable if he and that demon parted ways. Just a little more of my hard-earned knowledge of the deep, dark secrets the demons keep from the human race—the brain damage is brought on by abuse, and sometimes even legal demons didn't treat their hosts all that well.

With a pang, I thought of my own brother, Andrew. He'd hosted Lugh's brother, Raphael, for ten years, and had spent weeks in a state of catatonia when Raphael was gone. The good news was that he'd recovered. The really horrible, shitty news was that Raphael had recently possessed him once again.

I forcibly dragged my mind back to the problem at hand. What had I been saying? Oh, yeah. "If he's a—" I stopped myself, thinking that using the word "vegetable" right now might not be very sensitive. "If he's catatonic when the demon's gone, he can't corroborate a thing. It's not just my own ass I'm protecting, it's yours, too. You and your husband would be accessories. I'm sorry, but I just can't do it. And if you find another exorcist who agrees, you can be ninety-nine percent certain you're about to get scammed. No one's going to risk a murder charge, not when the pool of suspects would be so small."

There are only a couple hundred exorcists in the United States, and many of them would have alibis. I imagine if someone were stupid enough to take the Brewsters' money, they'd find themselves behind bars in no time.

"So what do you suggest I do?" Claudia asked bitterly. "Just write my son off as dead? Watch that . . .

that *thing* live out my son's life?" She shuddered. "I can't do that. I *won't*." A tear snaked down her cheek, and she angrily swiped it away. She didn't strike me as the kind of woman who cried easily, but it's amazing how much pain family can cause.

She stood up, snatching her purse from the seat beside her. My heart ached with sympathy, the situation with my brother making me feel her pain all the more keenly. Now, some might argue that the world was better off without one more God's Wrath wacko tromping around burning people alive, and I might even agree with them. But I'd rather see that wacko in a brick-and-mortar prison than imprisoned helplessly within his own body.

"Look, don't do anything drastic," I advised as Claudia strode to the door.

She stopped and looked over her shoulder at me. "I'll do whatever I have to do to free my son. He's had a hard enough life already. I won't abandon him."

I patted the air with my hand. "Yeah, I get that. I've got a, um, friend in the police department." Calling Adam a friend was a world-class stretch, but I didn't have any other way to describe him that wouldn't take five minutes of explanation. "Let me talk to him and see what he suggests."

"The police have already said they can't help me."

"I know, but my friend might be able to pull a few strings. Maybe at least get them to look a little more closely at the case and see if they can find any evidence of coercion."

Actually, Adam was the Director of Special Forces, the branch of the police department responsible for all demon-related crime. He also had a habit of playing fast and loose with the law, which meant he might be able to get things done that a more by-the-books cop couldn't.

Claudia looked skeptical but managed a nod of acquiescence. "Thank you. I will, naturally, compensate you for your time."

I could have used the money, but I didn't feel right charging her when Adam was going to do all the work. "No need for that. If I end up performing a legal exorcism for you, you can pay me then. Meanwhile, can I have your assurance that you and your husband won't try anything illegal while I'm looking into this for you?"

She hesitated, then agreed with a nod. "All right. I appreciate your help, and I'm sorry I asked you to risk yourself like that."

No, she wasn't, but I couldn't entirely blame her, so I accepted the apology.

While I debated how to approach Adam, I distracted myself by getting on the Internet and seeing what information I could scrape up on the Brewster family.

I wasn't expecting to find anything particularly interesting, or even particularly relevant. But I found a lot more than I bargained for.

Claudia Brewster was exactly what she looked like—an extremely successful career woman. She'd gotten an MBA from Harvard and had eventually brokered that into a position as vice president of a management consultant firm here in the city. Her husband,

Devon Brewster III, was old money, and I could see no evidence that he'd ever worked for a living.

But that wasn't what caught my interest. It turned out there was a hell of a lot about Tommy Brewster that Claudia had failed to mention. Starting with the fact that he wasn't her biological son.

It appeared no one knew for sure who Tommy Brewster really was. When he was three years old, he was found at a horrific crime scene, where a rampaging demon had killed four people. A cop had heard the screams and come running. The demon had grabbed Tommy and was about to smash his head against a wall when the cop reached them. The cop had shot the demon in the head, killing its host and saving Tommy's life.

The story got stranger from there. The police were unable to identify any of the four people who'd been slaughtered, though blood tests proved that two of them were Tommy's parents. Tommy was too traumatized to tell the police anything, not even his name. He'd gone into the foster-care system and had eventually ended up with the Brewsters, who'd adopted him when he was ten after he'd lived with them for several years.

The police weren't idiots. They knew the demon who'd killed Tommy's parents wasn't dead—the only way to kill a demon is to burn its host alive with the demon still in it—and they knew it was possible it would return to the Mortal Plain to finish the job it had started. When Tommy had gone into foster care, social services had been very careful to cover their tracks and make it impossible for the demon to locate him.

So, how did I learn all this information about him if it was such a secret? Because Tommy had posted the whole sordid story on his MySpace page, along with enough anti-demon invective to get his profile deleted if anyone bothered to complain about it.

It was possible the story was a load of shit. I'd looked up the stories about the slaughter, and there was no denying it had occurred and that a small child had been found at the scene. That didn't mean Tommy was that child. Still, if it was true, that would explain Tommy's devotion to God's Wrath. It *wouldn't* explain why the hell he'd posted so much information on the Internet.

Unless he was trying to attract the attention of the demon who'd killed his parents. Perhaps he was looking for revenge? It seemed a little far-fetched. After all, he'd been only three when it happened. Chances were he barely remembered anything. At least not consciously. However, I'd seen how powerful the subconscious could be.

I knew Adam could find out for sure if Tommy Brewster was who he said he was. And if his story turned out to be true, then his case became even more suspicious.

Who was the demon who'd slaughtered those four people and would have slaughtered Tommy if not for a policeman's timely rescue? Why had the demon gone on such a rampage? And could it possibly be a coincidence that shortly after Tommy Brewster turned twenty-one—the age at which he could legally register to host a demon—he turned up possessed?

The demons had shown far too much interest in this kid's life. My gut instinct said it would behoove me to find out why.